The W

Katherine Hastings

THE WILDER WIDOWS

For information contact :
http://www.katherinehastings.com

Ebook ISBN: 978-1-949913-24-8
Paperback ISBN: 978-1-949913-25-5

First Edition: December 2020
Editing: Tami Stark
Proofreading: Free to Be Creative Co.

www.katherinehastings.com

Four Widows. Four Wishes. One Wild Adventure.

When Sylvie's husband passed away, she'd barely hung her black dress back in the closet when three widows from Wilder Lane showed up on her doorstep. Who had time to properly mourn when an adventure spanning the globe awaited her?

After putting their own needs on the back burner to raise their families, Sylvie, Doris, Alice, and Marge struggle to find purpose now that their children are grown, and their husbands are gone. Loneliness pushes them together while they knit away the rest of their days. Then one night, a whiskey-filled pact catapults these ladies onto the adventure of a lifetime.

Each widow gets one wish, one wild adventure, she's dreamed of doing her whole life. With their wishes tucked away on notes inside their knitting basket, they pull them out, one at a time, vowing to do whatever it takes to help each other fulfill their wildest desires.

Hilarity ensues as these four diverse women stretch their boundaries to go where no widows have gone before. They stare death in the face, have cops hot on their tail, and shed away the responsibilities they've shouldered their whole lives. The Wilder Widows soon find out their lives aren't over... in fact, in this second act, their lives are just beginning.

SYLVIE

CHAPTER ONE

"Goodbye, Susie. Thanks again for everything." I waved while she pushed the hospital bed down the walkway to the van parked out front.

"Take care of yourself, Sylvie," she called back. "I really am sorry for your loss. Bruce was a good man."

Leaning against the doorway, I crossed my arms and watched Susie and Virginia lift the bed into the back of the van. With one last wave, they climbed inside. It was surreal watching them drive away, knowing I would likely never see them again. They had been a staple in my life this past month while Bruce slipped away. Their job had been to keep him comfortable, but they'd been as much a support system for me as they had for him. Making it through the horrors of the last few weeks would have been impossible without their comforting words and their knowledge of caring for someone in their final days.

With a heavy sigh, I stepped back inside and closed the door behind me. As it clicked shut, it sealed out the sounds of the engine driving away and the birds chirping at the feeder just outside. Silence settled over the empty house, and for the first time in months, there were no sounds other than my own breathing.

In. Out.

In. Out.

I no longer heard the soft beeping of the machines and the buzzing of equipment keeping Bruce comfortable. No longer did I hear the nurses' hushed whispers while they worked to adjust his medication or the blaring television because Bruce had refused to get a hearing aid years ago when he'd needed it. No one called my name, asking me to change the channel or bring them something to drink.

Silence. Just silence.

But it didn't last long. The doorbell rang and caused me to jump. Craning my head, I peered out the bay window overlooking the entry, but the covered awning hid away the surprise visitors. Part of me welcomed guests to bring noise to my life once again, the silence still unsettling. But the other part of me was exhausted from the past few days of people smothering me with their comfort after I said goodbye to my husband. The doorbell rang again, and I suppressed my groan and went to answer it.

When I opened the door, three older women stood squished together, each gripping something in their hands. Though I recognized them from seeing them around the neighborhood, I didn't know them personally.

"Hello, Sylvie, I'm Doris," the short round one said while she tipped her head and gave me the sympathetic smile I'd grown accustomed to since Bruce passed. "This is Alice and Marge." She pointed to each woman at her side. "We all live just down the road, and we wanted to check in on you."

"Thank you. I'm hanging in there," I answered while I looked to the other two. They all appeared a little older than me, but the similarities ended there.

Alice, the tall one with sleek modern-styled silver hair and legs up to my ears, mimicked the sympathetic smile. "You have my sympathies."

"Me too," grunted Marge, the one with a face like a pug.

"We're all widows, so we know how you're feeling. In fact, we call ourselves the Wilder Widows because, well, we all live on Wilder Lane." Doris gestured behind her to our suburban street. "Since you're a widow on Wilder Lane now, we wanted to welcome you to the group."

"Oh." I raised my brows. "I didn't realize there was a widow's group."

"We get together and do stuff since we're all bored and lonely." Marge shrugged.

"Lonely? Speak for yourself." One of Alice's meticulously groomed eyebrows rose in a challenge. "I'm not *lonely*, Marge. I've still got plenty of suitors to keep me occupied." She pursed her rose-colored lips and peered down her nose.

Marge rolled her eyes and grumbled beneath a long exhale.

"Anyway," Doris interjected, puckering her face while she scolded Alice with a look. "We just wanted to welcome you to the club." A wide grin spread across her chubby cheeks.

A widow's club? How had I never known such a thing existed? I supposed it was because until five days ago, I wasn't one of them. But now I stood in my doorway with three widows staring at me, awaiting my answer.

"I appreciate the invite. I'm not really sure what to think. I'm still trying to process what to do now that Bruce is gone, but—"

"That's why we're here. To help!" Doris grinned wider and pushed past me into my house. Trying to hide the shock in my eyes at the intrusion, I let her pass before gesturing for Alice and Marge to enter as well.

Marge hoisted the covered dish in her hands. "Where should I put this?" Her rough voice matched her unladylike exterior. Perhaps with a little make-up and a new hairstyle she could pass for a woman in one glance, but that dark grey bowl-cut and her bulging eyes had made me look twice the first time I'd seen her walking around the neighborhood. It had taken several long stares before I'd decided she was, in fact, a woman and not a short old man.

Still trying to process the invasion into my sanctuary, I pointed to the kitchen island. "You didn't have to make me anything, but you can set it there."

"I didn't make it. My mother did. It's lasagna."

Mother? Judging by the look of her, she was easily seventy years old. Either her mother was ancient, or she'd been very young when Marge was born. My own parents both passed away already, and I had only just turned sixty.

"Really, you didn't have to bring anything." In fact, I wished she hadn't. More sympathy casseroles than I'd ever be able to eat in this lifetime took up every inch of my fridge.

"I brought muffins. Fresh baked!" Doris pulled back the embroidered napkin lining her small basket. Steam rose off the muffins, and the intoxicating smell tempted the appetite hiding since Bruce's death.

"They look and smell wonderful. Thank you, Doris."

"Blueberry." She waggled her eyebrows then placed the basket beside the lasagna dish.

"I've got whiskey. You'll need it." Alice pulled a bottle out of the colorful Vera Bradley bag dangling from her arm.

"Oh!" I appraised it and smiled. "Well, thank you."

"I told you not to bring whiskey, Alice," Doris scolded. "Sorry. She doesn't bake." The last phrase was said in a whisper as if not baking was a mortal sin best not mentioned.

Shaking my head, the first smile in days started on my lips. "No. It's fine. Really. I appreciate it, Alice."

"It's the good stuff. Laphroaig Single Malt Whiskey. Cask strength. This will take the edge right off." She set it beside the muffins and smiled, revealing perfect white teeth fit for someone of her beauty. Even at her advanced age, with her impeccable style, sparkling green eyes, and fashionable shoulder-length silky hair, she likely still turned heads of men half her age. She looked considerably younger than the other two widows standing in my living room, but from the unnatural smoothness of her skin, I suspected it was more medical enhancement than her being closer to my age. But the longer I looked at her, the more I questioned her age, now wondering if perhaps she was younger than me.

"I appreciate you all stopping to check in on me. I'm surprised we've never met, though I'll admit I've seen you around. You ladies walk around the block together some afternoons."

"It's part of our widow's club. We help each other stay in shape... or try, I suppose," Marge said, gesturing to her ample belly. "I eat a lot of lasagnas. I'm Italian, and my mom likes to cook."

"And I love to bake, so that's where this is from." Doris wiggled her large hips and giggled.

"I drink." Alice shrugged.

There wasn't an ounce of fat to jiggle on her fit figure. I wasn't overweight, and I could still turn a head or two, but standing next to that leggy creature had me thinking more walking would do me good. Or perhaps more drinking if that's what was doing it for her.

Rolling her eyes, Marge impaled her with a look. "You even drink *on* our walks, Alice. Don't think we don't know what's in those 'sports drinks' you won't let us try."

Scoffing, Alice returned her scowl. "Only because I don't want your cooties, Marge."

"I don't have cooties. If anyone has cooties, with the way you carry on with your pool boy, it's you!"

"Don't forget the gardener. And my yoga instructor." A sinister smile curved her lips and caused Marge to widen her eyes, though with the size of them in their natural state, it was surprising they could get any larger.

Doris stomped her foot. "Ladies! Behave. You're scaring poor Sylvie here."

She wasn't wrong.

"May we?" Doris asked, gesturing to my couch. Glad she waited for permission this time, I nodded and followed them to the living room.

They sat down and perused me once again with sympathetic gazes.

"I hope you don't mind us barging in, but we wanted to check on you. You're one of us now. We widows need to stick together." Doris touched my leg, giving it a light squeeze. "There will be all sorts of things you'll need to learn. How to pay bills. Figuring out life insurance. Garbage day. Changing light bulbs. It's a lot, but lucky for you, we have it all figured out. All you need to do is ask!"

She pressed her glasses up on her nose, and I realized then who she reminded me of. My grandma Mildred. The glasses were similar, but it was the hairstyle that reminded me of her most. Soft grey hair pulled into a loose bun perched on top of her head was the only way I'd ever seen my grandma wear her hair. Today, as well as the few times I'd seen Doris around the neighborhood, she'd styled her hair exactly the same way.

"How sweet of you all to think of me. But actually, I've been doing most of that stuff on my own for some time. Bruce hated the day to day stuff, so I handled the finances, and he wasn't particularly good at house projects either. I learned long ago how to take care of myself, but I appreciate the gesture."

Doris slapped her leg. "Well, what a modern woman you are! When Harold died five years ago, I was lost. He was the first husband of ours to go, and it took me months to figure things out. That's why I've made it my mission to make sure every Wilder Widow gets the support she needs straight away. We just want to help."

"Well, I don't know how to do any of that stuff, but I have people if you need them," Alice said. "Lots of people."

"Just don't sleep with them like Alice does," Marge taunted.

"Stop it!" Doris swatted a hand at them then turned back to me with her sweet smile. "You'll get used to them. I promise we are a lot of fun to have around. And we could use a new face in our group."

Glancing at their eager faces, my mind raced with a storm of conflicting thoughts. *Do I even want to join this group of strange women?* My first thought was no, but when I contemplated the lonely days stretched before me, I considered it. My life here hadn't exactly turned out like I'd planned after Bruce moved us here from the city for his big promotion. I'd left my friends and marketing career with the goal of starting my own boutique marketing firm here. Those plans had gone up in flames when his health declined shortly after the move. My aspirations got swallowed up while I took care of him, and I'd barely made a single friend since we'd arrived here. Now I had no company to run, no friends to hang out with, and my daughter, Rachel, lived across the country in L.A.

"We meet three times a week and alternate houses," Doris went on. "Though with you in the group, it will be four times a week. Our schedules are flexible since none of us work or have husbands or children at home for that matter. So, let's plan Monday at Marge's, Wednesday at my house, Friday at Alice's, and let's do Sunday after church here."

Struggling to keep my jaw from sagging at her assumption, I bit my lip while I felt the weight of three sets of eyes boring into me. Not wanting to be rude but unsure if I wanted any part of this, I nodded my head.

"Wonderful! You'll need to have treats and coffee for our meetings. Alice will bring her own booze." Doris gave her the side-eye, and Alice just shrugged.

I kept nodding to avoid hurting their feelings, but now I wished I'd shaken my head instead. Although I did miss having female friends to hang out with, spending four days a week with these women might end up being more than I prepared for.

Already planning the numerous excuses I could use to get out of our meetings, I forced a smile. "I look forward to it, ladies."

"We Wilder Widows need to stick together!" Doris grinned. Her enthusiasm labeled her the leader of this crew, and it made sense since she'd been the one to hunt down Marge and Alice like a widow-sniffing bloodhound. I wondered if, like myself, they'd originally wanted nothing to do with it, but Doris's insistence finally wore them down. Whatever the reason they stayed together, it seemed I was one of them... at least for now. If this went the way I imagined it going, I would need to fade out of the group sooner than later.

"I really appreciate you all stopping by, and I look forward to getting to know you more. But I'm exhausted from the past few days, and I think I need to lie down for a bit."

"Of course." Alice stood quickly. "We'll get out of your hair."

"We completely understand what it's like to bury a husband." Marge rose, but at a much slower pace than agile Alice.

"Say no more." Doris touched my leg again before joining them. "I left our numbers and addresses in the basket with the muffins. Call if you need anything. Since tomorrow is Friday, we meet at Alice's house at eleven in the morning. It's the biggest house on the lane at the end of the cul-de-sac. You can't miss it. We hope you can make it."

"I look forward to it," I lied.

They started toward the door, and then Doris stopped and turned back. "Are you sure you're okay alone? I know I didn't want to be alone for even a second after Harold died, so I'm happy to stay the night if you need some company."

"Thank you for the offer, but I'll be all right."

"Are you sure? We can have a slumber party." Her eyes lit up. "Maybe the girls could stay too! A widow's welcome to our newest member!"

Marge grabbed her arm and pulled her forward. "Cripes, Doris! Leave the poor woman in peace."

Stifling my laugh, I followed behind them. "Really, I'm fine. My daughter stayed the last few nights and flew home yesterday. Last night was my first night alone, but I managed fine. It's time for me to adjust to my new normal."

"It takes a little while, but you'll get used to sleeping alone." Alice grabbed Doris's other arm and tugged her toward the door, then paused and peeked over her shoulder. "Unless you don't want to. I've got people for that as well." She waggled her eyebrows, and I finally let a little laughter escape.

"Thank you for coming by, ladies. I'll see you all tomorrow."

"Goodbye!" they echoed while they stepped outside. I closed the door behind them and stood pressing against it for a few moments before exhaling a breath and walking away. When I passed my bay window, I saw the three of them with linked arms walking away down the street. An odd assortment of women, to be sure, and I didn't know how I fit in yet. But when I turned back to my empty living room,

I decided there was no harm in meeting with them a few times. I could always find a way out if it turned out they were intolerable.

Though I'd used the exhaustion excuse to get them out of the house, it wasn't a lie. Burying your husband *was* a lot to handle, both emotionally as well as the logistics of planning everything. Rachel and Bruce had never been terribly close, so she'd handled his death without a ton of emotion, and with her job in upper management, she'd jumped right in to help organize everything from flowers to choosing his casket. But now that he was gone and buried, the hospice workers cleared out, and Rachel and my old friends from the city safely back home, I suddenly had nothing to do but rest.

After letting the quiet settle over me once again, I started through the house. Memories of our life met me with each step I took. Photos on the wall of us with Rachel. That trip he and I took to Hawaii. Our wedding photo. His football memorabilia from when he had won that championship in college; the same night we'd met while he celebrated the win in that bar down on Sealy Street. Our forty years of life together were now only frozen moments of time forever encapsulated in the mementos we'd created. Dragging my fingertips across the trophy, I kept moving while I tried to clear away the fog that had settled over my life these last three years. The three years we'd spent battling his cancer.

Everything looked different now. Our home was no longer a makeshift hospital with nurses and machines scattered throughout the living room where Bruce had spent his last few months. It looked like it did before he got cancer and our lives turned upside down. The floral couch I picked out for our thirtieth anniversary was back in place after I'd stored it to make room for his hospice bed. His La-Z-Boy, the one he'd spent the better part of a decade in, sat alone in the corner where I'd condemned it because of its hideous clashing brown upholstered fabric. We'd argued over it for weeks before our armistice when I'd allowed it in the living room, but not within ten feet of my beautiful couch.

While I looked over the room now resembling a more normal space, I noticed the crooked coffee table. I walked over and tugged the edge to straighten it back out. When I stepped back to examine the room, it appeared as if everything else was back in place. Nothing was missing... except Bruce.

I walked over to Bruce's La-Z-Boy and stood over it, remembering how many times I'd stood right here holding his beer or snacks, sometimes with my hand on my hips demanding he get up and take me for a walk or out to dinner. Usually, he'd waved me aside to get out of the way of the TV, and I'd stormed off in a huff threatening to move us back to the city where I had friends and a career to entertain me. But he'd ignored my pleas, and I'd never made good on my threats. Now he was gone, but that damned ugly chair was still here.

Sliding my hand across the worn corduroy fabric of his recliner, I moved around it then lowered myself into it. Since I hated the sight of it, I'd always refused to sit in it, but while I leaned back against the overstuffed headrest, I realized now why he'd wanted it so badly. Damned if it wasn't the most comfortable chair I'd ever sat in.

While I sunk into the cushions, I closed my eyes and let the tension from the last few days, and months... and even years since his diagnosis, slip away. Like a gentle hug, the chair eased away the anxiety of being on my own. I reached down and pulled the lever, and the footrest popped up. As I reclined, a little groan escaped my lips. For years I'd promised on the day he died I'd have this hideous thing hauled away, but perhaps I'd keep it after all.

Pulling the afghan blanket over my body, I let the exhaustion take me while I drifted off. Visions of my life with Bruce flashed through my mind while the darkness came, but the last thing I saw before falling asleep were the three faces of the Wilder Widows, and I wondered what tomorrow may bring.

CHAPTER TWO

"And *that* is how you make a chain edge cast-on." Doris held her knitted square up like a trophy. "See? Elastic but still firm."

Alice, Marge, and I sat across from her in my living room, each holding our piles of yarn and knitting needles in our laps. I looked down at my own attempt after trying to keep up with Doris's tutorial, but it looked nothing like her example. Glancing over to Marge's work, my eyebrows shot to my hairline. Mine at least resembled the example while Marge appeared to have knit an ugly knot. She caught my expression and furrowed her already sagging brow.

"What? It's close," she grumbled, then jutted her chin at mine. "And it's not like yours is good, either."

Hers wasn't even close to Doris's perfect technique, but she was right... neither was mine. We both looked over to Alice but saw the knitting needle and yarn untouched in her lap. Her hands were otherwise occupied by the martini she'd brought over in a thermos and poured into one of my glasses.

She set aside the untouched yarn and took a drink before answering our stares. "I'll have one of the staff do it for me later."

"Alice! It's not supposed to be for your *staff* to do. It's for you to learn!" Doris shook her knitting needle at her.

"If I want something knitted, I'll just buy it."

"But then you won't learn how." Doris held up her example again. "Don't you want to learn how to do this?"

"Not even a little." Alice scoffed and poured more of the martini from the silver thermos into her dwindling glass.

With a huff, Doris sat back. "Fine. Forget it. I give up. I've tried and tried, but you just aren't interested. No more knitting lessons."

"Whatever will we do?" Marge deadpanned.

Doris scrunched up her face and shoved her project into the small yarn basket she'd brought with her. It was smaller than a purse and had a hand-knit cover over it with a lace and scalloped trim she told us she'd custom created. Making our own matching yarn baskets was next on our lists of projects, and something none of us had any use for or desire to make.

This was my second week of Wilder Widows meetings and the third time they'd been at my house. Each time we got together, we filled the several hours we met with projects and time-sucks. With Doris in charge, we knitted and baked. Each time Marge was at the helm, we watched her ancient mother make Italian food, then sat around the table and ate it. At least at Alice's house, we occupied our hours with massages and pedicures. Once again, it was my turn to entertain, but I had nothing to offer. I didn't knit or bake. There was no one to rub us into comas. Other than marketing, I had no artistic talents or special skills, and there was no sense in teaching these ladies the art of closing a marketing deal. So, with my lack of skills to show, Doris stepped up with knitting.

Again.

While we sat in bored silence staring at the ceiling, I struggled to find the words to tell them this Wilder Widows club wasn't for me. Knitting, baking, and walking around the neighborhood was not how I envisioned spending my golden years. The money I had inherited from my parents, and the money Bruce and I had saved, was more than enough to keep me comfortable for the rest of my days, but I never imagined being retired at sixty. I'd always thought I'd be a career woman until at least my seventies. But now, the thought of starting a new career didn't inspire me the way it once did, and I felt lost with what I wanted to do with all my newfound free time. But the one thing I knew is this wasn't it.

"See. If we don't knit, there's nothing to do," Doris challenged after the silence went on too long.

"There is plenty to do other than knit, Doris," Marge said.

"Like what?" I asked, genuinely interested.

Silence settled over us while everyone contemplated the answer.

"Nothing. That's what's left for us. Nothing," Alice finally said. "I've got my money, my boy toys, and still… none of it matters. I'm bored senseless."

"It's just me and my mom. She cooks, and I eat." Marge slumped forward. "I've got nothing to do either."

"I miss having children and a husband to care for," Doris answered, and a slight quiver shook her lower lip.

I wasn't even sure what I missed, but I knew this wasn't the answer to filling the void. "Is this really it for us?" I gestured to the knitting basket. "Our husbands die, and we spend the rest of our days visiting each other's houses, knitting, and struggling to find something to do?"

"What's wrong with knitting?" Doris stiffened up.

"It's boring as hell," Marge answered, mirroring my thoughts.

"Well, I happen to like it," Doris spat back.

"Good for you, Doris." Alice rolled her eyes. "So knit. But for God's sake, stop trying to force us to do it."

"Force you? I was just trying to give you something to do!"

"We'll do anything as long as it isn't knitting," Alice said, then took another sip.

"Well, fine! I guess I'll just go home and knit alone. Excuse *me* for thinking we needed to be here for each other." Doris started to stand, but I rose first and stopped her.

"I wasn't trying to offend anyone. Please don't go, Doris."

Stopping when my hand closed around her shoulder, she turned back to me. "I was just trying to help."

"I know you were, Doris. Sit. Please. I'm sorry I offended you. It's just... this isn't what I expected to do with my retirement. I'm not really sure what I had planned, but I know it involved more excitement than knitting."

Following my instructions, she settled back down onto the sofa and clutched her knitting basket to her chest.

"This really is boring, ladies." Marge sat back, crossing her arms. "I mean, I appreciate having you in my life, but Sylvie is right. There must be more to life than what we're doing. We're not twenty anymore, but we're far from dead."

"Damn straight," Alice agreed. "I should at least be traveling or something."

"Why aren't you?" I asked, genuinely curious.

Alice opened her mouth to answer but closed it and shrugged.

With a snort, Marge snickered. "Because she'd miss me too much. That's why."

"Oh yeah. That's it." Alice scoffed.

"So why?" I asked again.

"I guess I don't want to travel alone." She paused, and her voice softened as she finished. "And I don't have any friends who would go with me. Other than you ladies, I don't really have anyone in my life."

As I watched the hardness in her eyes soften for a split second, I felt sad for her. Rich, beautiful, and yet still left unfulfilled in her life. I didn't want to end up like that. I wanted to use this time in my life to do amazing things.

Just what they were, I had no idea.

"See. Because she'd miss me." Marge's smirk tightened.

"Well, there must be more than this," I said. "We just need to put our heads together and figure it out."

"Like what?" Doris asked.

"I'm not sure." I shrugged. "But something."

They stared at me with anticipation as I sat down beside Doris.

"It's funny. I spent my whole life raising my daughter, taking care of my husband, and working my ass off to have enough money to retire and live the good life. But now that I'm here, I feel like I missed my life. All those years spent in service to others, and now that it's finally my time with nothing standing in my way, I'm not utilizing the freedom."

"I hear you, sister." Alice raised her glass. "I had dreams—big ones. But then the little bun in the oven pushed them aside, and I never got to live the life I wanted. And now it's too late." She sighed and downed her martini.

"I certainly wasn't planning on being a suburban housewife," Marge said. "I had big dreams myself. Adventures I wanted to go on. But, with Percy's war injuries, and then raising our daughter, we didn't ever go on any."

"Bruce and I traveled every so often, but between our jobs and raising Rachel, we didn't get out to see the world like I'd always wanted."

"Am I the only one who enjoyed just being a wife and mother?" Doris asked. "I never yearned for anything else. I really loved it. All of it."

"It's not that I didn't like being a mother," I answered, "but between being a wife, a mother, and my career, I didn't get a lot of time for just myself to find things I'm truly passionate about. Now I feel like I'm running out of time."

"Running out of time?" Doris laughed. "You're what, fifty-five or sixty?"

I nodded. "I just turned sixty-one."

"You're like a spring chicken! I'm over ten years older than you," she said. "I'm surprised you aren't clucking instead of speaking."

"A babe in the cradle," Marge added, shaking her head. "What I wouldn't give to be sixty-one again. Things really start to go downhill fast once you hit seventy. Everything aches."

"I'm not a spring chicken." I snorted.

"You're not too old to have some fun, Sylvie. I still have fun and," Alice leaned forward and whispered, "don't tell anyone, but I'm older than you."

We all faked a gasp, and Marge clutched her chest. "Say it ain't so, Alice! You're not forty like you've been telling everyone?"

Alice swept a look across the three of us as she lifted an eyebrow. "I can pass for forty."

"In the dark," Marge taunted.

Narrowing her eyes at Marge, Alice continued. "None of us are too old to have some fun."

"We're not all gonna bang the pool boy, Alice." Marge rolled her eyes.

"Don't say bang! Disgusting!" Doris scolded and covered her ears.

"That's not what I meant." Alice shook her head. "Not that I don't recommend it." She waggled her brows.

"Take your hands off your ears, Doris!" Marge shouted so she could hear. Doris pulled her hands down. "You can listen again. We're not still talking about banging."

Her hands shot back to her ears.

"Oh, cripes." Marge waved at her. "Uncover your ears! No more banging talk, you prude!"

Doris peeled one hand from her ear, pausing to make sure the sex talk was over.

"How did you ever manage to make six kids, Doris? The turkey baster?" Alice tipped her thermos upside down, but no more clear liquid poured out. "Shit. I'm out."

"The regular way. With love." Doris lifted her chin.

"You banged. That's how you got babies." Marge laughed.

"Gross!" Doris cupped her hands over her ears again.

"Bang bang bangity bang bang *bang!*" Alice shouted loud enough there was no way Doris's hands blocked out the assault.

Giving up, Doris removed her hands and sat back. "You're all going to hell."

"At least we'll have each other." Alice smiled and reached out, squeezing Marge's hand.

"We'll be warm and toasty. Together." Marge blew Alice a kiss before their sinister laughter merged.

"Laugh now. It won't be funny when the flames of hell are licking at your feet."

"Oh, don't you worry, dear Doris. I'll seduce the devil, and he'll give Marge and me a penthouse suite. I'll be the reigning queen of hell in no time flat." Alice smirked and crossed her legs the opposite way, drawing attention to the lean, long lines that stretched up to her A-line skirt. I'd have killed for legs like that even back when I was twenty. Knowing her legs were one hell of an asset, she rarely covered them up, insisting on skirts and dresses all the time.

"It's *hell*, Alice. Your worst nightmare. You'll be short, fat, and will have a face that not even a mother could love." Doris returned the smirk when she saw the confidence falter in Alice's expression.

"I've been in hell. 'Nam. Whatever's down there will be a walk in the park." Marge pointed at her feet.

"You were in Vietnam?" I asked, startled by the statement.

"Yes, mam. First Lieutenant Margherita Moretti at your service. It's where I met my sweet Percy."

She'd only mentioned her husband, Percy, a few times, but never had she mentioned her time served in war. Interested to hear more, I leaned forward, pressing my elbows into my knees. "If you don't want to talk about it, I completely respect that, but I'm curious what you did over there."

"Two tours, which was two years, I served as a nurse. A lot of that was right in the thick of the fighting."

"Was it scary?" I asked.

Blowing out a puff of air, Marge nodded. "Terrifying. But with my nursing degree, it was my privilege to do what I could, so I enlisted in the Army. 'Nam itself was hell, but I loved the thrill of adventure and even the occasional bullet whizzing past. I miss that rush. I never wanted to be a boring old lady."

"Hear, hear." Alice lifted her empty glass then frowned. "I'm all about skipping the knitting and having some girl talk, but if we're going to chat about our pasts, I will need something else in here."

Excited to hear more about Marge's life, and perhaps have a little fun, I tried to mentally catalog my alcohol. "I'm afraid I don't keep much booze around. Bruce had beer, but after he got sick, he couldn't drink, so I stopped too out of respect."

"Well, shit." Alice's frown deepened.

"Good. You should try water, Alice. It's better for you." Doris gestured to her own glass.

"There's plenty of water in vodka." Alice arched a brow.

"I could go for a drink myself. What about that whiskey Alice brought you?" Marge asked, and three sets of eyes turned to me.

I'd forgotten about the bottle Alice had delivered during their first visit. "You're right! I still have it!"

"Well, then. What are we waiting for?" Alice grinned.

After looking to Marge and getting her confirming nod, I glanced over to Doris. She pursed her thin lips tight, and worry lines deepened on her face.

"Do you want some, Doris?" I asked.

"I don't think I should." She shook her head.

"Oh, come on. Do it!" Alice begged.

"Do it, Doris. Do it." Marge grinned.

She shook her head harder. "I don't think so."

"Come on, you sissy. You know you want the whiskey. It will be fun!" Marge kept on.

"I don't like peer pressure!" Doris looked ready to crumble beneath the taunting stares.

"I'll just pour you a glass, and you can drink it or not drink it. Your choice." I walked to the kitchen and found the bottle in the cupboard where I'd stashed it. After pouring four glasses of whiskey, I carried them back on a platter and set on the coffee table. Alice snatched hers up without hesitation, and Marge followed suit. Doris and I exchanged a nervous glance before I plucked mine up as well.

"It's been ages since I've drank, much less had whiskey." I gave the glass a sniff. A shudder traveled up my spine when the strong smell of alcohol permeated my nostrils.

"I've never had whiskey," Doris admitted, staring at it like the devil himself sat on the edge of the glass taunting her.

"Go on, Doris. It won't kill you." Unfazed by the straight whiskey, Alice gulped down a swig.

Marge and I took a simultaneous sip, both of our faces puckering while we choked down the fiery liquid.

"Cripes, that's strong!" Marge sputtered.

"It's pure whiskey. What'd you expect?" Alice laughed and took another swig like a pro.

"Wow." I exhaled a breath ripe with whiskey. The warmth traveled through me, and just as Alice predicted when she gave it to me, it already started taking the edge off.

The three of us stared at Doris while she shifted on the couch. "I don't know, girls. I don't think it's a good idea."

"Doris. We can only knit and walk so much. Let's have some fun!" Marge leaned forward, pushing the glass toward her. "Our husbands died. Our lives are nearly over. We earned this shit."

Biting her lip, Doris reached out and slid the glass into her hands. After one sniff, she fanned her nose and pulled a face. "I can't! It smells like gasoline!"

"That works in a pinch." Alice smiled. "This is much smoother."

"Go ahead, Doris. You won't die." Marge took another sip of her own, this time masking the bitter face I knew she was dying to make.

Plugging her nose with one hand, Doris closed her eyes and lifted the glass to her lips. We watched with bated breath while she took a large swig. The moment it passed her lips, her eyes shot open, and she coughed, nearly spitting out the fiery whiskey I knew burned a trail down her throat.

"Geez Louise!" she shouted.

"Atta girl, Doris!" Marge said.

"Well done." I smiled and lifted my glass in a toast. "To the Wilder Widows."

"To the Wilder Widows!" They mirrored, and our glasses clinked together.

CHAPTER THREE

"Holy cripes, I'm hammered," Marge said, reclining on the sofa. The mostly empty glass dangled in her fingertips, threatening to tip out the last remains of the whiskey.

"I feel funny." Doris teetered beside her, a hiccup punctuating the sentence.

Squinting one eye to see better, I looked to Alice who seemed the only one unaffected by the half-empty bottle of whiskey sitting on the coffee table. "I feel so relaxed." I sighed. "It's been ages since I've been this relaxed."

"I told you girls whiskey was the answer. *Now* I'm into these Wilder Widows meetings." Alice grinned.

"I vote we do this for every meeting." Marge matched her smile.

"I don't think I've ever been drunk before," Doris said.

"Ever?" I asked, turning my squint toward her.

"No. I had wine on occasion and a few sips of beer once or twice, but I've never gotten drunk. My body is a temple, and I don't think the temple should be drunk."

"I think the best way to honor the temple is to bathe it in booze." Alice waved a hand over her impressive figure. "Like an offering to the Gods."

Snickering, I took another sip of my whiskey. "I've been drunk many times, but it's been a while. I forgot how fun it is. This kind of reminds me of high school when my girlfriends and I snuck some of my dad's brandy and got drunk and told each other secrets."

"Oh! Secrets!" Alice lit up. "Let's do that!"

"Do what?" Marge asked.

"Tell each other a secret."

Doris shook her head. "I'm not sure about that. Secrets are secrets for a reason."

Alice scoffed. "It will be like our Wilder Widows whiskey confessional. Like church, Doris. Just think of us as priests. Wouldn't God want you to be honest?" She arched a brow, and Doris bit her lip while she processed. "I'll even go first."

"You will?" I asked while I tried to think of what secret I wanted to share.

Alice leaned forward, and we followed suit, excited to hear what she had to say.

"When I was younger, I was a showgirl in Las Vegas. And one night after a show, a big Hollywood celebrity invited me to his table. You probably know of him... Harry Hayes."

Of course, I knew who Harry Hayes was. He was the heartthrob I dreamed about when I went to bed in my teens—me and every other teenage girl on the planet.

"Yes, yes. And then you slept with him," Marge said and sat back. "This isn't a secret. You tell this story to anyone who will listen."

Narrowing her eyes, Alice scoffed and sat back. "Well, it's a good story."

"A *secret,* Alice. That's the rule." Marge challenged.

"I have no secrets. I'm an open book." Alice crossed her arms. "You probably don't either."

Marge glared. "I've got secrets."

With a scoff, Alice rolled her eyes. "Like what? You wore a skirt once?"

Marge took a breath and then slammed the rest of her whiskey. When she set the empty glass down, she took a deep breath and blew it out. "I think I'm a lesbian."

"What?" Our three voices merged into one shout while we all whipped around to look at Marge.

"Yep. I think I'm a lesbian."

"You *think*?" Alice asked, her eyes as wide as mine. "Isn't that something you should *know*?"

Marge only shrugged. "I never acted on my feelings, so I can't say for certain, but I definitely think I may be a lesbian."

Doris clutched her chest. "But what about Percy? You can't be a... lesbian," she whispered the last word like she'd head straight to hell with the rest of us if she said it too loud. "You were *married,* Marge!"

"Yeah. I think Percy batted for the other team as well."

"Double beards?" Alice nearly spit out her drink with the explosive laugh. "You two were double beards?"

"What's a double beard?" Doris asked.

"A beard is a woman a gay man uses to make the world think he's straight," I said, still struggling to conceal my shock. Turning back to Marge, my eyes widened. "Did you both know about the other?"

Marge shook her head. "No. I only suspected. We met in 'Nam, and I'm pretty sure he had a thing for boys. But he proposed, and with a face like this I knew I wouldn't be getting another proposal, so I said yes."

"But, you had a *baby!*" Doris was barely hanging on.

"We did it. Twice. That was all it took to make a baby."

"Wait a minute." Alice closed her eyes while she let the sentence resonate. "Are you trying to tell me that in the last, what, fifty years, you've only had sex *twice*?"

Marge nodded.

Alice feigned passing out before sitting straight back up. "How are you even alive? I would *die* without regular sex!"

"Well, considering she's a lesbian and not attracted to men, I can see why doing it wouldn't be high on her priorities," I said.

"No interest whatsoever," Marge agreed. "And neither did Percy. We did it once on our wedding night and once when we decided we wanted to have a baby. Lucky for us, we got knocked up on the first try."

The color started to return to Doris's ashen face. "Heavens to Betsy, Marge! What was your marriage like?"

"Best friends." Her gruff demeanor disappeared behind the sweet smile remembering Percy induced. "We were the best of friends."

"So you, a lesbian, married a gay man, and you two just lived like roommates?" I asked.

"Well, I'm not sure I'm a lesbian. Maybe I'm just asexual."

"I don't believe in asexual." Alice scoffed. "Everyone likes sex. You just haven't found the right person yet."

"I'm not a lesbian, and I didn't like it. I never even had one of those... you know," Doris whispered.

"What?" Our voices rose once again in echoed shock.

"What do you mean you didn't like it?" I asked. "You never had an orgasm? Never?"

Deep crimson crept down her cheeks while she shook her head. "I'm not comfortable talking about... you know. Just forget I said anything."

"Too late now, Doris." Alice grinned like the Cheshire cat. "Spill."

"I'm not spilling!" Doris shrunk beneath her stare. "Let's just focus on Marge. She's the lesbian!"

The statement sent our heads swiveling back to Marge.

"I'm not *sure* if I'm a lesbian. I just suspect."

"Well, are you attracted to me?" Alice asked, leaning forward to give her a seductive stare.

Marge puckered her face. "No."

"Then you're not a lesbian," Alice stated with certainty.

"How do you figure?" I asked.

Her manicured hand swept her lithe body. "Well, hello! Because look at me. If she liked the ladies, she'd certainly want some of this."

Laughing, I shook my head. "That's not accurate, Alice. Just because you look like that doesn't mean she's instantly attracted to you."

"I was the first time I saw you." Marge shrugged.

Alice sat forward, and her face illuminated from the admission. "You were?"

"Then you talked, and that fantasy went out the window."

"Go to hell, Marge." Alice crossed her arms and lifted her chin.

Doris, Marge, and I burst into laughter while Alice feigned her anger.

Leaning forward, Doris whispered. "So, how does one know for sure if they're, you know... a lesbian."

"I'm not sure. I never really thought about acting on it," Marge said. "I had feelings for some ladies when I was younger, and in that day and age, it wasn't acceptable, so when I met Percy, I decided to just get married and pretend they'd never happened."

"That's sad, Marge," I said. "You never really got to find out if you are a lesbian, and maybe could have found a wonderful woman just perfect for you."

"I'm not sad about it. Percy was my best friend. Even though the romance wasn't there, I wouldn't have traded a second of our life together for a tryst with a beautiful woman."

I sighed at her statement, and this time it was my eyes brimming with tears. "That's beautiful, Marge. You two were lucky to have each other."

The waterworks started, and the three of them stared at me with scrunched brows. Every time I tried to choke back the tears, they only came out harder.

"Now look what you did. Your lesbianism made her cry!" Doris huffed.

"No." Shaking my head, I wiped my eyes. "It's not that."

"What's wrong, Sylvie?" Marge reached over and rubbed my back.

While I struggled to shove the secret I wanted to scream back into my mouth, the whiskey took hold of my tongue. "I hated him. Bruce. I hated him so much, and I was happy when he died."

The moment the truth tumbled out, I wanted to shove it back in. For almost forty years I carried it in silence, a weight that nearly crushed me to death.

"Now *that's* a secret." Alice let out a long-exhaled sigh. "You hated him? Really?"

Nodding, I sniffled and peered up at them, terrified to see the looks of shame I was certain would bore through me. They blinked at me in stunned silence.

"I shouldn't have said that. I didn't mean it." I tried to backpedal.

"Yes, you did." Marge touched my back. "It's okay to say it."

"If you hated him so much, why did you stay?" Alice brushed a stray piece of hair from her bulging eyes.

It was too late to take it back, and saying it out loud for the first time in my life lifted the weight I'd shouldered alone and carried for Rachel. "I wanted my daughter to have the family life she deserved. And by the time she left for school, I'd grown complacent. Then we moved here. With no friends and no career to keep me occupied away from him, his volatile personality became even more apparent. I knew I couldn't stay married to such a miserable person any longer. But when I finally gathered the courage to leave him, he got cancer. Then I was stuck. Who leaves their dying husband?"

"Shitty luck." Marge sucked the air through her teeth.

The sentence caused me to snort, and I nodded. "It *was* shitty luck. And it's been three years since he got diagnosed. Three long years living with the man I couldn't stand, a man who's constant complaining and temper only worsened with the illness. Three years watching him deteriorate and praying for the end, then cursing myself for wishing he would die. Three long years."

Doris finally closed her slack jaw. "I'm so sorry, Sylvie. That must have been awful for you."

Nodding, I wiped the last tear drying on my cheek. "Yeah. It's been a long, miserable life with that crotchety man. And now I'm here, sixty-one years old and alone."

"I never really loved my husband either." Alice shrugged. "His money, yes. But him? No. Though he wasn't a bad man, I just didn't love him. He was no Harry Hayes."

"I loved my Percy." Marge sighed.

"Yeah, but like a friend, you lesbo." Alice rolled her eyes. "It's different."

Tears glistened over Doris's eyes. "Well, I loved Harold. With all my heart."

"You're lucky, Doris," I said. "I wish I could have felt that way about Bruce. But I was stuck with him."

"Yeah, kids now these days have it easy with their drive-through divorces and their gay-loving ways." Marge scrunched up her nose. "It wasn't like that for us. You got married to someone of the opposite sex," she said, pointing her finger for emphasis, "and you stayed married. Period. Nowadays, I'd be out of the closet, Sylvie would be divorced, Alice would be a swinger, and Doris... well, Doris would still be Doris."

Doris just shrugged and nodded.

"I was a swinger a couple times." Alice smirked. "Fun times."

Blowing out a breath, I sat back. "There were many times after divorce became more acceptable that I thought about leaving, but I stayed anyway. And then when I was finally ready... cancer."

"Well, now they're all gone, and all that's left is us." Alice took a swig straight out of the bottle. "Just us. Bored old ladies who let their entire lives pass them by."

"I still can't believe this is it for me," Marge grumbled. "Getting drunk with a bunch of old ladies. The adventurous life I had planned is gone. Gone."

"Don't say that, Marge." I tried to comfort her with a touch, but the whiskey made me miss, and I patted the air instead. "We aren't too old. Other women our age still get out there and live their best lives. We've just become complacent in ours, but I'm determined to find fun stuff to do. No more knitting."

"I love knitting," Doris pouted, hiccupping again.

"You knit your little heart out, Doris. That's the point," I said. "These are the golden years. We should be able to do whatever the hell we want. We earned it."

"We *did* earn it!" Marge raised a triumphant fist before her arm went limp and fell back at her side. "All those years living as housewives and mothers, and what do we have to show for it? Nothing, that's what. Now it's *our* turn to do what we want, damn it! Our turn!"

"Amen, Marge. Amen." Alice hoisted the bottle.

"I don't feel like I missed anything," Doris slurred. "My whole life, I wanted a family. A husband. Grandkids. I never even thought of another life."

Marge grunted. "But now what, Doris? They're all gone. Your kids live across the country. They come to visit with your grandkids once or twice a year. And your husband is dead."

Doris's eyes glistened while she stared at Marge in disbelief. Her chin puckered as she fought the tears.

Alice tossed a pillow and smacked Marge in the head. "Christ, Marge! Way to destroy Doris's cheery outlook on life!"

Marge looked to Doris, who had a single tear dripping down her flushed cheek.

"Well, it's true." Marge shrugged.

"It is true," Doris whispered, her voice shaking with the weight of her admission. "They're gone—all of them. And I have nothing left. I'm all alone." The sobs shook her body. "And sometimes... sometimes when I'm feeling lazy, I buy baked goods at the market and pass them off as my own!" The sobs turned to wails.

"You what?" we echoed.

"My secret." She sobbed. "It's that I'm a fraud. A fraud!"

"The scandal!" Alice teased. "Doris, you are a treacherous thing."

"Going straight to hell with us." Marge shook her head, and Doris's sob deepened.

Alice shot Marge a look. "Now look what you did!"

"No," Doris said between sniffles. "She's right. You're all right. I'm a fraud, and we gave up all our good years in service of others, and now they've just abandoned us. We're alone. Old. It's over."

"It's not over." I reached over and rubbed her knee. "We won't *let* it be over. There's no way I'm going out like this, rotting away the rest of my days after I gave up my whole life married to that asshole."

"So, what do we do?" Alice asked.

"What we should have been doing all these years. Whatever the hell we want!" Slapping my thigh, I stood up. "We are each going to write down one thing we wish we would have done and put it there." I jutted a finger to Doris's knitting basket. "Then we make a pact that no matter what is on that note, we help each other do it."

"An adventure!" Marge's eyes bugged out even more. "I want an adventure!"

Teetering while I tried to stand, I pointed to her. "Yes! An adventure. Exactly. What do you say ladies? Are you in?"

"Anything we want?" Alice arched a brow.

"Anything." I grinned.

"I'm in!" Alice set the whiskey down, and we all turned to Doris. "Doris? You in?"

While she chewed on her bottom lip, her eyes darted between us.

"Well?" Marge leaned in.

"What the heck! Let's do it!" Doris clasped her hand over her mouth and stifled her giggle.

Without waiting, I stumbled to the kitchen and grabbed the notepad and pen I used to write my grocery list. Ripping off a piece of paper for each of them, I passed them out, and one by one, we wrote down our wishes.

"Ready?" I asked, folding up my own.

"Ready," they mirrored, each clutching their own note.

Grabbing Doris's knitting basket, I dumped out the contents onto the floor.

"Hey! Where am I supposed to put those?" Her face scrunched while she looked at her beloved knitting supplies in a heap on the floor.

"I know where you can put them." Marge waggled her eyebrows, causing Doris to scoff and sit back.

"Alright, alright." I waved my hand between them then set the empty knitting basket on the coffee table between us.

With a glance at each other, we all smiled and dropped our wishes in. I grabbed the lid and put it over the top, and we all sat back and stared at it.

"Today we start living our lives. The lives we were meant to live." Crossing my arms, I pursed my lips and raked them all with my confident gaze. Today I was going to start living again.

CHAPTER FOUR

My head pounded like a marching band had set up shop in it. Hangovers of this magnitude were a thing of the past. A college staple I hadn't felt in decades. While I struggled to open my eyes, I heard a groan behind me. Then I noticed the weight pressing down on my legs.

"What the?" When I blinked open my eyes, I saw Doris sprawled across my legs, our two bodies filling every inch of my couch. A long string of drool dangled from the corner of her mouth, inching its way toward my pants. As I glanced around my living room, flashes of the night flooded back as I made out the crumpled forms of Marge and Alice still passed out as well. The hideous brown fabric of Bruce's recliner enveloped Alice like a cocoon, and Marge lay sprawled at her feet in an awkward heap on my rug.

"Ouch," I whispered while I pulled my leg free of Doris's head just a moment before the drool made contact. The movement startled her awake, and she sat up with a start. I was grateful she took her drool with her, and it didn't land on my beloved couch.

"What's going on?" Her wide eyes shot around my living room, and I was certain her mind was trying to piece together the evening, much like mine. "Am I? Did we sleep here?"

"Whiskey. That's what's going on," Marge grumbled from the ground. The word whiskey pulled the color straight out of Doris's face. "I feel like shit." When she opened her eyes, I saw the same red hue in them that Doris sported as well.

"Good morning," Alice sing-songed and stretched. "Whoa. You slept with Doris? Maybe Marge isn't the only lesbian in this room."

Doris gasped, but Marge and I just laughed. "How are you so chipper?" I groaned as I rubbed my throbbing temples.

After a long yawn, she shrugged. "I feel fine."

Marge flopped onto her back, covering her eyes with an arm. "That's because you spend your life either drunk or hungover. This is normal for you."

"Why does my mouth feel like this?" Doris smacked her lips together. "I can't swallow!"

"Cottonmouth," Marge mumbled. "Drink something. There may be some whiskey left."

"Don't say whiskey," I groaned, and the thought of it made my stomach churn.

Just as I forced down my own gag, Doris retched beside me.

"Bathroom! Go! GO!" I shouted as I shot up and pushed her off the couch.

Covering her mouth, she bolted to the bathroom, and a moment later, I heard another familiar sound. It was the same one I'd heard Bruce making for months during his chemo. After the toilet flushed, she emerged from the bathroom, horror and shame worn plain on her green-tinged face.

"I threw up," she whispered, wiping her mouth. "Why did I throw up?"

"Whiskey." Marge shook her head.

Once again, that word churned my stomach, and Doris spun on her heel and disappeared back inside the bathroom. When the retching returned, Marge chuckled from her post on the floor. "That was too easy. Should we go for three?"

"Don't," I scolded, leveling her with a glare. "If you make her puke on the carpet, you're cleaning it up."

"If she pukes out here, I puke. You'll be cleaning that up as well." Alice peered down at her over the arm of the chair.

"Party poopers."

Doris stepped out again, pausing this time and giving a backward glance at the bathroom door. "I think I'm done. Why am I throwing up?"

Alice and I shot a look to stay Marge's tongue.

Though it had been a while since I'd been hungover, unlike Doris, I at least recognized what it was. "I forgot you'd never been drunk. This is a hangover. Just drink some water, dear. It will help."

Alice leaned back in the recliner. "Grab us all one while you're up."

Doris shuffled around the kitchen then returned with four glasses of water on a tray. The glasses clinked together as her hands shook, and the vibrations only increased while she tried to set them down.

"Careful there, Shakes Hoolihan," Marge said while she sat up and helped guide the tray to safety.

"Why are my hands shaking?" Doris stared at her trembling extremities.

"Whi—"

"Marge! No!" I shouted.

Alice smacked Marge on the arm. "You'll be fine, Doris. Just drink your water, and maybe a little hair of the dog will get you right again."

"Eat dog hair? No!"

Alice rolled her eyes. "Hair of the dog, Doris. Like a Bloody Mary. Ooh! What do you ladies say we head to my house, and Agnes can whip us up mimosas and bloodies?"

"I think I'm never drinking again." I groaned.

"Me neither." Marge nodded before gulping her water. "And I should really get home. My mom is probably worried."

"Oh, your mom! Is she okay being left alone for a night?" I asked.

Marge grunted. "Oh yeah. We just live together for the company. It's not like I have to take care of her or anything. She still insists on doing everything for herself. Stubborn woman doesn't need a damn thing from me. But I still bet she's worried I didn't come home."

"You're seventy years old and you still have a curfew." Alice snorted.

"I don't have a *curfew*. It's just that I never stay out, and she's probably got the neighborhood watch searching the bushes already."

"There's no one at home to worry about me." Doris sniffled.

Alice shrugged. "My staff is used to me not coming home. But Agnes really does make the best Bloody Marys. Marge, just call your mom. Tell her you're not dead in a ditch and let's go! Why not? What else do we have to do today?"

"Never. Drinking. Again." I shook my head.

"Oh, come on, ladies. We just started having fun in this widow's club. Don't wuss out on me now."

"I think one night of binge drinking was plenty, Alice," I said. "My head is pounding, Doris still looks green, and I don't trust Marge not to make her puke again. Knitting is starting to sound good."

"How can I knit with my hands like this?" Doris lifted her hands, and we stared at them for a moment while they trembled. "I can't knit! How can I knit?"

"We're *not* knitting." Marge slammed her empty glass back down. "I'm not going out like that."

"Wait..." Alice started, and I watched her eyes raking my living room. "Didn't we make some kind of a bucket list of wishes last night?"

The memory of our moment of solidarity crashed back into my mind. "Yes! We did!"

"Where is that basket?" Alice stood and searched around my living room. "Here!" She reached down behind the couch and came up, clutching the colorful basket.

"Oh, yeah!" Marge laughed and pointed. "I forgot about that."

"What are you doing with my knitting basket?" Doris asked, scrunching her brow.

"Remember, Doris? We all wrote down one crazy wish we want to do before we die."

"We did? I don't remember that." The lines in her brow deepened. "Wait. Where are my knitting supplies?"

"On the floor." Marge pointed to the pile of yarn and needles.

"My stuff!" Doris hustled over to it and dropped to her knees, pulling the remnants of her knitting supplies into her lap. "It's a mess!"

Alice tossed up her hand. "Forget the knitting shit, Doris. What's important is these wishes in here. The wishes we *promised* to help each other fulfill."

"We were drunk. We're not actually doing that, Alice." I scoffed. "Are we?"

"To hell we aren't!" Marge stood up, and Alice stepped to her side, nodding in solidarity.

"We are?" I tried to remember my wish and then snorted when it came back to me. "We really are?"

"Hell yeah, we are. We made a pact. A Wilder Widows pact. And we are doing it. A promise is a promise."

Marge crossed her arms and nodded in agreement.

Alice stood firm at Marge's side. "We've all got life insurance from our dead husbands and nothing but time on our hands. Why not, ladies? It's time for the Wilder Widows to get a little wilder! We're doing this."

When I remembered my wish, I realized it was something I'd always wanted to do, and something I still could. It wasn't too late. Was it? The same excitement I'd felt when I wrote it down bubbled up inside me again.

"I don't remember what I wished," Doris said, setting her knitting supplies on the table. "Let me look and see what it says."

"No!" Alice turned away, clutching the knitting basket to her chest. "We open one at a time, drawn at random. And no one can tell anyone what their wish is until it's pulled."

"But I don't know what mine is!" Doris stomped.

Alice tipped up her chin. "Good. Then it will be a surprise to you as well. It's what your deepest desire was with whiskey as your truth serum."

The moment she said 'whiskey,' I watched Doris's now-returning color drain away once again. She bolted for the bathroom, the sound of the slamming door prefacing the retching that started again.

"You said it this time, not me." Marge smirked and gave Alice the side-eye. "She's surprisingly fast." Marge stared at the spot Doris had just been.

"Yes. Quite nimble," Alice agreed, pinching her brow.

Doris emerged a moment later, clutching her stomach. "I'm never drinking again."

"We all say that at some point, Doris. You'll get the hang of it." Alice stepped over and slung an arm around her shoulder, guiding her back to our group.

"So, are we really doing this?" I pointed at the knitting basket.

Marge and Alice responded with enthusiastic nods. We all turned to Doris, and she shrank beneath the weight of our stares.

"But I don't know what I wished for."

"All the more fun for our adventure." Excitement flickered in Marge's eyes. "I need this, Doris. I need an adventure. What do you say?"

After a moment of shifting her eyes between us, she nodded. "Okay. I'll do it!"

Grins stretched across all our faces as we agreed to our pact. Suddenly I felt the weight of Bruce, of my marriage, my anger over all the wasted years, sloughing away while excitement took its place. Excitement about the journey ahead of me and the obstacles no longer in my way. Excitement to gaze into the past and find the me who was once there, was still there, and introduce myself to her once again.

"So, what do we do?" Marge jutted her chin at the basket.

"We each take turns picking. One wish at a time. When we've made it come true, we pick the next. And no peeking." Alice passed a warning gaze across us. "Deal?"

"Deal," we responded in unison.

"So, who goes first?" Doris asked, the color finally creeping back into her skin.

"I think since we're at Sylvie's house and it was her idea, she should pick," Marge said.

The weight of their stares nearly crushed me into the carpet, but I nodded and stepped in front of Alice. With a gentle lift, she pulled off the top of the yarn basket, and I closed my eyes and reached inside. The crisp edges of folded paper found their way into my fingers, and I pulled one out. When I opened my eyes, I saw the elegant pen strokes of the name.

Alice.

"It's me! It's me!" She nearly dropped the yarn basket when she started jumping up and down. Excitement that dwarfed my own radiated out of her green eyes.

Carefully, I unfolded the note.

"Well? What does it say?" Marge and Doris leaned in while Alice straightened up, her elegant neck stretching tall while she gazed down at us.

When I saw the answer to that question, my jaw dropped open, and my eyes shot up to meet Alice's. One dark silver brow arched, and a sinister smile pulled up her lip.

"You've got to be kidding, Alice." I lifted the note, but she only shook her head, crossing her arms while she stood immobile.

"A pact is a pact. You promised to help me achieve it."

"What is it?" Marge squinted while she tried to read the note.

"A promise is a promise." I smiled and felt the butterflies take off in my stomach.

"It would be a shame not to let the world get a load of these babies one last time." She gestured to her long legs and cocked a hip.

"What does it say?" Doris leaned over my shoulder.

After taking a deep breath and getting a confirming nod from Alice, I read the note. Her wish. The desire we promised to help her achieve. "Headline as a Las Vegas Showgirl."

ALICE

CHAPTER FIVE

Even in the daylight, the lights of Las Vegas outshined the sun. They flickered and pulsed with the same energy that filled the town I remembered so well. A town filled with my hopes and dreams, and the very town that snatched them away from me. While we drove down the strip, the same excitement ignited inside me that had the day I arrived here when I was only eighteen years old. With nothing but my face and these legs in my arsenal and not a penny to my name. I'd arrived on these very streets after hitchhiking my way from Iowa the day after I'd graduated high school. And now, thanks to the Wilder Widows, I was back.

It was no surprise Sylvie drew my name first. I was always the first at everything. First girl in my class to kiss a boy, first one to crash a car, first one to lose my virginity, and now I was the first widow to live out her wildest dreams. Thoughts of feeling the spotlights shining on me once again sent butterflies fluttering around my stomach.

"It's so shiny!" Doris said while she peered out the tinted window of our limo. "Everything sparkles!"

"I think I'm going to have a seizure." Marge shielded her eyes from the perceived assault.

"I came here once with Bruce. He got hammered and lost fifteen thousand dollars of our life savings." Sylvie rolled her brown eyes and slumped back against the seat. "He was such an asshole."

Laughing, I pulled myself away from the window and turned to the three ladies sitting across from me. "Welcome to my home."

"Wilder Lane is your home." Doris frowned.

"No. Wilder Lane is where I've lived, but Vegas..." I sighed and let my gaze drift back out the window, "Vegas is my home."

"So, you haven't been back in how many years?"

I didn't want to say it. Saying it only reminded me of how old I'd become. How far away I was from the starry-eyed girl who'd arrived on these streets with dreams of fame and fortune. Dreams of applause and admiration. Dreams that I once again dared to let flicker back to life inside me. "Over forty years."

"Cripes, you're old." Marge chuckled.

"Shut it, Marge. I still look *good,* and that's a hell of a lot more than I can say for you."

She crossed her arms, and her scowl only deepened the creases on her drooping face. I often wondered when I looked at them what my face would look like if I'd followed in their footsteps and aged naturally. Just the thought of lines on my taut skin sent a shudder coursing through my spine. No. Not me. Being a dancer, there were many things in life I was graceful at, but aging wasn't one of them. I'd be clinging to my youth for as long as my doctors could continue fighting the gravity trying to pull down every inch of me.

While I looked across them, I wondered what they would look like if they would only listen to my fashion advice. Doris and Marge hadn't changed a bit since I'd met them, and Sylvie, while much better looking and younger than the others, was also terribly out of style. I stared at the sea of colored cardigans and slacks across from me, then I smiled.

"I have an idea," I said while visions raced through my mind.

"Why are you looking at us like that?" Sylvie stared back at me.

"We're getting makeovers."

"Makeovers? Oh no. No, no, no." Marge shook her head, and soon Doris joined.

"Oh, come on, ladies! This journey is about doing something different. Exciting. New. What better way to start it off than with a new look?"

Sylvie pursed her lips and gave me a contemplative shrug. "I have been thinking about a new hairstyle." She tucked a piece of her limp long hair behind her ear. It shimmered with a blend of grey and her natural blonde. "Maybe a little shorter? With layers?"

"Yes! I love that!" I nodded enthusiastically.

"I haven't changed my hair in thirty years." Doris shook her head. "I like it like this."

"Doris, you look like the old maid from the card game. It's time for a change."

Marge snorted. "*That's* who you remind me of! I could never put my finger on it."

"I do not look like the old maid!"

We all looked to Sylvie for her opinion. She tilted her head while she appraised her. "You look exactly like my grandma, who also looked like the old maid. Sorry, Doris."

Doris scoffed and touched the bouffant of hair knotted into a bun on top of her head. "But it's how I've always worn it."

"Exactly." I pointed. "We're changing things up. Starting with your looks. James?" I called through the open window to the driver.

"Yes, Miss Addington?"

"Take us to Barneys, please."

"Of course, Miss Addington."

Marge shook her head, and the mop of dark grey hair brushed her eyebrows with the movement. "I'm not getting a makeover."

"You need one more than any of us. If Walter Matthau was still alive, people would mistake you for him and stop you on the streets to ask for your autograph."

Sylvie snorted and burst into laughter while she stared at Marge. "I'm sorry, but now I can't unsee it."

"I do *not* look like Walter Matthau."

"Well?" Doris tipped her head and squinted. "You kind of do."

Before Marge could argue, the limo turned and slowed to a stop. "We're here, Miss Addington."

"Come on, ladies. Shopping. Hair. Makeup. Let's go."

The pull of my city was too strong to wait for James to open the door. I hopped out and took a deep breath, inhaling the smells that hadn't changed in all these years.

Las Vegas.

My home.

****

"You're all set, Miss Addington," the store clerk said as she handed me my receipt. After three hours of shopping, we'd each headed off with a stylist for our hair and makeup. It'd been two hours since I'd seen the Wilder Widows, and anticipation at their transformations caused me to tap my foot impatiently. If I was back in my town, I wasn't going to be seen with a bunch of old ladies. Though I appreciated being the best-looking one of the bunch, I didn't need their slacks cramping my style.

I glanced in the mirror and appreciated the new highlights in my hair. Though I'd left the style the same, the fresh cut and color brightened up my complexion. I saw a slight crease starting between my brows and leaned in closer to examine it.

"Damn it," I whispered, then wondered if I would have time to stop for Botox before my big showgirl debut.

"Well?" I heard Sylvie behind me and turned. Where a plain older woman once stood, a vibrant and fashionable woman took her place. Her long, straight hair now brushed across her shoulders with feathered layers and blonde highlights where the grey had been, gave it multitudes of volume and movement. The new makeup paired with the chic new outfit made her look at least a decade younger. Younger than me, in fact, and suddenly I regretted my decision to help them with their appearances. But one backward glance in the mirror and I knew I was still the hot one, though she gave me a run for my money.

"You look incredible, Sylvie! Like a new woman!"

"I feel incredible! Thank you, Alice. I needed this. A whole new me for a whole new life."

"Exactly." I reached out and squeezed her hand.

"Holy shit," she whispered as she peered over my shoulder. I turned to follow her stare and lost the battle to keep my jaw tight when my eyes clapped onto Doris.

She shuffled in front of us, swiping a hand down her new outfit. "Do I look all right? I feel weird."

"Doris, is that you? You look incredible," I breathed. It wasn't just the new clothes causing me to struggle for my next breath. The bouffant had been replaced with a short, layered style no longer resembling the old maid. Contoured makeup brought out the features in her face, and for the first time since I'd met her three years ago, I noticed how beautiful her eyes were. A dark blue now contrasted with the sweep of cobalt shadow at the corners of her lids.

"It's okay?" she asked sheepishly, pressing her hand up into her hair. "I feel bald."

"You look beautiful, Doris. I can't even believe you're the same person!" Sylvie kept shaking her head. "And wait! Your glasses! How can you see without them?"

The new pink blush brushed across her cheeks deepened to crimson while she looked down at the ground. "Actually, I have perfect vision. I just thought glasses made me look smarter, so I've worn them for years."

"What?" I choked. "You wore fake glasses?"

Biting her lip, she nodded. "The stylist you set me up with told me I look younger without them and made me put them in my purse."

"Your stylist was right," Sylvie said. "You really look like a different person."

"Fake glasses? Really, Doris?" I laughed.

"No one thinks I'm smart!" she argued. "Smart people wear glasses."

"No, Doris. People who can't see without them wear glasses. Glasses don't make you look smarter. They make you look like you have vision problems." I rolled my eyes. "Fake glasses."

"Well, now I feel even dumber than I look." She sighed.

Sylvie stepped forward and pulled her in for a hug. "You aren't dumb, Doris. And you look beautiful."

"Thanks, Sylvie."

"Who died?"

Marge's voice startled me, and I turned around, excited to see the third transformation. But when my eyes raked over her, I cocked a hip and heaved a sigh. "Seriously, Marge?" I waved a hand over her. "You look exactly the same."

"I do not. I had a makeover just like you all did." Her gruff face scrunched up while she scowled.

"Doris had a makeover." I waved my hand over her dramatic change. "Sylvie had a makeover." Another wave of my hand emphasized Sylvie's new look. "You look exactly the same."

"You do look the same, Marge," Doris agreed.

Marge shook her head. "No. These are new slacks, and this is a new shirt."

"They are the same as your old ones," Sylvie said.

"But these are new. Those were old. And my hair? Can't you tell?"

I tipped my head and examined the same cut she'd had since I knew her. "What? Did they use a different size bowl when they cut it?"

Marge let out an exasperated breath. "No. My part. It's on the opposite side!"

The laughter snuck out my nose while I tried to choke it down. "Your part? *That's* your makeover? And what part? It's a bowl!"

"Well, she parted it differently. Maybe it already went back." She shrugged.

I shook my head. "If anyone asks, you're our grandma."

"Fine by me."

"Fine." I turned to the other two widows. "Well, what do you ladies say we take our fine selves to the show?"

"You found one?" Sylvie asked.

"I did. I had the concierge help me, and we ordered tickets. He said there is a show tonight at eight o'clock. Which is," I looked at my watch, "in only one hour. We need to go and watch it so I can see if it's the show I want to be in."

"You do know you can't just march up on stage and dance when you find the show you want." Marge arched a brow.

"We'll figure out the logistics later. For now, I just want to get back to the theatre and see a show. It's been too long."

"I hate theatre," Marge grumbled.

"There will be beautiful, mostly naked women dancing, Marge. You should love it, you lesbo."

Her eyebrows rose, and then she nodded. "Let's go."

We made our way back to the limo where James hurried to open the door. Chatter filled the ride to the venue, but I could only stare out the window in silence. The lights. The people. The excitement. Vegas used to come to life at night, and from the looks of the streets filled with bodies, it hadn't changed a bit.

"Look at that woman!" Doris pointed. "She's practically naked!"

"She's a hooker," Marge said. "That's basically the mandatory uniform."

"A streetwalker? A lady of the night?" Doris gasped and clutched her chest. "But it's not even all the way dark yet!"

"They're hookers, Doris. Not vampires." Marge rolled her eyes, and I chuckled to myself.

"You okay, Alice?" Sylvie asked when we pulled up. "You've been quiet."

"Just thinking." I took a stilling breath when James opened the door. It brought back memories of my years here when this door would open, and fans would cheer while the dancers poured out. I missed the sound of them as I climbed out absent the cheers. Instead of glittering dancers filing out behind me like clowns in a clown car, the three little widows were my entourage.

Even though I wasn't dancing tonight, I still felt the jitters that used to preface my dancing in the early years. When I claimed our tickets from will-call and headed toward the entrance, they only amplified. The ladies trailed behind me while I searched for the doors to our section, but I was too in awe of the atmosphere to speak to them when they continued with their constant barrage of questions. The crowds gathered, and the lights dimmed and flickered, warning us the show was about to begin. I looked to the usher dressed in a formal red uniform similar to the old days and remembered how they used to join us after the show on occasion at the parties we dancers flocked to.

"Alice? Do you know where you're going?" Doris asked for the fourth time, and this time I huffed a breath and turned to face her.

"Yes, Doris. It's section twenty-two. This one." I pointed toward the numbers above the door.

"Tickets?" the young usher asked when we stepped up. He was handsome, and I thought back in my dancing days, I would have flirted with him mercilessly only to leave him hanging when the high rollers came calling.

Too excited to see the show, I forwent my usual routine of flirting with handsome men and handed him my ticket. Then I saw my trembling hand and snatched it back before anyone noticed. Glancing over my shoulder at the girls to make sure none of them witnessed my weakness, my excitement, or maybe it was fear, I was glad to see their eyes all roving around the elegant room instead of fixated on my momentary lapse of confidence.

"This way," the usher said, and I motioned for the ladies to follow. When we stepped inside the theatre, my feet stuttered to a stop. The dark stage caught my eye first. I remembered standing at the edge of the curtain, staring at the dimly lit stage, just waiting for the moment the lights flicked on and beckoned me to dance beneath them. Now I viewed the stage from a different angle, from the audience, but still, I waited for the moment the lights would flood the darkness and the stage would once again call my name.

"Here you are," he said, gesturing to the fourth-row seats I'd managed to snag.

"So exciting," Sylvie whispered in my ear while we made our way to our seats. "Are you excited?" She took her place beside me. Marge sat on my left, and Doris landed just beside her.

"It's just research," I lied, unsure why I couldn't let on how overwhelming this was for me. How much pain and resentment I felt sitting in the seats instead of standing on the edge of the stage. I could picture them—each girl standing in her spot, stretching, preparing. I knew the excitement they felt, whether it was their first time on stage or whether it was the one girl who proved herself over them all. The one girl who would shine the brightest. The star.

The girl who was supposed to be me.

The lights flashed on, and I blinked as fast as my heart raced while I let my eyes adjust. One by one the dancers fluttered out, a sea of long legs much like my own. The sparkles on their costumes glimmered in the light, and my breath trapped in my throat while I took them all in. Their movement. Their beauty. The smiles they wore not knowing that one day this could be gone, and they could end up alone with nothing but the remnants of their shattered dreams.

"I'm taping it so you can learn the routine," Sylvie whispered, and I glanced over to see her phone pointed at the stage.

"Thank you," I whispered back, letting my eyes snap back to the stage and the dancers kicking and leaping in unison.

Then she appeared. The star. Her feathered headdress towered above her, and I fought the tears, remembering how proud I was the day they gave it to me. The day I became the star of the show. When they placed it on my head, the weight of it had surprised me, but I had lifted my chin and straightened my spine, proud to be the one to bear the burden.

She danced to the center of the stage, and I recognized the steps while she moved with precision and grace. The routine was different, but I could envision every move before she flowed into the next. I fought the urge to close my eyes and fade away into the memories of dancing on stage. The ones I saw each night when I closed my eyes. Instead, I kept them open, trained on the dancer I should have been.

Anger seethed inside me at the envy I felt. *I* was the one people were supposed to be envious of. I was the beautiful one. The talented one. And later in life, I was the rich one. It was my life everyone wanted, yet now I felt the cold grip of envy wrapping around my soul. I would give up all the money and all the jealousy bestowed upon me for just one moment to stand on that stage again and feel what that dancer felt. To relive my youth and feel myself come to life once again. To go back. Everything here transported me back, and I wanted to stay there, trapped for all eternity in a moment in time.

Even the smell was the same. A bouquet of perfumes, sweat, and determination. It was an aroma I would bottle and inhale every minute of my life if it could ever be replicated. But it couldn't. It was a smell derived from years of hard work, sacrifice, and a desire to shine brighter than the sun. And I hadn't inhaled it in over forty years. As I watched the show, I let the smells and sounds transport me back to a time when I thought I was invincible. A time when I thought

I held the world in the palm of my hand. Instead, I ended up living in a subdivision... alone and unknown.

When the show ended, the crowd launched to their feet, and their cheers rose into a chorus I would never forget. The sound of applause. Appreciation. Adoration. The soundtrack reserved for only the chosen few. The ones who fought through the pain of training eight hours a day. The ones who clawed their way through the rubble to come out on top. The ones who sacrificed everything for the dream of hearing it. Tears stung my eyes while I remembered the feeling of standing in front of it, the sound waves wrapping around me like a warm hug. When I watched the star take her bow, I envied the fact she got to feel the strongest embrace. An embrace that was stolen from me just before I could enjoy it myself.

"Those ladies have legs for days," Marge said as she sat back down. "I definitely think I'm a lesbian. I've got those feelings... down there."

Even though I usually had a cocky comeback for everything Marge said, I was too busy fighting my tears to say anything.

"You okay?" she asked. "I'm waiting for your backhanded comment."

"I'm fine," I said, barely able to choke the words out.

"I got the whole thing on tape." Sylvie shoved her phone in my face, and I saw the dancers replaying on the small screen. "Now you can watch it and learn all the moves."

"Thank you," I said, but I knew I didn't even need the tape. Even after all these years, I could still memorize a routine in a glance.

"Place is clearing out. We should go." Marge bumped me with an elbow, and I nodded my response.

One by one we filed out, and I listened to the girls chatter about the incredible show. Silence was all that I could muster while I tried to battle the anger ripping apart my insides. I'd expected to feel excitement at seeing the show and the chance to dance again, but instead, all I felt was regret.

"Over there!" Doris shouted, pointing to our limo.

James saw her waving and grinned before opening the back door. "Welcome back, ladies. Did you enjoy the show?"

"Oh, yes!" Doris nodded as she climbed in. "It was incredible. So shiny!"

"We did, James," Sylvie answered and ducked inside.

"I used to be one of them." I cast a backward glance over my shoulder at the theatre.

"And you will be again." Marge's hand squeezed my shoulder, and I caught her unusually sympathetic gaze.

Pressing my lips together into the biggest smile I could muster, I squeezed her hand. "Thank you, Marge."

"Just don't expect me to take my eyes off the third girl on the left to watch you instead." She blew out a puff of air before dipping inside the limo.

Finally, laughter snorted out my nose, and I shook my head while I let the sadness wash away.

"Where to, Miss Addington?" James asked before closing me inside.

"Back to the hotel."

"Can we gamble downstairs before going to bed?" Sylvie asked as the door closed.

"We wouldn't be the Wilder Widows if we didn't get a little wild in Vegas." I grinned, and the limo pulled out.

CHAPTER SIX

"Oh! I won!" Sylvie bounced beside me while she swept her winnings into her arms. "I never win!"

"I lost. Again." Marge scowled as the dealer moved her chips away.

While they gambled, I still struggled to sort through the feelings battling inside me since we left the show. Anger. Excitement. Fear. More excitement. More fear. They rose and retreated like the tide, and I started to question my one wish. Did I still have what it took to own the spotlight? Or would I be laughed off the stage, a washed-up dancer clinging to a dream she should have kissed away decades ago? A fear greater for me than even death itself.

I'd spent the better part of my life dreaming of returning to Vegas to reclaim my rightful place, but now that I was here, I started to lose my faith.

Not that I would ever admit it to the three widows who made up my whole world.

Another thing I'd never admit.

No. To the rest of the world, I had everything. Money. Looks. Prestige. All the things I hadn't had when I grew up poor on that farm. My entire youth had been spent being teased for my home-sewn clothes, the way I smelled like cow shit when I rode on the bus each morning, and my long, skinny legs that earned me the nickname Gumby. The very same long legs that I used to waltz right out of that crap town and into the spotlight. But even though I had cried alone in the bathroom every day at recess, I never once let them see my tears.

Then I'd blossomed in middle school, my looks earning the envy of every girl and the adoration of every boy. I'd stopped playing with the cows before school so I didn't smell like a cow pie, and I'd mastered the art of sewing and made clothes that looked like they came straight out of the catalogs I fashioned them after. I'd turned my life around and emerged from my youthful cocoon as a beautiful butterfly.

Those bullies soon became my 'friends,' though I never trusted a single one as far as I could throw them. And after a life mucking cow shit, I had pretty strong arms. I always knew they weren't my real friends, and neither had been any other woman since. Like my high school friends, women flocked to my side throughout my life but always waited for me to falter. Hoping someday they'd see me knocked from my throne.

Then after Ed had clutched his chest and dropped dead at my feet, leaving me alone once again, Doris and Marge had knocked on my door and extended an invitation to join them. One I'd, of course, scoffed at. Me? In a Widow's Club? Ridiculous. But in reality, I'd yearned for friendship my whole life, and for the very first time, I found it. I had friends. Real ones. The kind who weren't secretly hoping I would fail. Whispering behind my back. Smiling at me through gritted teeth as they told me how pretty I looked that day.

Doris and Marge may not have been the exclusive women I'd spent my life rubbing elbows with at cocktail parties, but Marge hadn't been wrong when she'd said the reason I hadn't traveled was her. It was them. Now that I'd found them, I couldn't imagine a life where I didn't spend it with the only people who truly had my back. Women who held me up instead of trying to push me down. The kind of women who would fly to Vegas with me to help me realize my one and only dream.

And I loved them dearly. So much more than they would ever know.

"I'm on fire!" Doris proclaimed, and I turned to see her walking toward me, waving.

"What? You win ten cents?" I gestured to the voucher flapping in her hand.

"Almost five dollars." She hoisted it like a trophy.

Sylvie tossed her chip up in the air and caught it with ease. "I just won a thousand."

"Oh. Wow!" Doris widened her eyes, then glanced down at her voucher and slumped. "I thought five dollars was good."

"It is." Marge's scowl deepened. "I'm in the hole."

I slipped an arm around her shoulder and squeezed. "You'll get 'em next time."

"Can I offer you some drinks?" We all spun to see the aged cocktail waitress standing in front of us with a tray of brightly colored drinks topped with colorful umbrellas. The color of the drinks couldn't compare to the bright makeup painted across her face. Makeup that, like her high hair, belonged back in the eighties. Marge pulled from my arm, and her scowl softened as she locked eyes with the waitress.

"Yes. Um, yeah. Thanks. Looks, uh... looks good." Marge stumbled over her words while she swiped at the back of her neck and shuffled from side to side.

Arching my brow, I watched Marge dissolve into a puddle of mush under the batting lashes of the waitress at least a decade younger.

"Go ahead. Take one," the waitress said, her sparkling eyes still engaged with Marge's bulging ones. "On the house."

"Don't mind if I do!" Doris said, unaware of the silent seduction happening before her.

Sylvie took a drink, but her side-eye confirmed she also saw the sparks igniting between Marge and what I could only assume was a retired showgirl.

"Thanks. Yeah." Marge plucked a drink from the tray. "I don't normally drink, you know, like fruity drinks. But these look, uh... you look good."

You? I nearly let the laughter I held in slip out while Marge's face flooded with a red deeper than the cherry sticking out of the drinks.

"They. I mean, uh... *they* look good."

The same flush filled the already over-blushed cheeks of the waitress while she dropped her eyes to the ground before fluttering them back up again. "I'll be sure to come by with more when you're done with that one."

"Yeah. Great. That'd, uh, be great. I'll just be here. Yeah."

"Okay," she said and turned away, casting a sweet smile over her shoulder before disappearing into the crowd.

Sylvie and I stared at Marge while she stood with eyes glued to the last place the waitress had been. Finally, Marge blew out the breath she'd been holding and deflated.

"Hey! She liked you!" Sylvie bumped her with an elbow.

"She did? You think?" Marge spun back and raked us with those oversized orbs.

"You were practically doing it on the floor." I let out the laugh I'd been holding.

"She's so hot! Wow!" Marge clapped her hands on her head and closed her eyes before snapping them back open and staring back at us. "You really think she liked me?"

Hot isn't the word I would have used to describe that particular waitress, but she'd definitely been into Marge. Sylvie and I nodded in unison.

"What's going on?" Doris asked after sucking a long sip of her blue drink through the straw. "Who's hot?"

"How did you not see that?" I shook my head.

"See what?"

Sylvie smiled. "Marge met a lady."

"What? Where?" Doris swiveled her head around.

"A hot lady!" Marge added.

"Where?" Doris kept sweeping the crowd.

Exhaling a sigh, I shook my head. "The waitress, Doris. Marge and the waitress definitely want to get it on."

Her mouth dropped open as she struggled for words. "Wait. You mean *met* a lady?"

Marge waggled her brows and nodded. "Yep. My first lady."

"Wait. So, you really do think you're a..." Doris leaned in and whispered, "lesbian?"

"Quit whispering it, Doris! It's not taboo. It's lesbian. Lesbian. Lesbian! LESBIAN!" I shouted and grabbed the attention of our entire section of the casino.

"Shhhhh, everyone is staring!" She tried to clap her hand over my mouth, but I screamed the word through her cupped hand.

"Say it loud and proud, Doris! Lesbian!"

"Okay, okay! Shhhh. Enough!" she scolded and released the grip on my mouth. "Just stop shouting!"

"Say it without whispering, or I'll shout it again." I pursed my lips and gave her a warning smile.

"I'm just not—"

"LES—"

"Okay! Okay!" She swatted me with her hand. "Lesbian. There I said it without whispering."

"One more time. With meaning." I grinned.

With a heavy sigh, she looked straight at Marge. "Marge is a lesbian. And I'm okay with that."

"Atta girl." I patted her on the back.

"Well, I only *may* be a lesbian. I'm not sure yet."

"Not sure?" Sylvie argued. "You and that waitress were flirting. Hard."

"Yeah, but that's just flirting. I don't think I'll know for sure until I... you know."

"Coochie canoodle?" I asked.

"Oh God, gross." Sylvie cringed.

"I was thinking more like kiss a woman. But yeah... that. I don't think I can know for sure until I try to... know you."

"Coochie canoodle."

"Alice, stop!" Sylvie laughed and slapped my arm.

"What?" I shrugged. "That's what they'll be doing."

"I may be a lesbian, and even I'm horrified by that term." Marge shook her head and shuddered. "Let's just call it 'lady loving.'"

"Same thing," I said with a shrug. "So, are you going for it?"

"I wouldn't even know how to start. Not only have I never hit on a woman before, but I haven't flirted since I was in 'Nam. And even then, I was terrible at it."

"Well, you were doing very well already," Sylvie encouraged. "She was responsive."

"You think?"

Sylvie and I nodded in unison.

As we finished our nod, the waitress emerged through the crowd, and her eyes moved straight to Marge. A shy smile curved her hot pink lips and caused Marge to flush once again. She looked to Marge's full drink before casting one last glance and moving back through the crowd.

"Oh yeah." I laughed. "She's into you. And you'd better drink that sucker down, so she has a reason to come back over."

"Good idea!" Marge took a sip of her drink, and it caused her face to pucker. "What the hell is this? Cripes. It's so sweet I think my teeth are gonna fall out."

"Drink it anyway. Drink it for love." I egged her on, and Marge took a long sip through the straw.

"Love hurts."

"Isn't that the truth." I sighed and remembered how much pain love had brought into my life.

"You okay, Alice?" Sylvie asked, noticing my sullen expression.

"Yes. Fine," I said, but I could see she didn't believe me. "A table. Let's sit." I gestured to the table a group of ladies just vacated. The four of us hurried over to secure our seats before someone else swooped in.

"Alice, you've been weird all night. Spill." Sylvie hadn't let the short break in our conversation make her forget her astute observation.

Taking a sip of the fruity drink, my face puckered as much as Marge's had. "Good God. Someone get me some vodka."

"Spill." Sylvie leaned forward onto her elbows.

"Fine." I sighed. "I'm pissed off."

"Pissed off?" Marge scoffed. "This was *your* idea. You wanted to come here, and you know, dance again or whatever. Well, we're here."

"I'm not pissed I'm here *now*." I shook my head. "I'm pissed I haven't been here the whole time. This is where I belong." I waved my hand at the sights and sounds around us. "On stage. *That* is where I belong. And I missed it. I missed it all, and I'm just..."

"Pissed," Sylvie said, and I saw the recognition in her eyes. "I get it."

"You do?"

"Yeah. I had a lot of dreams that Bruce stood in the way of. It's tough not being able to go back and get a redo."

"I just didn't realize how hard it would be to see the life I missed out on."

"So why *did* you miss out on it? You haven't told us what happened." Doris asked, happily sipping her drink.

Memories of heartbreak and shattered dreams crashed back into me like a semi-truck. "I got knocked up."

"Damn kids," Marge grumbled and took another excruciating chug of her drink.

"I came here fresh off the farm and out of high school. I'd seen a program with showgirls on TV when I was a kid, and I was in awe of them." I drifted off while I remembered how I'd watched them move on stage, admiring their grace and beauty. They took my breath away. "Some kids had dreams of being a doctor, or a scientist, or a writer. But not me. The minute I saw them dance, I *knew* that's what I wanted to do. I wanted to shine on stage just like those women I'd seen on the television. So, I begged for dance lessons until my parents agreed. And you know what? I was good. A natural they said."

"And you certainly got the legs." Sylvie gestured to my stems, and I crossed them the other way.

"It was a mix of hard work and genetics. But yes. I got the legs. And I had the drive. So, I danced my way through high school. Every talent show. Every musical. I was there. Dancing. And the day I graduated, I didn't bother to go to the parties. I knew I'd never see those people again. I'd be too busy being a star."

"So, you came to Vegas?" Marge asked, still struggling to down her drink.

"I packed a bag an hour after graduation and marched out to the road. Hitchhiked the whole way here."

"You could have been murdered." Doris shook her head.

"It was a different time then." I shrugged. "And I wasn't murdered. I got here safe and sound. It took me a year of cocktail waitressing and auditions before I got picked to be a showgirl. God, the excitement I felt when they said yes."

I pressed my chin into my palms while I remembered those feelings that still felt as fresh as if I'd just heard the words 'You're in' again.

"It was a dream come true. All those hours of training and practicing, and finally, I was in. I spent a year as a dancer, living the life and enjoying every second of it. But what I really wanted, what we all wanted, was the center of that stage. The lead dancer. The star."

"Did you get it?" Sylvie asked.

I nodded, remembering again how it had felt to hear them call my name. "I did. After a lot of hard work and dedication, I finally did. They fitted me for my costume, and the choreographers taught me a special routine. I spent weeks training, just waiting for the day the new show opened, and this time it would be me standing in the brightest spotlight."

"And then you got pregnant?"

"Turns out I already was." I sighed. "A couple months before I had been chosen as the star, I'd been out at the casino with the girls after a show. The casino owners used to pay us extra to take sweeps through in our costumes, mingle with the customers, and we always met tons of men. And lots of celebrities. Like once it was Harry..."

"Cripes, Alice. We all know you banged Harry Hayes!" Marge rolled her eyes, and Doris cringed at the word banged.

"Well, I did," I scoffed. "And you know what? He liked me—a lot. In fact, I was pretty sure he was the one. He said he was coming back for me in a few months after he got done shooting his movie. He left for the set, and a month later, I met Ed. He was here on business, and he was handsome. So handsome." I drifted off, remembering his flashy white smile and those dark, sexy eyes. "As handsome as Harry Hayes, even. And he was smitten with me. He chased me all over town."

"If he was handsome, I can't imagine you ran far." Marge chuckled.

"Shut it, Marge. I was smitten with Harry, but after a few too many cocktails, I succumbed to the passion I felt for Ed. We had a tryst. A one-night stand in his hotel room. It was nice, and I had a good time, but my heart was already off with Harry. The next morning, he gave me his number, but I left. No intentions of seeing him again. That was until the day before my big debut."

As I told them the story, I relived it all over again. The excitement. The anticipation. Then the devastation of having it all ripped away from me.

"They were doing the final fitting for my costume, and it didn't fit. The director screamed at me for putting on weight, and I'd noticed it too. But I had been starving myself, and still, my stomach got bigger. It was then I realized I was pregnant... and so did the director. He fired me on the spot. Said he'd wasted all his time and talent on me and told me to get the hell off his stage. My understudy took the stage the next night, and I never got my turn in the spotlight."

"Oh, Alice. How awful." Sylvie reached over and took my hand. "You were so close."

"I was right there, Sylvie. I was right there."

"So, you called Ed?" Doris asked.

I nodded. "I did. I had no money saved up and no job. And being knocked up, who would want me? I couldn't go home to the farm, and Harry would never be interested in a has-been showgirl with a bun in the oven, so I dug out Ed's number and called him up. He came to Vegas, we got married, and that was the end of that. The end of my dreams."

"But you got a beautiful baby out of it." Doris pressed her lips together and gave me her best smile.

"I did. I'm not saying I hated having a baby, and Celeste was a blessing, but I never wanted to be a housewife. A kept woman. I wanted to get on that stage in the headdress and be the star. I just wanted to be the star."

"And you will again!" Marge pummeled the table, causing Doris to jump. "By God we're going to get you up on that damn stage if we have to do it at gunpoint."

"Nobody's pointing guns at anybody," Sylvie reasoned.

Doris shook her head. "Guns scare me!"

"But how *are* we going to get you up on that stage?" Sylvie stared at me.

"This time, I have something I didn't have the last time I came here to be a showgirl."

"What's that?" Marge asked before enduring the last full swig of her fruity drink.

"Money." I grinned. "This time, I have money, and I bet I can pay my way for a one-time spot in that show."

Marge contemplated the statement. "You think they'll let you up there? You know, now that you're old?"

"I'm not *old*. And I've still got these babies." I lifted my legs high in the air, giving them a first-hand look at the stems women of any age would die for.

They all took an appreciative sweep of my legs, and then Marge looked back up at me. "Yeah, you've got the gams, but can you still even dance? I mean, those moves looked hard. I just think we may need a gun. Percy taught me how to shoot when we were in 'Nam. I can handle myself if we need it."

I slammed down the rest of my horrible drink and stood with the same grace that earned me the top spot over forty years ago. Looking behind me to make sure I had room, I mimicked the dancer I'd envied on stage tonight. My feet responded to every request, and my still-agile body bent and moved with the same precision as I'd had after spending my life training it. When I finished my impromptu show, I did a high kick and watched my high heel clear Marge's head, finishing with my calf resting on her shoulder.

"Oh, I can still dance." I smiled while the Wilder Widows stared wide-eyed at my leg, still resting on Marge. A smattering of clapping broke out around us, and I turned to see some people passing by who had caught my spontaneous show. I slid my leg off Marge and took a bow, relishing even the few echoes of applause before they dissipated and left me standing once again at our table.

"Damn, Alice." Marge blew out a breath. "How in the heck do you still move like that? Even though your plastic surgeons try to defy it, you've got to be at least sixty-five years old! Or seventy? Eighty? *Ninety?*" Marge kept counting higher as her eyebrows lifted. "How old are you anyway?"

"A lady never tells. Just because I'm not on stage anymore doesn't mean I stopped dancing and training. I haven't missed a day dancing since I was fifteen years old. And I'll be dancing until the day I die. All the kinky sex I have doesn't hurt my flexibility either." I pressed a hand on my hip and smirked.

"I've never been able to lift my legs that high." Sylvie stared at my legs while I stood beside her. "Seriously. Not even as a teenager. It's remarkable you can still move that way. Seriously. How old are you, Alice?"

"None of your business." I lifted my chin and ignored their frustrated groans. I'd never admit the number to anyone that wasn't holding the scalpel to make me look the age I felt. "Now, if you all don't mind, me and my gams are going up to my penthouse to practice that routine so when I take the stage, I'll be sure to shine."

"Do you need the video I took?" Sylvie fumbled through her purse for her phone.

"I think I remember most of the routine, but my memory may not be what it used to. I'd love to watch it."

"Here you go," she said after sending it to me. "Should be in your phone now."

"You ladies have a nice night. I'll meet you at nine for breakfast, and we'll figure out how to get me up on that stage after I've aced this routine."

"I'm going to play the penny slots." Doris stood, taking her bucket with her.

"I'm going back to the table I can't seem to lose at. Good night, Alice." Sylvie started off.

Marge's eyes drifted across the room and landed on the cocktail waitress still eyeing her up. "Well, go on, Marge. Go get yourself another drink and talk to the woman."

"Are you sure? I'm not good at this like you are, Alice."

I pressed a hand on her shoulder. "What do you have to lose, Marge? If it doesn't work out, you'll never see her again. And if it does, well, you can finally find out if you're really a lesbian."

"I'm scared, Alice."

"You dodged bullets in Vietnam. You said you wanted excitement and adventure. That over there," I pointed to the colorful waitress still eyeballing her, "is excitement and adventure. Get in there, soldier."

Pursing her lips together, I watched her muster up her gumption. "Okay. I'm going in."

"Good luck." With one last pat on her back, I sent her off to the grinning girl waiting for her in the corner before I headed up to my room to make sure I could nail every step of that dance routine.

****

"Over here! Alice! Here!" Doris waved frantically from the corner table at the casino restaurant. I waved back and limped my way past the breakfast buffet to their table.

"Good morning, ladies."

"Are you hurt?" Doris asked, gesturing to the awkward way I moved to get into my seat.

"It's nothing. Just a little sore from the extra practice last night." Sore was an understatement. Every muscle screamed at me that I was well past my dancing prime. I still trained every day, but for only an hour. It had been decades since I'd danced for six hours straight.

"Alice, you look terribly uncomfortable." Sylvie pursed her lips.

"It's nothing. When you're a professional dancer, this is how you feel all the time." It wasn't a complete lie, but I didn't want to let on that I'd overdone it last night while trying to perfect the routine I'd danced until four in the morning. I finished my slow sit down and waved at the waitress passing by. She acknowledged me with a nod and disappeared around the corner. I noticed the fourth seat at our table was empty. "Where's Marge?"

Sylvie shrugged. "We haven't seen her yet. We thought maybe she'd be down with you."

"Oh really?" I smirked. "Did she land that waitress last night?"

"We never saw her after you went up. I have no idea," Sylvie said.

"Oh stop!" Doris waved a hand at us. "She's just all talk. She's not really a..." Doris leaned in to whisper, but my scolding stare sent her back in her seat, and she finished in her normal tone. "Lesbian."

"We don't know if she is or isn't, and neither does she. I'm hoping she got some answers last night."

"Me, too," Sylvie agreed. "She sure did look cute all flustered."

"I've known Marge for three years, and I've never seen her blush. She was like a schoolgirl with a crush last night."

The waitress came up behind me and interrupted my chuckle.

"The buffet is help yourself, but can I get you something to drink?"

"We'll take four screwdrivers."

"Alice! It's nine in the morning," Doris scolded.

"Fine. Make them mimosas."

The waitress gave me an appreciative smile and walked away before the ladies could argue.

"If Marge doesn't get here soon, I'll drink hers for her. God knows I'll need it to help ease the muscle pain."

"Speak of the devil!" Doris waved over my shoulder, and I turned to see Marge walking past the restaurant doorway. She paused, and the little waitress appeared behind her.

"Get. Out," I whispered when I saw them turn to face each other. Marge reached out and tucked a piece of the waitresses' disheveled hair behind her ear. The three of us watched in silence while Marge leaned in, sliding her hand along the woman's back and bending her backward into a knee-quaking kiss.

Our gasps merged into one while Marge kissed the waitress like a returning war hero seeing her long-lost love again. With one more peck on the lips, Marge stood her up, bid her goodbye, and marched into the restaurant with a grin so wide I thought her face may tear.

"Good morning, ladies." She slid into her chair beside me while we all continued our slack-jawed stares. The waitress arrived with our mimosas, and by the time she finished placing them on the table, our jaws were finally snapping shut.

"You old cougar!" I laughed and punched her in the shoulder. "You did it, didn't you?"

The stoic look on her face shattered as she broke into another grin. "It turns out I *am* a lesbian! I'm a HUGE lesbian!"

"All right, Marge!" I cheered, lifting my glass.

"And I *do* like sex! In fact, I love sex!"

"I'm so happy for you!" Sylvie lifted her own glass.

"I knew you weren't asexual. I told you that you just hadn't found the right person."

"Roxy is amazing. She's just incredible. We spent all night... you know." She waggled her eyebrows.

"Bow chicka bow wow." I sing-songed as I shimmied my shoulders.

She let out a long sigh, and her eyes shimmered with a newfound sparkle. "We talked all night, and... lady loved, and it was incredible. In fact, I think I'm *in* love."

"Well, you know what they say lesbians do on their second date, don't you?" I smiled, and only Sylvie laughed, knowing the answer.

"Bring a U-Haul." Her laughter mingled with mine.

Marge blew out a puff of air. "It isn't a joke if it's true. I'd move in with her tomorrow if she'd let me. I told her I'd come back after we get done doing our wishes."

"We couldn't be happier for you, Marge." Sylvie reached out and touched her hand. We all looked over to Doris, who still stared at her with wide eyes. "Doris? Do you have anything you'd like to say to Marge?"

"I'm sorry. I'm just shocked. I've known you for so many years, and I just had no idea."

"Neither did I, really. I wondered, but I didn't know. Now I *know*." She closed her eyes and sighed, that new softer side of Marge surfacing once again.

"Well, I am happy for you, Marge. You deserve happiness." Doris joined us in raising our glasses. "Here's to Marge and... lesbian lady loving!"

The three of us exchanged a sideways glance and dissolved into laughter.

"See! I can be wild, too. I said it! I'm not a complete prude."

"To lesbian lady loving!" I raised my glass high. We clinked them together, and each took a long swig of our mimosas.

"Well, now that we have Marge's lesbianism sorted out, we need to figure out how to get me on stage. And I think I know just how to do it."

They leaned in as I told them the plan I'd concocted last night while I'd done more high kicks than I had in decades.

CHAPTER SEVEN

The four of us stood outside the theatre staring up at the marquee lights.

"Does everyone know what they're doing? You've got your parts?"

The three of them nodded.

"Good. We've got one last shot at this. One shot to get me back up on that stage."

Everywhere I'd tried today had turned me down with laughter that had caused my face to heat up to scalding. I'd been laughed out of every show I'd tried to infiltrate today, and it seemed the producers weren't going to budge on letting me dance my way back into the spotlight again.

Laugh? At *me?* The damn indignity and horror to be begging for a spot in the center stage. A spot where I *belonged.* Even though I'd offered them some serious dough, every door had slammed shut in my face.

I scoffed. "Too old. I'll show all of them *too old* when someone lets me up there to dance."

"Damn ageist patriarchy," Marge grumbled. "Bastards wouldn't know talent if it high-kicked them in the face."

"Thanks, Marge. Damn ageist patriarchy is right. But screw them. We'll just make our plea straight to the most important person in the show." I paused and crooked a smile. "The star."

With all the producers giving me a resounding no, our only remaining hope was to try to bribe the lead dancer to step aside. Now we just had to sneak in and find her.

"We've got your back, Alice. Lead the way." The soldier inside Marge resurfaced as the look of determination tightened up her face.

"Let's go." I led the way into the theatre through the crowd gathering in the concession area. Single filed, we moved toward the backstage entrance, and I tried to keep my cool when we reached the bouncer blocking the door. I knew how seriously they took security for the girls, and even a few harmless old ladies would have trouble breaking through the barrier.

"Sorry. No one is allowed backstage," he said as he stepped further into the opening, crossing his arms tight, which caused his oversized muscles to bulge even more.

"We're just here to see her granddaughter, Sarah. She invited us to the show." I pointed past him and kept walking, acting like we belonged.

He blocked my attempt. "Sorry, ma'am, but no one is allowed."

Ma'am. Ugh. That word never stopped making me cringe. I brushed it off and looked up at him, flashing my most seductive smile. "Please, sir? It's her birthday, and we really do need to get back there and see her. We flew all the way from Iowa, and we just *have* to get back there." I dragged my fingertips along his forearm, but his clenched jaw told me he was immune to my charms.

"No one gets back there. I'm sorry. You'll need to take your seats. The show starts in ten minutes."

"But sir," I said, trying again. "She'll be so happy to see us. Please? It's her birthday, and we're here to surprise her."

He only clenched his jaw tighter and shook his head. No luck. I glanced back to Marge and gave her the go-ahead.

Plan B.

"Uh-oh," she said as she shuffled her feet. "It's happening."

"Oh no. Your irritable bowel syndrome?" I feigned my horror.

"The buffet," Marge groaned. "I shouldn't have eaten all that shrimp."

"Don't do it, Marge! Just hold it!" Doris pressed her hands on top of her new hairdo.

"I can't. It's coming. Bathroom. Now. Now!" Marge danced back and forth, clutching her rear.

"Just go in your Depends!" Sylvie shouted to her, but Marge shook her head furiously.

"I forgot them. I forgot them!"

"No Depends? Shit!" I turned to the bouncer who watched the scene play out with terror-filled eyes. "We need a bathroom. Now!"

"It burns! It burns!"

"Now! She needs a bathroom NOW!" I grabbed his tight t-shirt.

"In the lobby!" He pointed.

"It's too far! No time! No time!" Marge cringed, tightening the grip on her pants. "Now! It's gonna happen!"

"Holy shit! There! Just down the hall! Go!" The bouncer leaped out of the way, and we hustled Marge past while she groaned and shuffled, still clutching her rear.

When we made it around the corner and out of sight, we struggled to suppress our laughter as our snickers merged into one.

"Marge, you could have been an actress." I grinned while we continued past the bathroom sign on our left. "That was an Oscar-worthy performance."

"I can't believe it worked," Sylvie whispered as we pressed together and kept on hustling down the long, abandoned hallway. It wouldn't be long before the bouncer came looking for us.

"Do you know where to go?" Doris asked, and I paused, listening.

"This way. I can hear the girls." We followed the voices, and the giggles got louder as we closed in on the dressing rooms. When we turned the corner and spilled out into backstage, the nerves I'd been suppressing crackled back to life.

It was decades later, and the energy remained the same. The excitement. The anticipation. It was palpable, and it seeped back into my soul. The girls raced around snatching costumes off the racks and struggling for space in the lighted mirrors. Dozens of sets of legs matching mine hustled around while they squealed with the same excitement I felt.

"Wow. It's crazy back here!" Sylvie said while a dancer blew past. "Is it always so busy?"

I nodded. "Always. It's part of the fun. The getting ready. Makeup. Hair. Costumes. It never got old."

"So how do we find her? The lead dancer? That's the one we need to talk to, right? Which one is she?" Marge asked.

I swept my gaze through the horde of women and then down the hallway to the door with the golden sign. "There. She's the star, so she'll be the only one with her own dressing room. She's in there."

We moved through the dancers to the door that said, 'Shelley.'

"She's in here?" Doris asked.

I nodded, remembering how it felt the day I was the one assigned my own personal dressing room. Part of me had been sad to be pulled from the commotion of the other girls, but most of me had been elated to have the prestige of my own space. I was certain this dancer felt the same. I knocked on the door.

"Enter!" her voice sing-songed, and I took a breath before I turned the knob.

We stepped inside, and I saw her reflection as she dusted highlighter across her cheeks. She looked up and caught us staring at her in the mirror, then turned around to face us.

"Who are you?" she asked, furrowing her infuriatingly smooth skin. I remembered when my skin looked like that without the help of doctors.

Marge closed the door behind us and sealed us inside the room.

"Hi, Shelley. We hate to intrude, but I have an offer for you," I said, stepping toward her.

Worry lined her face while she examined us once again. "What are you doing in here? This is my dressing room."

"I know. I was you once, the star of the show, and I would have been furious if a group of strangers barged into my dressing room just before curtain call."

"Well then, you should probably know to get out." She arched a painted-on brow.

"I'm here to ask you not to dance tonight."

"Why would I do that?" she asked, standing up and facing me.

"Because I'll give you five thousand dollars to stay in your dressing room and let me take center stage."

"What?" She choked and then dissolved into laughter. "You must be joking." But I didn't join her in laughter, and soon, her face dropped. "You can't be serious? You're not serious."

"Sweetheart, I'm dead serious. And in about forty years, you're going to look back and remember this moment and understand exactly why I'm standing here offering you five thousand dollars to sit in your room tonight and let me back on that stage."

"This is crazy! Our routines are rehearsed for weeks before we take the stage. You can't just take my spot!"

I lifted the corner of my lip and then broke into the first steps of her routine, spinning to a stop to see her slack-jaw as she appraised me.

"Not bad. How old are you?"

"None of your business. So, what do you say? Five thousand dollars, and you just stay in here." I pulled the stacks of cash out of my bag and watched her eyes grow at the sight of all the crisp green bills.

While she stared at the money and chewed on her bottom lip, I held my breath.

"No. I can't. I'm sorry."

"Ten thousand," I spit out.

"No. I worked too hard to get here, and I'm not losing my spot. They'll fire me, and you know it."

"Just say we kidnapped you or something." Marge joined me at my side. "We can lock you in your bathroom."

Her eyes dropped to the money, but then she shook her head. "No. I've worked my whole life to earn that spot. I'm not going to risk it so some has-been can steal my spotlight. No. The answer is no."

Has-been? Heat flushed to my cheeks while I narrowed my eyes. "I may be a has-been, but I watched you dance last night, and I could have danced circles around you back in my prime. Hell, I can dance circles around you even now. Take the money, and I'll show you."

She lifted her pointed chin. "Not a chance in hell. I'm the star, and I won't let you take my place. Now get out."

Despite the fury stiffening my spine at her harsh rejection, I knew I would have done exactly the same thing. No amount of money could have coaxed me out of the spotlight.

"Fifteen thousand." I tried anyway.

"I'm calling security." She started toward the door, but Marge blocked her.

"Please. Just let me dance," I begged as I looked over to her costume hanging from the rack. "I just want to wear it one more time."

"Get out!" she shouted and tried once more to get to the door. This time Sylvie blocked the attempt.

"Please," I begged. "I want to dance just one more time."

"Security!" she shouted, but Marge leaped forward, trapping the word with a hand over her mouth.

"Marge! What are you doing?" I shrieked as I saw her manhandle the terrified dancer.

"I told you she'd say no, and we needed a gun!"

The moment she said 'gun,' the dancer's eyes nearly bulged out of her head.

"Marge! We said no guns!" Doris swatted at her as the dancer ceased her struggle.

"I don't have a gun. But this hussy is going to get us all arrested!"

The minute she admitted she was unarmed, the dancer resumed her fight. Marge muscled her backward, and I stood watching in horror as she shoved her inside the private bathroom and pushed the door shut.

"Help! Security! Help!" The dancer cried, but the door muffled her pleas so no help would be on the way.

"Marge! What did you do?" I tried to keep my breathing calm but watching Marge lean against the door to contain the restrained dancer sent my heart to speeds faster than I knew it could sustain.

"I can't hold her long! Alice, hurry up and get dressed. Do it!"

I jumped at her commands and hurried over to the costume that sparkled even in these dim lights. When I reached out and touched it, the sounds of the struggle and Doris screeching behind me all faded away. Tracing fingers around the crisp edges of the sequins and rhinestones, and then along the soft feathers pluming out behind it, I was instantly transported back to my youth. Back to the day they gave me my costume, and I knew that finally, I would be at the center of the stage.

The star.

"Quit dickin' around, Alice! Step on it!" Marge huffed while she struggled to keep the door shut.

I snapped out of my nostalgia and turned around. "We can't do this!"

"We're already doing it! I'm not going to jail again for nothing!"

"Again?" Sylvie gasped.

"Just... not now!" Marge shook it off. "Put on the costume! I can't hold her much longer!"

"We're going to jail! We're all going to jail!" Doris fell apart while she paced back and forth in the dressing room. "I'll never survive it!"

"We're not going to jail, Doris!" Sylvie grabbed her by the shoulders and shook. "We made a promise—a pact. And we are getting Alice up on the stage, and we are *not* going to jail. Now snap out of it!"

Light peeked out from the crack in the bathroom door when it pushed open. "Help!" The dancer's voice flooded into the room just before Marge slammed it back shut.

"I'm losing it!" Marge shouted. "Someone's gonna hear her if you don't get your ass in gear!"

Sylvie leaped to her side and leaned up against it. "Hurry up, Alice!"

I turned back to the costume and took a stilling breath. Sure, this wasn't how I intended things to go, but I deserved to be in this costume. I deserved the spotlight. It was stolen from me, and damn it, I was stealing it back.

While they struggled to contain the dancer, I stripped off my clothes, slid on the shiny underwear, and fumbled to close the back bra. When I looked down to see my tidbits glimmering in rhinestones again, I couldn't wipe the grin back off my face. "I still look good!"

"Hurry up!" Marge demanded.

Jumping back to get dressed, I slipped on the plumed tail feathers and reached into my purse, pulling out my crystal covered shoes. The ones I'd stolen the day they'd kicked me out, and the ones I'd held onto all these years hoping that someday I could wear them on stage again. While I slid the sparkling stilettos on, I cringed at the way my muscles screamed from the movement. I was still sore from all those hours of rehearsing this routine, but I powered through while I slipped my swollen feet into the shoes that had been made just for me.

"Ouch," I mumbled while I rose to standing, my feet screaming for relief. But pain had no place in a dancer's repertoire. We danced through it, and tonight I would force my feet to move even though I could already feel the straps cutting through my skin.

The lights in the dressing room flashed, and my heart stuttered to a stop. "This is it! Curtain call!"

"Let me out! Now!" The dancer pushed harder at the door, but Marge and Sylvie put their weight into it.

"I need help with the headdress. Doris, get over here."

Doris paced the room, mumbling to herself while she chewed on her nails.

"Doris! Now!" I commanded, and she jumped at the sound of my voice. "You need to lift it onto my head."

"Okay, yeah. Coming." She hustled over, and I picked up the feathered headdress, carefully lowering it into her grasp.

When it settled into her arms, she nearly dropped it. "Geez Louise! It's so heavy!"

"You have no idea. Now hurry up." I squatted down in front of her, cringing as the pain in my thigh muscles demanded my attention. But I ignored it while I crouched low and prepared for the weight of the one thing I still yearned for all these years.

I felt it settle onto my head. It wasn't the physical weight of it that nearly pushed me all the way to the ground; it was the responsibility that came with being the bearer of the headdress that would set me apart from all the others.

"Wow," Doris said while she stepped back, and I rose. "You look incredible, Alice."

"I do?" I asked, then turned to see myself in the full-length mirror. Tears burned behind my eyes when I caught my reflection. No longer did a housewife, a mother, a widow, and a has-been look back out at me. The reflection in that mirror was me. The dancer. The beautiful, talented, driven woman that arrived in Las Vegas all those years ago. The reflection in the mirror finally looked the way I still envisioned myself. The reflection in the mirror was a star.

"Hot damn, Alice." Marge whistled. "If I hadn't just met a lady last night, I may have made a run at you myself."

"Yeah?" I smiled and wiggled my tail feathers at her.

"Incredible, Alice. You look incredible." Sylvie sighed then returned her attention to the door, still struggling against her.

The lights flickered again. We had only minutes left.

"It's time." I lifted my chin and channeled all the confidence I could muster.

"So, what happens now? You just run out on stage?" Sylvie asked.

"I need to go get in line. I'll just keep my head down and slip into her spot. With any luck, she's the last spot since she's the star, so hopefully, the dancer in front of me will be too focused on herself to notice I'm an imposter."

"And what about this one?" Sylvie jutted her chin at the door. "The second we let go, she's getting security."

"Can you move that in front of the door?" Marge asked me and pointed to a wooden dresser I knew I couldn't budge.

"It's too heavy. It would take all four of us to push it, but you two can't let go of that door."

"I'll move it." Doris stepped to its side and cracked her knuckles.

"Doris. It's got to be two hun—"

She leaned down and pressed her palms into the side, grunting while she pushed the dresser across the carpet.

"Holy shit," I whispered as I watched her face turn red, but she never let up speed.

"Here I come!" She kept pushing and slid the dresser in front of the door while Marge and Sylvie jumped out of the way. When it slid to a stop, she leaned against it, puffing, and then stood up to catch her breath.

The three of us stood gaping at her, and finally, Marge broke the silence.

"Cripes, Doris. What are you? The Hulk?"

Doris only shrugged. "I bake a lot. The stirring and kneading are a surprisingly good arm workout." She gestured in the air as she stirred her invisible bowl.

The lights flicked again, and we all jumped.

"Oh my God. This is it. It's time."

"We'll be in the audience cheering you on! Good luck, Alice!" Sylvie pulled me in for a hug.

"Break a leg." Marge gave me a nod.

"We'll see you after!" Doris waved, and I watched them file out the door.

While I stood in the dressing room alone, I wondered if I would have felt this way if I'd have been given a chance to star in my own show all those decades ago. There was so much fear inside me now. Fear I didn't think I would have had back then. Fear I was too old. I would forget the routine. Fear that security would pull me off the stage and toss me in the clink. But as I stood there watching the lights flash for the final time, I pushed it aside and reminded myself I deserved this. My whole life, I had trained for my chance to shine, and it was stolen from me. Well, this time, no one was taking it away.

CHAPTER EIGHT

Ignoring the muffled pleas of the dancer, I opened the door to the backstage and lowered my head, my oversized headdress hiding my face. Careful not to draw too much attention to myself, I followed the sounds of the audience until I saw the dancers lined up, each one in their own zone, while they rehearsed the routine in their heads one last time. When I saw no open hole awaiting the star, I knew her place was at the back of the line. I hurried to my spot and took a deep breath while I did the same thing as them, closing my eyes and practicing the steps in my mind one more time while I stretched.

"Jesus, Shelley. I thought you were going to miss... Who the fuck are you?"

I opened my eyes to see my line neighbor's shocked expression.

"Shelley is sick. I'm her replacement."

"What? Where's her understudy? If she's sick, it should be Donna here."

"Donna's sick, too. Diarrhea." I sucked the air through my teeth.

"I have never seen you before. What the fuck is going on?"

"I'll be great. Just worry about yourself."

"Hey! Someone get Roger!" she called to a man behind us. "Find out what the hell is going on and who the fuck this woman is!"

Panic of my discovery took my already racing heart to speeds rivaling my favorite vibrator. While it hammered against my ribcage, I watched the man disappear around the corner. *Shit*. I didn't have long. I stared out past the dancers onto the dark stage, pleading for the lights to turn on. To beckon me to dance beneath them once again. To turn on before this Roger fellow came and ripped me from my dream.

Again.

As if they could hear my silent plea, they responded, and the darkness flooded with light. The music broke the silence and merged with the applause I lived to hear.

"Showtime," I whispered to the girl beside me, watching her face drop. "You're a professional. Just get out there and do your job. Don't worry about me."

Before she could argue, the line of ladies leaped forward, each woman moving with grace and elegance as she took the stage. I started my counting, letting the music creep back through me until my neighbor followed behind them.

"5, 6, 7, 8..." I counted and then let my feet do what they were born to do.

Dance.

When I emerged from the curtain and felt the heat of the spotlight saturate my skin, it was all I could do not to stop and open my arms, enveloping it with the same embrace it bestowed upon me. But my feet kept going, they already knew the routine, and even with the screaming pain from the too-tight heels and my mind fluttering away, they kept time and danced me to the center of the stage. When I arrived, I danced to a stop and waited. I waited for the moment I knew was coming.

I heard the click above and felt the extra heat penetrate straight through me. The spotlight. The one reserved for the star. It shined directly on me.

The crowd cheered as we started dancing again. The sound of heels clicking on wood sent me back in time to the days where this was my life. My body moved without thought, the routine already committed to my muscles. My heart soared along with my legs while I kicked my way back into the line, finding myself in the center beside the one dancer who knew my secret. She cast me a sideways glance while maintaining her smile, and I slid my arm onto her shoulder, grateful she was a pro who cared more about the performance than the fact there was an imposter beside her.

But I wasn't an imposter, I thought, while I kept time with the women more than half my age. The imposter was the woman I'd been all these years. The wife who stood on the sidelines, supporting her husband while he climbed his way to the top of the company. The mother who pushed aside all her dreams to make sure her daughter got to live hers. The widow who spent her nights with random men chasing the adoration that could only be found in one place. The place I now stood. The place I belonged. No. I wasn't an imposter. I'd just been away from home for too long.

The song ended, and the applause rose again. It washed over me like a cleansing wave, the echo of the cheers sliding inside my soul and filling the cracks I never thought would heal. The lights dimmed as we waited for the next set, and for a moment, I could see out into the audience. I could see the sea of faces all staring at the stage—all staring at me. And then my gaze stretched across the crowd, and in the back beneath the exit lights, I saw them—the Wilder Widows. Three matching grins met me, and Doris waved. Even though I couldn't break my pose and wave back, I gave them a slight nod. A thank you for helping me relive the dream I hadn't given up on so many years ago.

Movement at the side of the stage caught my eye, and I turned to see the dancer we'd locked away pointing at me with a swarm of bouncers at her side.

"Shit," I whispered while I kept my smile. This routine called for me to exit stage right, straight into the arms of the authorities, who would certainly lock me away. And even though this moment in the spotlight was worth a lifetime in jail, I wasn't ready to be done yet. And I wasn't going to go easily.

The music returned, and with it, the dancers began their routine. My part was to stay with them, then dance my way off stage and return with a costume change. But there would be no costume change tonight. The only other costume I was getting into if I went out that way was an orange jumpsuit. And orange wasn't my color.

I broke from the line and high-kicked my way to the front of the stage. The dancers behind me kept their timing though I knew every one of them struggled to process what to do. Hours and weeks of rehearsals told them my job was to dance off stage. Yet here I was, fan kicking my way back to the spotlight. But they were pros. Trained, dedicated professionals who would dance around a fallen comrade if needed.

While they continued the routine behind me, I let my body explode into a series of moves that caused the audience to roar with applause once again. Every muscle in my body screamed for relief, but I kicked and leaped through the pain. Their cheers worked like painkillers, numbing the agony as I let their adoration wash over me like a soothing bath. My rogue routine continued until the music came to a stop. I landed in my pose and puffed while I struggled for the breath that wouldn't refill my lungs. If last night was training, this was the marathon.

Before my body could collapse from the exhaustion, I saw the sea of bodies rise to their feet. Cheers and whistles refueled me while I closed my eyes and tried to memorize the sounds. This was my first and last performance as the star I had always wanted to be, and I wanted to remember every single second of it. As the applause started to die down, I glanced back over to the side of the stage. The glare from the lead dancer burned brighter than the spotlight. Several police now gathered at her side, and she challenged me with an arched brow.

"Shit." I glanced back at the Wilder Widows still cheering in the back. It was now or never.

"You've all been wonderful! Thank you! Thank you!" I blew kisses to the audience and then leaped off the stage into the aisle. Gasps flooded the room while I sprinted between them, waving and smiling as I bolted toward the back to the widows who watched my approach with wide eyes. "Go! Go!"

"Cripes! Cops!" Marge pointed behind me to the officers rushing the stage.

"Go!" I screamed again as I crashed into them.

"I can't go to jail! I won't survive!" Doris screamed as she rushed outside with us. "I won't make it!"

"Just run, Doris! Run!" Sylvie shouted as she found her stride beside me. We tore down the sidewalk, the feathered plumes of my headdress tugging against the wind that blew past my head when we reached top speed. I clung to it and held it in place.

"Ditch the headdress!" Marge screamed. "It's slowing us down!"

"Never!" I shouted back. I'd waited too long to wear it to discard it on the ground like trash. I ran on, clinging to it tighter while my feet screamed for mercy, but I pushed them even harder. The feathers for my tail touched my calves as I kicked up my heels behind me, running at speeds I hadn't hit in years. Hell, I was a dancer, not a runner. This may have been the fastest I'd ever gone.

Gawking bystanders jumped out of the way, and I saw cell phones pointed in our direction while we raced to the limo just around the corner.

"What the hell? You gotta love Vegas!" I heard a man's voice say as we blew past. Three old women and a Vegas showgirl tearing down the street.

"There! James!" I pointed to the limo where I saw James leaning up against the hood. "James! Start the car! James!" I screamed, but I choked on the words as I struggled for breath. Finally, he looked up, and his widened eyes resembled all the spectators of our sprint to safety.

"I'm not gonna make it," Doris puffed beside me, her pace slowing.

"Come on, Doris!" Sylvie grabbed her hand, tugging her forward to where James jumped into the driver's seat of our limo.

"Run, soldier, run!" Marge barked. "The enemy is at our heels! Stopping is death! Run! RUN!"

Doris dug in and returned to our side. We slammed into the side of the limo, and Sylvie fumbled to open the door.

"Hurry! Open it!" I shouted, then pushed her out of the way, whipping open the door myself. One by one, we dove inside, and I had to squish my headdress through the door. Marge brought up the tail, slamming the door to seal us in.

"What the hell?" James asked as he looked into the back seat.

"No time! Go! GO!" I screamed, and he stepped on the gas.

The tires squealed, and we all collapsed in a heap from the quick movement.

"Holy shit! I did it!" I wheezed as I struggled to catch my breath. "I did it!"

"Cripes, that was close."

"That was the most excitement I've had in my whole life!" Doris fanned her face.

"Let's do it again!" Sylvie said before coughing as she finally took a deep breath.

"We did it! We did it! I was a star!" I pushed the button above my head, and the wind swept into the back of the limo as the moonroof opened. I stood up and wiggled my costume out the top, the breeze whipping me in the face as I emerged out the moonroof, clutching my headdress to keep it from blowing off.

The onlookers we'd just run past stood lined on the streets watching as the limo raced past them. "I'm a star! I'm a star!" I screamed at them, my smile so wide I worried I'd get a bug in my teeth. But even that wouldn't have wiped it away. Because tonight I was finally the star I'd always known I could be.

When we made it safely off the strip, and I had screamed my stardom to anyone who would listen, I dropped back down into a pile of feathers and sat back against the seat.

"Well? Was it worth it?" Sylvie asked as she pulled the bottle of champagne from the ice bucket.

My answering smile said it all. "It was incredible. Everything I wanted and more."

"You were a star, Alice." Marge smiled. "And a criminal. But mostly a star."

I heaved a deep sigh. "Totally worth the jail time, but just in case, we should get the hell outta this town."

"Where are we going now?" Doris asked as Sylvie set out the champagne flutes.

"I think the answer is in the knitting basket." I grinned.

"Yeah? We're going again?" Sylvie untwisted the cage from the champagne.

"Of course we're going again! And this time, I'm spending the rest of our adventure as a STAR!"

The cork popping echoed through our limo, and we squealed with excitement while bubbles poured out the top. Sylvie filled the glasses, and we each lifted one into the air.

"To Alice. The star." She smiled.

"Thank you. All of you. I can't tell you how much it means to me I got to relive this part of my life. I'm excited to help you all achieve your dreams next."

We clinked our glasses together, and the bubbles tickled my lips before I slugged it down.

"So, who's next?" I asked.

"We need to pick to find out. The basket's right here." Sylvie pulled the hideous little knitting basket out of her oversized purse. "You got your wish, so you should pick next."

"Okay." I reached out, and Sylvie lifted the lid. When I slipped my hand inside the basket, I felt the tiny pieces of paper brushing against my skin. I closed my fingers and pulled out my hand, and looked down at the writing on the outside.

Doris.

"Ooooh! Now we get to find out what Doris's whiskey-filled wish was!" I laughed as I held it up.

"Oh my!" Doris fanned her face. "I can't even imagine what I wrote. Probably baking classes."

"It better not be baking classes." I arched a brow.

They all held their breath while I unfolded the piece of paper. After I curled it open, I read the writing and then furrowed my brow. "I want to have a hootie." I read the note then looked up at Doris. "What the hell is a hootie?"

The color drained from her face as she clasped a hand over her mouth.

"What's a hootie, Doris?" Sylvie asked, tipping her head.

"Geez Louise! I need a redo!"

"Doris. What the hell is a..." My eyes lit up while I struggled to choke back my laugh. "It's an orgasm, isn't it?"

"Don't say that word!" Doris covered her ears.

"It *is* an orgasm!" I howled with laughter. "You call it a hootie?"

"Stop!" Doris shook her head as she turned an unnatural shade of head. "I was on whiskey. And we'd just been talking about it, and... well, I never had one. And yes, I call it a hootie. But that's not my wish! I need a new one." She reached for the note, but I snatched it away.

"Nope. This is your wish, and whiskey wishes never lie. If you want an orgasm, we're getting you an orgasm." Marge nodded her head decidedly.

"Stop saying that word!"

"Orgasm!" I shouted. "Orgasm, orgasm, orgasm! You'd better get used to that word because that's exactly what we're going to get you. Every woman deserves orgasms in her life."

"Hell, I need one of those too." Sylvie laughed.

"Well, Marge here is a lesbian. Maybe she could just take care of both of you, and we could move on to the next wish." I chuckled, and Marge impaled me with a look before her stern expression faltered as she suppressed a laugh.

"If Doris wants an orgasm...a *hootie,* we need to do it right. We need to find her a nice, sexy stud who can rock her world like Roxy rocked mine last night." Marge waggled her brows.

"And where exactly are we going to find this stud?"

We all sat in silence while Doris slumped back in her seat. Then Sylvie's face lit up.

"I know where we can find a stud for Doris. There's one city in the world known for love. And since they invented the good kind of kissing, I bet they invented one hell of a hootie too." She pursed her lips and waited for us to catch up. When I did, she nodded along with me.

"Where? Where are we going?" Marge asked, and Doris shared the same confusion.

I knocked on the partition window, and James opened it up.

"Yes, Miss Addington?"

"First off, thanks for the rescue back there. Stellar getaway skills."

"Why thank you, Miss Addington. It looks like you ladies had a hell of a time."

"That we did, James. But now we're going to need you to swing by the hotel and grab our bags, then take us to the airport."

"Absolutely, Miss Addington. Are you heading home?"

I matched Sylvie's mischievous smile and shook my head. "No, James, we're not. We're going to Paris."

DORIS

CHAPTER NINE

In all my seventy-one years on this earth, I never thought I'd see anything as beautiful as Paris. The lovely rivers and bridges were a treat to my eyes, and the tiny cafes dotting the street looked like something straight out of a movie. I'd always had a secret dream to see it, but visiting Paris wasn't something I thought someone like me would ever do. But as soon as Alice said it, I knew this would make a wonderful wish. Even though I had no intentions of doing that thing they had been pressuring me about since we read my wish in Las Vegas, I did want to see every nook and cranny of the City of Love.

"What about him? I bet he could curl your toes." Alice pointed out the limo's window and gestured to the handsome gentleman strolling down the cobblestone street.

"Stop it!" I swatted her arm as the heat rushed back to my cheeks. A flushed face had been a constant feeling since I'd heard Alice read those horrifying words I'd written, and one I knew I'd better get used to since the three Wilder Widows wouldn't stop needling me about my... hootie. I cringed just thinking about it. "We're in Paris, and it's beautiful. And I'm *not* going to... you know, with any strange man. So just stop it!"

"'Don't stop' is what you'll be saying when you're having your hootie. At least that's what I said to Roxy." Marge grinned, and I wanted to crawl inside the seat and disappear beneath the black leather. Knowing they were picturing me, you know, was more mortifying than that time I forgot to take my curlers out when I ran to get more eggs at the store.

"Are you all done yet? Can we stop worrying about that thing I wrote, and just enjoy the fact that we're in Paris? Paris! Never in my wildest dreams did I ever think I'd be in Paris."

Sylvie sighed and stared back out the window. "I've always wanted to come here. It's beautiful."

The limo continued winding down the idyllic streets until we pulled up in front of a grand hotel. When it stopped, Alice pulled her purse into her lap. "This is the best place to stay in Paris. Ed and I came here a couple times when he was traveling for work."

Even though I'd wanted to pay my own way, since Alice insisted on staying at all the best places and flying first class, she'd picked up the bill for our plane tickets and suites in Las Vegas, and now in Paris. Though we all had some savings and life insurance money from our husbands, none of us could have afforded to travel in the kind of luxury Alice demanded. And even though it made me feel a bit guilty, I was grateful to get to enjoy the luxurious things I'd never imagined someone like me could experience.

The limo door opened, and we all filed out, each stopping to stretch while the driver grabbed our bags. I'd spent more time on planes this week than I had my whole life before this, and every muscle in my body ached from all the travel. I noticed Alice take a tender step and wince when she landed on her left foot.

"Still bothering you?" I asked while we started inside.

"It's nothing. I'm fine." She dismissed my comment with a wave, but her unnaturally smooth skin crinkled as she grimaced with each step.

Marge furrowed her brow while she watched Alice hobble toward the hotel entrance. "Maybe we should get you some crutches. You look uncomfortable."

Alice scoffed and spun to meet us. "I will *not* be caught dead in Paris on some hideous sticks. They won't go with any of my outfits. I'm just a little sore from my return to the stage. I'll be fine."

She spun on her heel and started off, one awkward step at a time. After exchanging a glance, the three of us followed. When we arrived at the counter behind her, Alice was already barking orders at the front desk receptionist. Being the most seasoned traveler of our bunch, she took over booking all our flights and hotels, and I was grateful we had her. I wouldn't know the first thing about reserving a room or plane tickets. Harold and I rarely traveled except for the occasional wedding or to visit our grandkids, and when we did, he always took care of the arrangements. Now Alice handled it, and I was glad this wasn't one more skill I'd need to learn as a widow. Figuring out taxes and paying bills had been more than enough for me.

This whole trip had been such a whirlwind. It was hard to believe this was real and not some bizarre dream I was having after taking cold medicine. When I'd started this Wilder Widows club, I had intentions of knitting circles and baking tips. Hopping on a plane and jetting around the world was never part of the plan. But as nervous as I was to step out of my comfort zone and join these women, I had to admit I was having the time of my life.

"We'll need those four rooms next to each other if you can," Sylvie said while she helped Alice sort out our reservations.

"Maybe put one of them on the opposite side of the hotel." Marge chuckled, and we all furrowed our brows. "You know, since Doris will be having a hootie and hollering away. I don't need to have that sound burned into my mind for eternity. Keep her room away from ours."

With a gasp, I clutched my chest, and my eyes darted to the receptionist who only pinched her brows together and continued clicking away at the keyboard. At least I didn't think she understood Marge. Alice and Sylvie burst into laughter, and their mirth-filled eyes raked over me once again.

"Stop it!" I hollered in hushed tones. "All of you, stop it! I'm not having a," I leaned in and whispered lower, "*hootie*. It's not happening. I want a room next to all of you. I'll be scared all by myself!"

I could see the enjoyment in their glimmering eyes at how uncomfortable this made me. While I wanted to crawl out of my skin again, they only seemed egged on by the horror I knew I wore plain on my face.

"Lighten up, Doris." Alice smirked. "We're just having a go at you."

I crossed my arms and did my best to level them with a glare, hoping I was getting my point across but knowing it probably fell short. Scolding had never been my strong suit. Harold was the firm one with the kids while I tried to bribe them with baked goods. I narrowed my eyes and tried anyway. "Well, stop it. I'm going to get on a plane and go home if you don't stop."

"We're just teasing." Sylvie reached out and touched my arm. "All in good fun."

"Well, it's not. I'm not comfortable with it at all." I lifted my chin and pursed my lips, hoping that maybe, just maybe, they would stop.

"Fine. Four rooms together," Alice said to the receptionist, who never stopped typing.

"Oui. Four rooms, all side by side, Miss Addington." His thick French accent caressed every word. "Should I have your bags brought up?"

"Yes. Merci," she answered while she took the keycards from him. "Come on, ladies. Let's go get refreshed before we hit the town."

We followed the concierge to the elevator and rode up in silence. When we got to our floor, one by one we filed down the hall and broke off to enter our rooms. Mine was last, and I followed him through the door, stopping to catch my breath when I saw the beautiful room before me. Elegant curtains dangled from the windows framing a spectacular view of Paris. The four-poster bed was far more elegant than any I'd ever slept in with its innate carvings and crisp linens. Every inch of this room screamed luxury. When I traveled with Harold to visit the kids, we always stayed at a Super 8 since he got a discount, and this was a far cry from that.

"Will you be needing anything else?" the concierge asked while he waited at the door.

"No. Thank you. It's beautiful."

A long pause kept him at the door, and I remembered then I'd seen the others slip him some money on their way in.

"Oh! Hold on!" Remembering this wasn't a Super 8, I fumbled through my purse and opened my wallet, pulling out a few dollar bills. "Thank you."

"Merci." He bowed before closing the door behind him.

Alone at last, I fell back on the bed with a sigh. I glanced out the window and watched the fingers of sunlight stretch across Paris, and it took my breath away. How was someone like me, a suburban girl from Minnesota, in a luxurious hotel room in Paris?

A knock on the adjoining door startled me, and I almost slipped off the bed.

"You in there having a hootie?" Marge asked from the other side, and I heard the laughter peppering the words. "Don't be too loud. I gotta call and let my mom know I landed safely. Don't want her to think I'm staying in a brothel."

"Stop it!" I tossed a pillow at the door and climbed under the covers. Her laughter trickled under the door before it quieted.

"We're going for lunch in an hour. Take a nap. You'll need your energy for later. For your... hootie."

"Heavens to Betsy, Marge! I'll come over there and pummel you with my rolling pin!"

"You didn't pack your rolling pin. At least I hope you didn't."

I hadn't, in fact, packed my rolling pin, though I'd thought about it. You never knew when you may end up needing to do some baking, and only my grandmother's rolling pin got my dough as smooth as I liked. While I listened to Marge tittering on the other side of the door, I wished I'd put it in my bag.

"Good. Night," I spat and pulled the covers up over my head. Even with my heart racing from the embarrassment of her picturing me doing... that... it didn't take but a minute for the exhaustion of the travels to push me off to sleep.

****

"Oh, man. I wish Roxy was here to try this. It's delicious," Marge said, her full mouth mumbling the words while she tried to chew the second course of our lunch, a decadent cheese smeared on the baguette. It was even better than the first course, which was some of the best food I'd ever eaten.

"This sure beats hot dish." I moaned my pleasure while chewing the creamy delight.

"What the hell is hot dish?" Alice hoisted her empty champagne glass and gave it a shake to attract our waiter's attention.

"Haven't you ever had hot dish?" I asked.

"I've had food that is hot and in a dish. Is that hot dish?" Alice set her glass down after receiving an acknowledging nod from our waiter.

I shook my head, swallowing the last bite of my food. "No. It's a dish I used to make for my family all the time. You take tater tots—"

"Tater tots?" Marge arched a brow.

"Yes. Tater tots, cream of mushroom soup, some ground beef, and I liked to throw peas in mine. You know, for nutritional value."

"Oh yes, because peas are going to make that so nutritious." Alice rolled her eyes and shoved another bite of cheese in her mouth.

"I can't believe you've never had hot dish! Pretty common where I'm from in Minnesota. Although every family has their own interpretation. It was Harold's favorite, so I made it for my family every Sunday night."

Memories of my days as a wife and mother flooded back into me. I could still hear my children's laugher while they raced in the door after a Sunday football game in the park, tripping over one another while they dropped their dirty clothes and raced to the table for the fresh-baked cookies I would have waiting. Harold would greet them with a smile from his post in front of the television, and I would swipe my hands across my apron before pulling them each in for a hug. One by one, I would squeeze each of my six children, pausing to inhale the smell of their hair while they wiggled free for more cookies.

After making them each wash up, they would file down the stairs and join us at the old oak table that had been in my family for two generations. Harold would turn off the television, and my family would gather around the table, our laughter and stories filling every nook and cranny of our home.

My family.

Even though it was only Harold who'd passed away, the distance between all of them scattered around the country often made me feel like I was the last one left. What I wouldn't give to fall back in time and live forever in the moments where my home was filled with more than just me and my knitting supplies.

"I've made it this many years without eating a tater tot, and I'm certainly not going to start now." Alice crinkled her nose, but her soured expression brightened instantly when the waiter appeared with her mimosa.

"It actually sounds good." Sylvie shrugged, and a nostalgic glow rolled through her eyes. "My mother used to make a rice dish with cream of mushroom soup and chicken. Oh, it's been years since I've had it."

"I love me some tater tots, but it ain't as good as this. No way, no how." Marge smacked her lips and then popped another bite of food in her mouth.

"Nothing is as good as this," Sylvie agreed and took a bite as well. "You have excellent taste in restaurants and hotels, Alice. You haven't steered us wrong yet."

"Do you know what else I have excellent taste in?" She arched a brow and jutted her chin toward the handsome waiter in the next section over. "Men."

Sylvie snickered. "I don't doubt that one bit."

"What do you think of that one, Doris? I bet he could give you a hootie."

There it was again. That unbearable heat scalding my cheeks. It surprised me I had any skin left after the number of times they'd heated my cheeks to an inferno.

"You're redder than the roses in your garden." Marge snorted.

"We aren't talking about this anymore."

"You're right. Talk is cheap. It's time for action. Excuse me!" Alice waved toward the waiter. "Excuse me!"

When I saw him look up at her and start our direction, I choked down my piece of cheese. He was a tall drink of water with blue eyes and dark hair framing a chiseled face. And he couldn't have been over thirty-five. Half my age. "What are you doing?"

A cat with a canary held nothing to the sinister smile pulling up Alice's lips. "What I do best. Picking up men."

"Don't!" I whispered, leaning across the table and tugging at her Chanel jacket. "Stop it!"

With a quick shrug, she dislodged my hand and gave him a wave.

Marge sat back and crossed her arms. "This oughta be good."

"Alice, Doris looks pretty uncomfortable. Maybe we should ease up." Worry lines creased Sylvie's face while she looked me over.

And she was right. Alice was taking this one step too far. Heck, we were one step too far about a mile ago.

As the waiter approached, my heart hammered inside my chest. The last time it rattled my ribcage this hard was when I got the call Harold had a heart attack. I didn't like the feeling then, and I didn't like it now.

"Bonjour, Madame. How can I assist you?" he asked when he arrived at our table.

It was all I could do not to get up and run, knowing the things Alice was capable of.

"Bonjour." She smiled, her long, manicured finger crooking to him and encouraging him closer. Holding her gaze, he leaned in.

Even at her age, I watched her seductive gaze spark desire behind his eyes. It matched the promises brewing behind hers. A soft pink flush crept across his cheeks as he closed in on her space.

"How can I help you, Madame?" he asked, his voice mirroring her seductive tone.

I watched in awe as she traced her pink nail across his cheek, finishing beneath his chin and pulling it closer. She was like a siren sitting at the edge of the sea, charming sailors right into the rocks. And from the way his eyes sparkled, it seemed he would steer his ship straight at them if it meant getting a chance to have her make good on the promises flickering behind her eyes.

"What is your name?"

"Gabriel."

"Well, Gabriel. Do you know two things in this world that get better with age?"

"Wine and women," he answered so quickly even Alice was taken aback.

She recovered and matched his coy grin with her own. "Very impressive, Gabriel. And very true."

"Is there something I can," he paused and perused her with a gaze that had me ready to recite the rosary, "do for you?"

"Actually, Gabriel. My friend over here is looking to have a good time in Paris. If you know what I mean."

When their gazes broke apart and clapped onto me, I nearly tumbled out of my chair. "Alice!"

"Alice," Sylvie warned. "What are you doing?"

The warning and my obvious discomfort didn't dissuade her. "Doris needs to loosen up a little. Do you have any ideas how we could make that happen?"

I tried to melt into my chair, disappear from under his probing gaze. It wasn't just that a man other than my husband was looking at me like that, but more that I wasn't as beautiful as Alice or any other woman a man like him could have fawning at his feet. Sure, Alice could be his mother... heck maybe even his grandmother... but she was stunning. Confident. Sexy. The way men of all ages eyeballed her when she walked into a room was something I'd never felt in my life. And while this waiter raked me up and down, insecurity and embarrassment churned inside me until I could almost explode. Even though I would never lay with a man who wasn't my husband, the thought of him turning up his nose at me was almost as bad as the thought of him considering doing what it was Alice insinuated.

"Your friend is beautiful."

Beautiful? Did someone call me beautiful? I studied his face to make sure he was looking at me and not someone behind me. I glanced over my shoulder just to make sure. When I looked back at him, those blue eyes were still staring straight at me. *Me? Beautiful?* Harold called me pretty on occasion in my youth, but this was the first time in my life anyone had ever called me beautiful. The shock of his words sent a heatwave to my cheeks so intense I wanted to dump my ice water on my head.

"Isn't she though?" Alice grinned. "Well, Doris? What do you say? Should we see if Gabriel can meet us out for drinks later?"

Silence settled over the table, and for a brief moment, I pictured myself in his arms. I pictured kisses like I'd seen in the movies. Passionate and long. Kisses I'd never had with Harold. Ours were mechanical. Kisses shared between a husband and wife. What I pictured doing with Gabriel was anything but mechanical, and as I envisioned his tongue invading my mouth and his hands caressing my body, a wave of shame rose up and pulled me under.

Tears burst from my eyes, and I leaped up from the table, knocking over several glasses when I bumped the edge.

"Doris!" Sylvie called as I ran through the restaurant, but I ignored her and pushed through the crowd, eyes blurred with tears, searching for a place to hide. I heard Marge and Alice join in on the calls, but I saw a bathroom door and darted inside, racing into the stall and slamming it shut behind me.

CHAPTER TEN

"Doris?" Sylvie called into the bathroom. Her voice echoed and bounced off the stone walls, but I sat quietly on the toilet pretending I didn't hear her. "Doris? I know you're in here. Come out and talk to me."

"No." I sniffled and wiped a sleeve across my nose. "Just leave me alone."

Her kitten heels clicked across the floor, and her shadow stretched under the stall door when she stopped just outside it. "Doris. Let me in."

"Just go away."

"Alice was out of line. I'm so sorry we embarrassed you."

"It *was* embarrassing. And... it's more than that." I struggled to identify all the emotions churning inside me. Embarrassment topped the list, but others mingled with it, confusing me even more.

"What else is it, Doris? Talk to me. Open the door."

I swiped at a tear with the back of my hand. "Just go, Sylvie. I don't want anyone to see me like this."

"Fine. If you won't open the door, I'm coming under."

"What? Sylvie!" But before I could argue, her shadow contracted, and her head appeared beneath the stall.

"God, I hope they cleaned these floors," she said as she slid under. When she popped up in front of me, she dusted off her shirt and swiped a hand across her pants. "Now, tell me what's wrong."

I opened my mouth to speak, but only sobs came out.

Sylvie leaned down and pulled me into a hug. "It's okay, Doris. Everything will be okay."

"You in here?" Marge shouted from the doorway, her rough voice booming through the vacant room.

"We're in here, Marge," Sylvie responded.

"Where?" Alice asked.

"Third stall," Sylvie called.

Two more shadows appeared under the door.

"You coming out?" Marge asked.

I shook my head, and Sylvie answered back. "She's not coming out."

"Then let us in," Alice said.

"No. I just want to be—" Before I could finish the sentence, Sylvie unlocked the door and pressed against the slate grey wall. Alice and Marge squeezed in beside her and closed the door behind them.

"You alright?" Marge asked in the softest voice she was capable of.

"No." I sniffled again.

"I'm sorry, Doris." Alice reached out and touched my shoulder, but I shrugged it off. "I didn't mean to upset you. I was just trying to help."

"By pimping me out to some man in a restaurant?" I spat, shocked by the force in my own voice. "*That* is you helping?"

"Well, he's handsome, and I'm sure he could—"

"Enough about my hootie! I'm not having a hootie! Especially not with a stranger! I'm not like you. Sex is... sex is supposed to be special. Something shared between two people in love. A husband and a wife."

Alice submitted without a fight. "You're absolutely right, Doris. I've been too pushy, and this isn't who you are. I'm sorry I tried to force it on you and that I embarrassed you. I promise I won't push another man on you. It was all in good fun, and I see now I went too far."

"You did go too far." Even though my anger softened, I still tried to give her my best glare.

"We did," Marge agreed. "And I'm sorry I laughed at you."

"Thank you." I wiped the last of the tears drying on my cheeks. "I just... I can't just take a man to bed. *Especially* a young man like that. I'm old enough to be his grandma."

"That you may," Alice said, "but he thought you were beautiful. Even if you don't take him to bed, it must still feel nice knowing a man that looks like that still finds you desirable. At least it always does for me."

There. That unknown emotion reared up inside of me again, but this time I was able to identify it. *Desire.* For the first time in my life, I truly felt desire, and that just sent shame back to the top of my growing heap of emotions.

"I may be a lesbian, but I can still say he was a looker. You should be walking on cloud nine. He wanted to have his way with you."

"That's part of the problem!" I admitted, then buried my head in my hands. "I *did* like it. And I had... thoughts." I whispered the last word and peeked out between my fingers.

"Is that so?" One corner of Alice's lips rose and twitched in excitement. "Because if you want to–"

"No!" I ripped my hands from my face and shook my head. "No, I don't want to... you know. But the fact I even thought about it... well, it's shameful!"

"It's natural, Doris. Human. There's nothing wrong with desire," Sylvie said. "You have nothing to be ashamed of."

"Well, I've never felt desire. And now I have, and God is looking down, just shaking his head at me. He's so disappointed."

A snort slipped out of Marge's nose. "Really? People are starving, killing each other, and the world has gone to hell in a handbasket, but you think God stopped everything because you pictured yourself having sex with a hot waiter?"

"God sees all." I pointed up to the ceiling and pursed my lips.

"Well, that may be," Sylvie said, "but then he also sees your pure heart. He won't fault you for being human, Doris. And it is healthy. And natural. And I have a hard time believing you'll get to the gates of Heaven and get turned away because you pictured yourself in the throes with Gabriel, the waiter."

Her soft smile settled me, and I nodded my head, finally coming back to my senses. "Thanks, Sylvie. I needed to hear that."

"You're allowed to have thoughts, Doris."

"Really? You've never had impure thoughts?" Alice asked, tipping her head. "Never?"

My eyebrows shot to my hairline as I shook my head. "No. Never."

The bathroom door opened, and thudding footsteps approached. We remained silent, packed in our stall while we listened. A quick zip echoed through the room, followed by a loud stream of urine. When I heard the low cough of a man in the stall beside us, I clapped a hand over my mouth. The other three widows followed suit, and the four of us listened to the man beside us humming his tune while he finished his business. When he left, and the bathroom door thudded closed, we burst into laughter.

"Is this the men's bathroom?" Sylvie howled between laughs.

"That was definitely a man pissing." Marge snorted.

"I didn't look! I just ran in here! Heavens to Betsy, we're in the men's bathroom, aren't we?"

"This is probably the closest Doris is getting to a penis in Paris." Alice dissolved into hysterics, and the rest of us joined her.

When we'd finally composed ourselves, I took one last breath to refill my lungs deflated from laughter. Sylvie reached out a hand. I took it and let her hoist me up.

"Can we get out of here before some man comes in and takes a shit?" Marge wrinkled her nose. "I've been beside enough shitting men in 'Nam. It ain't pretty."

Our laughter converged again as we hustled out of the bathroom.

****

A bouquet of aromas from the fragrant flowers lining the park blended with the fresh bakery smells floating down the road. The four of us walked arm-in-arm as we made our way through the park across from the restaurant. Alice had paid the bill and made her apologies before meeting us outside and agreeing some fresh afternoon Paris air was just what I needed to recover.

Alice squeezed my arm. "I really am sorry about making you so upset."

"It's alright, Alice. I'm sorry I ran off like a ninny. This is just all so much for me to handle."

"You've really never had fantasies, Doris?"

I shook my head. "No. I mean, I've seen movies with some saucy scenes, but as far as putting myself in them? Never. It's just not like that for me. Sex was my wifely duty, but it was never something I considered enjoyable."

"I'm sad you never got to enjoy it," Sylvie said. "Bruce was no pro in the sack, but I found ways to make it enjoyable. And there were a couple men before Bruce far more talented." Her eyes closed momentarily while she inhaled a deep breath. "One in particular that I envisioned on top of me every time I needed a little help getting my hootie. Worked like a charm."

"I did it those two times with Percy, but if it had been like it was with Roxy..." Marge blew out a breath, "I would have spent the better part of my life in bed."

Alice smirked. "Nothing wrong with that."

Marge lifted her eyebrows. "Now I get why you're getting it on with everyone, Alice. I get it."

They exchanged a brief look of solidarity.

"I just don't think that sex is an important part of my life. It was a wifely duty. My husband is dead, so now it doesn't even matter anymore." I surprised myself that I had started talking so openly about sex. Until these three women dragged me on this adventure, it wasn't something I'd ever discussed with anyone. It still felt odd to talk about it, but each time we did, I cringed a little less.

"Doris, I know that we went too far back there," Sylvie said. "But I do think you're selling yourself short just closing that chapter of your life. You *are* beautiful—"

"Yeah, now that she doesn't look like the Old Maid." Marge chuckled, and Sylvie bumped her with an elbow and went on.

"Men notice you now, Doris, even if you aren't noticing them noticing you. Sure, that doesn't mean you're going to hop in bed with some waiter you just met, but you shouldn't discount meeting a man and falling in love again."

"Oh, I don't know about that." I shook my head. "I think that ship has also sailed. It's just me and my knitting now. And, of course, I have you gals."

"Bah!" Marge waved her hand in the air. "If I can find someone, *you* can find someone. I also thought my days were done, and I would just rot alone in my mother's house, but let me tell you, Doris... we aren't dead yet! It's time you think about moving forward into this next chapter of your life and opening yourself up to the possibilities."

Alice pursed her lips then smiled. "Wow. Look at Marge going full Tony Robbins."

"Can it, Alice. Meeting Roxy... changed me. I'm excited again. Life is filled once again with new opportunities and adventures. I hope that soon it is for all of you. I'm telling you, Doris... don't shut out the possibilities. Maybe you've got a Roxy waiting for you too."

"I'm not a lesbian!" I scoffed. It wasn't that I had a problem with Marge's sexuality, but the thought of it shocked me. In fact, I was still trying to process how a woman could be married for the better part of her life and then come out as a lesbian. And even though I had no intention of taking a strange man to bed, I knew with certainty it wasn't a woman I wanted.

"I didn't mean a *woman*. I meant a *someone*. For you, a man."

"Was there ever anyone besides Harold?" Sylvie asked.

I shook my head. "No. Never. Harold was literally the boy next door. We grew up together. Our freshman year of high school, he asked me to a dance and then to go steady. We were together ever since. Well, until three years ago when he died."

"Wow." Alice blew out a breath. "So, you had only one man your entire life. I can't imagine."

"There's nothing wrong with it," I defended. "It's the way God intended it."

Sylvie stepped closer to my side. "But what now? Does God think you need to spend the rest of your life alone? I can't imagine that's what He would want for you."

Pursing my lips together, for the first time in my life I thought about what life could be like with another man. Would he think I was beautiful? Kiss me with passion like I'd never known? Make my heart race the way Marge said hers did when she met Roxy? But what if he didn't like my cooking? Or heaven forbid he had something horribly wrong with him, like a gluten intolerance, and he couldn't enjoy my muffins. It was bad enough having to bake a batch of those abominations for every church outing now.

I shook my head. "I don't think I can. The thought of another man is too scary. I had my husband. My children and a life I loved. That was enough for me."

"But you can have that and more," Sylvie said. "Bruce is barely cold in the ground, and granted I hated that son of a bitch, I know there is still a chance for me to find love again."

That same nostalgic twinkle danced across her eyes for but a moment before dissolving once again.

"I find love all the time. In fact, I'm finding love with Gabriel tonight back at my room. He's coming by at ten." Alice's white teeth flashed in the bright sunlight.

"Alice! You're kidding?" Sylvie dissolved into laughter.

"Why would I be kidding? If Doris isn't going to climb him like a jungle gym, one of us certainly should."

"Alice! You're terrible!" I shouldn't have been shocked, but once again, she managed to drop my jaw.

"You only live once. Time you started embracing that as well, Doris. Not with one-night stands like I do but relinquishing your life to nothing but knitting isn't living. Marge is right. It's time to open yourself up to the possibilities."

"Possibilities." I let my gaze drift over the bright flowers peeking out of the ground. For a moment I wondered if it was possible, like those flowers, perhaps I could bloom again. "I never thought much about those. I was the oldest of four girls, and I spent most of my childhood babysitting and raising my sisters. Both of my parents worked, and I enjoyed taking care of them, so motherhood was a natural choice for me. But I knew when I had children of my own, I didn't want to be away at work all day like my mother. I wanted to be home with them and enjoying every second of their youths. Teaching them and loving them. Knowing this, I never thought about college or other possibilities. I married Harold two months after graduation and started having babies the following year. That was the life I wanted, and it's exactly the life I got. And I don't regret one second of it."

"But that was then," Sylvie said. "This is now. This is the second part of your life, and you need to just be open to more. Your children are gone. Your husband is gone. You deserve to find a new kind of happiness."

Despite Sylvie's good intentions, being reminded that I had nothing left felt like a slap across the face. But they *were* gone—all of them. And even though I missed them all, I was glad my children had found their own lives. Each had gone to college, and then they had all gone off in different directions. Katie, my oldest, lived in Orlando and was happily married with two grown children and a job she loved. Abbie got a job in wine sales and traveled the world. Cindy graduated college with her high school sweetheart and followed in my footsteps as a stay-at-home mom, and they had two beautiful boys. Joe got a job as an executive in New York and lived a big life in publishing. Peter met a sweet southern girl and moved to Atlanta to marry her, and now they have one little one just under a year old. And then my youngest, Lizzie. Always the free spirit, she finished college and ever since just swung from job to job, and boyfriend to boyfriend. Each one happy in their own lives, and each one far removed from mine.

Picturing them living their best lives caused me to smile, as it often did, but then the sadness of missing them pulled my lips back down. I was alone.

"So, if you aren't going to find yourself a young Parisian lover, what exactly is your wish, Doris?" Marge asked.

What was my wish? Even though I didn't remember writing it, apparently a hootie was my deepest desire. But sleeping with a man I didn't love wasn't something I could do. No. The real wish I had was impossible. "To travel back in time and be a wife and mother again. To be needed again."

That was it—what was missing in my life. No one needed me anymore. Even as a child, my mother needed me to help care for the younger children. Then I married Harold, and I got to take care of him. Cooking, cleaning, and making sure he could relax when he came home from a long day of work. And then my children. Each of them needed me. To be a mom. A chauffeur. A cook. A shoulder to cry. A hand to hold. And then, one by one, they each let go, each found their own way until it was just Harold left to take care of. And even that fulfilled me. Being a wife. But then... I was alone. No one needed me anymore.

"Oh, Doris." Sylvie slung an arm around my shoulder and pulled me in tight, causing the tears to slip past my heavy lids.

"I miss being needed."

"We need you." Marge closed an arm around my other shoulder, and the two of them sandwiched me with their warmth.

"No, you don't." I swiped away a tear. "No one needs me."

"Don't need you?" Marge squeezed. "If it weren't for you, who would pester us to get together for our Wilder Widow meetings? Without you, we never would have met."

My loneliness sent me to Marge's door a year after Harold died. I'd heard her own husband had passed away and, while I felt sad she was suffering from the loss, deep down, I was thrilled to have another widow to spend time with. Someone I could share all my new knowledge with. Someone who would maybe need me. I'd baked a batch of muffins and showed up on her doorstep that day, much like I'd done with Alice a couple years after that, and now Sylvie.

"And the muffins!" Sylvie grinned. "We *need* your muffins. There isn't anyone on the planet who can bake like you do."

Sniffling, I nodded. "They are really good muffins."

Alice stepped to Sylvie's side and reached her long arm around us both, increasing the pressure surrounding me. "I would be lost without you, Doris."

"And I would be lost without all of you. I'm sorry I'm always forcing you all to get together and knit with me. It's just that... I'm so lonely."

"Stop apologizing," Alice said. "We may grumble about it, but I, for one, love our Wilder Widows times together."

"Me too," Marge agreed.

"Me three." Sylvie smiled. "And look at where this little group you put together has taken us. We're in Paris, ladies!"

A heavy sigh lifted my shoulders, and I exhaled some of my sadness. "I love you, ladies. I don't know what I'd do without you."

"Nor us without you." Alice squeezed my hand. "But you still need to pick a wish, Doris."

"Can't 'Go to Paris' just be the wish?" I asked while we continued sauntering along.

"No," they mirrored.

"Your wish has to be wild. We're the *Wilder* Widows, after all! And we all know what your true wish is." Alice arched a brow.

"Don't start that up again! I'm not having sex with a stranger!"

"I know, I know!" Alice lifted her free hand in submission. "Wait a minute." Slowing down, she tugged all of us to a stop.

When she turned to face me, and I saw the mischief flickering in her eyes, I knew I should turn and run back to the hotel. Even though she was in impeccable shape and could easily outrun me on a regular day, with her bum foot, I was pretty sure she couldn't catch me.

"What is going on in that pretty little head of yours?" Sylvie tipped her head.

"I have an idea." There it was again. The cat that ate the darn canary.

CHAPTER ELEVEN

After a quick cab ride wound us through Paris, we followed along behind Alice until we stood at the door of a boutique shop situated along a small cobblestone street. I tried to read the pink script letters above the door, but I'd never learned French. "What is this place?"

Alice only smiled and pressed open the door, the small bell overhead jingling as we passed beneath it.

"Bonjour!" a women's voice called from the back of the small store.

"Bonjour!" Alice called back.

As the tiny brunette lady wound her way through the racks toward us, I scanned the bright colors surrounding us. Feather boas in a rainbow of colors brushed along my arm as I passed them by. Shelves filled with colorful objects stretched out along each wall, and I furrowed my brow while I tried to make out what they were. A children's toy store? Dog toys?

"What can I help you ladies with today?" The young woman asked, switching to English after she heard Alice's English response.

"We will just need a few minutes to browse, but I'll be certain to let you know if we have questions. And please, ignore the tantrum that's about to occur."

The woman's furrowed brow mirrored my own. *Tantrum?*

"Very well." She shrugged and turned, heading back to her counter. "I'll be over here if you have any questions."

When I turned back to face the Wilder Widows, I saw the same mischief twinkling in all three sets of eyes. "What's going on? What is this place?"

"Doris," Alice said, taking my hand in hers. "We know we were wrong to try to force a man on you. Sex is not something to be taken lightly."

I nodded along.

"But your deepest desire was a hootie."

I scoffed and opened my mouth to speak, but Alice raised her hand and stopped me.

"Now, now. Let me finish. There are other ways to have a hootie that don't involve a man. And we are standing in the store with every sex toy imaginable to make sure we accomplish our goal."

Slowly, my eyes widened as I scanned the store again. The bright-colored objects weren't dog toys or children's toys, after all. They were sex toys.

"Alice!" I shrieked and started toward the door.

Marge snatched me by the wrist and pulled me back to a stop. "Hold your horses, speed racer."

I stomped my foot on the ground. "I can't be in here! It's not right!"

"Doris," Sylvie said. "There is nothing wrong with enjoying yourself *without* a man. It's natural."

"These are *not* natural!" I struggled to take my next breath, feeling like I was in a funhouse as the walls closed in around me.

"Just take a breath, Doris." Alice exaggerated her own, and I inhaled and exhaled with her. "There. Better?"

"No!"

The clerk at the counter peeked over at us, but Alice reassured her with a wink. "Alright, Doris. Panic is over, and now we can talk about other ways you can get your hootie."

In all my days, I never imagined I would come to Paris. But even more surprising was the fact I was standing smack dab in the center of a house of pleasure. I could almost feel the disapproving gaze of God staring down at me shaking his head once again. "No. I can't."

"Before you bolt out of here to live a life devoid of all pleasure, just hear us out." Sylvie's serious expression startled me. For the first time since we landed, I realized they weren't just teasing me. This wasn't just a long, drawn-out embarrassing prank. They truly wanted to see me experience this.

"Why is this so important? I can't imagine that having a hootie is really going to change my life."

All three sets of eyes widened in response, and three heads tipped up and down at me.

Alice squeezed her eyes tight, opening them and letting her intense gaze penetrate mine. "Wars are fought over hooties, Doris. Marriages crumble, and careers destroyed all for hooties. People *die* for hooties, Doris. There's a reason for that."

"I'd die for another hootie from Roxy."

"I'm not leaving here without at least a few new toys. I need me a hootie, too." Sylvie smiled and plucked a plastic box from the shelf beside me. "Look, Doris. This one is a rabbit. You love rabbits!"

The strange-looking contraption resembled a bunny at first, but when I looked at it closer, I saw the phallic shape and knew what it was intended for. "Geez Louise! That's obscene!" I looked at it again. "And *huge!* Are they supposed to be that big?"

"Just like men, they come in all different sizes, sweetie." Alice pulled a smaller one from the shelf. "See, this one is a cute dolphin. And it's waterproof, which means bath time fun!"

I loved bubble baths, and now the thought of a dolphin sex-toy would forever haunt my me-time. "What does it even do?" I asked, not seeing the same recognizable phallic shape in this one.

"This one isn't for inside. It's for outside. It vibrates against your–"

"Okay! That's enough. I've heard enough."

"This would be a great one to start with, though." Sylvie tried to shove it in my hands.

"I'm not starting anything. I can't. I'm sorry. I know you all think I need to have a hootie, and it will change my life, but it's just not going to happen. I had sex enough times with Harold; if I was capable of one, I'm sure it would have happened. Maybe it *did* happen, and I just didn't notice!"

All three heads shook violently at me.

"You would know," Sylvie said.

"But maybe it—"

"You would *definitely* know." Alice laughed.

"Well, maybe I'm missing something down there, and I'm not even capable of having a hootie." Confident in my conclusion, I crossed my arms and gave them a stiff glance.

"Unless you are some strange medical marvel, you have the parts necessary for a hootie." Marge snickered.

Alice nudged Marge with an elbow. "Marge, you're the lesbo. Why don't you take a look? Pop the old hood and have a peek around to make sure all her parts are where they're supposed to be."

Marge and I answered with mirrored glowers.

"No one is looking down at my lady bits! I think I'm ready to go."

"Alright, alright," Alice submitted. "We tried. We'll stop now."

"Thank the good Lord," I said on a sigh.

"But you really are missing out." Sylvie pulled the dolphin toy from Alice's hands and tucked it under her elbow. "I'm taking this one with me."

"Good choice. I have it in pink and blue," Alice added.

"So, can we go now?" Shifting my weight, I looked to the door.

"Well, we can go, Doris, but we still need to figure out what your Wilder Widows wish is if you aren't going to have a hootie. A wild wish."

"I've never done anything wild in my life." I sighed. "I don't think I have it in me."

"Never? You've *never* done anything wild?" Marge scowled and shook her head. "That's even more reason to make sure you do something crazy."

My mind wandered, moving backward through my life, searching for any instance I'd done something crazy. Something wild and exhilarating. But each step back in time revealed only more and more of the same. Motherhood. Marriage. Responsibilities. There was no memory of any wild adventures. Except...

"Once!" Holding up my finger, I lit up, remembering the one time I'd done something wild in my life.

"Well? What was it?" Sylvie asked while she picked up another strange looking device and turned over the box to read the back.

"When I was sixteen, there was a dance. Homecoming, I think. It was just a few months after Harold and I started dating. After the dance, he and I went with a group of friends to the water tower. We climbed up to the top, and it was exhilarating! And then the girls I was with decided we should flash the town!"

All those feelings of excitement and terror bubbled back up inside me. I remembered how scared I'd been climbing to the top. How small everything had looked down below while I clung to the railing until the color drained from my knuckles. Harold had kissed me on the cheek that night for the very first time. After months of only hand-holding, he'd taken our relationship to the next level, and when I'd felt his lips on my cheek, my heart had raced even harder than it had when I'd looked out over the horizon.

I could almost feel the butterflies fluttering around again. It had been so long since I'd thought about that night, and now I felt like I could close my eyes and open them once again and be peering out over the little suburban town I'd called home.

"You naughty little minx, you!" Marge bumped my shoulder with a fist. "You flashed people! And here you let us think you were a prude."

Shaking my head, I snapped back to the present. "Oh no!" I tittered. "I never flashed anyone. The other girls did, but I couldn't. I turned away while they lifted their shirts."

"Wait a minute." Sylvie closed her eyes and lifted a hand. "Are you telling me you didn't even *do* the wild part of the night?"

"I told you! I climbed the water tower!"

Three sets of blinking eyes stared blankly back at me. Alice broke the stare and shook her head.

"Doris. Darling." Her soft ivory hand pressed into my cheek. "Climbing to the top of the water tower is not the wild part. Flashing people. That's the wild part."

"Well, it was wild for me." I scoffed.

As Alice stared me down, I saw it again. That light. The mirth. The idea coming to life, and I knew she was up to no good.

"Well, if sex toys and hooties aren't your wish, what if we say climbing to the top of the Eiffel Tower is your wish? Helping you relive that moment of your youth when you climbed the water tower."

I nodded my head as the smile spread across my face. "Yes! That sounds like a wonderful wish! Oh, yes!"

"And flashing Paris from the top."

My face dropped along with my stomach.

"Oh! Yes!" Marge clapped, and Sylvie bounced beside her.

"What? No!" Stepping back, I shook my head harder, but their heads nodded in response.

"Yes." Sylvie smiled.

"Yes." Alice put an arm around my shoulders. "We're going to the top of the Eiffel Tower, and this time you're going to do it. You're going to flash Paris."

My mouth opened and closed, but it felt like someone shoved a ball of yarn in my mouth. *Flash Paris? Impossible!*

"Doris. It's time." Marge narrowed her oversized eyes. "You need to break the mold. Step out of your comfort zone. Live a little. And we're going to be right by your side."

"And we'll flash Paris with you." Alice gave a sharp nod.

"We will?" Sylvie and Marge mirrored.

"All for one, and one for all. Doris, we'll do it with you. What do you say?"

I chewed on my lower lip while I thought back to the night I'd stood on that water tower. Deep down, I'd wanted to lift up my shirt and scream to the world. To feel the freedom those other girls experienced. But I had been too scared. And while the widows stared at me, I felt the same fear once again.

"Well?" Sylvie arched a brow. "If we do it, will you?"

Fear. Excitement. Exhilaration. More fear. Emotions I hadn't felt since I was seventeen flooded back into me. I wanted to say no. Say that God wouldn't approve, or I was too old, too insecure, or too scared. Instead, my head nodded.

"You will?" Alice's face illuminated even more than right after she got one of her chemical peels.

"Okay. I'll do it," I whispered, still shocked to hear the words coming out of my mouth.

"Really? You'll do it?" Sylvie beamed.

"I'll do it." This time I said it with conviction. This time I meant it. There would be no chickening out and turning away at the last minute, closing my eyes and letting another experience pass me by. This time I would feel the wind on my chest and the freedom that came with it. "I'll do it!" I shouted.

"Drop the dildos, Sylvie! We've got some flashing to do!" Alice grabbed my hand and pulled me out of the store, waving frantically at a cab.

CHAPTER TWELVE

"Why is the line so long?" Marge grumbled while we stood in the same row of people we'd been behind for the last hour, each waiting their turn to take the lift up the Eiffel Tower.

Sylvie answered. "Because we didn't plan on flashing Paris tonight and preorder our tickets."

"This is getting ridiculous. I don't do lines." Alice rose on her tiptoes and peered over the heads of the people waiting ahead of us. "We need to get up there before Doris chickens out. I'll be right back."

Before we could find out what she was up to, Alice disappeared into the crowds all waiting their turn to tour the impressive structure towering over us. Tipping back my head, I stretched my gaze up to the top again.

"This is a lot taller than the water tower," I said, staring up and feeling my confidence continuing its descent into darkness. Alice was right. Every minute we stood here was one more minute I had to change my mind. And after an hour, all that renewed enthusiasm I'd harvested in the naughty shop snuck out like a balloon with a pinhole in it. With each passing second, my courage deflated. "It's okay, ladies. We can just go. I don't need to–"

"No!" they echoed.

"You're not backing out. Not this time, soldier." Clasping my shoulders, Marge gave me a soft shake. "Forward. Always forward, soldier. And tonight, forward is taking you up there to show your tatas to the world." She jutted a finger toward the top.

Once again, my head nodded before I had time to come up with an excuse to get out of this. And did I want to get out of this? Deep down, I knew I didn't want to. For once in my life, I wanted to be wild. To shed my rigid rules and morals like a snake sheds its skin.

"If I can do this, so can you." Stiffening her stance, Sylvie went shoulder to shoulder with Marge.

"Okay. I can do this."

"You can do this." Marge gave one last squeeze and released her grip.

"Widows! Wilder Widows!" Alice screeched over the din of voices flooding the space surrounding us.

We turned to see her waving frantically beside a tour guide near the entrance. After exchanging glances, we slipped out under the ropes and hurried toward her.

"Hurry up, girls!" she called as we got closer. "I got us in!"

"Of course you did. You're Alice," Sylvie said between huffed breaths when we arrived. "I would expect nothing less."

"Ladies, meet Alexandre. He'll be our guide." Alice waved a hand over the middle-aged man who could barely take his eyes off her to acknowledge us.

"So, we're really doing this?" I struggled to swallow over the lump in my throat.

"Yes!" they echoed, and Alice reached out and grabbed my hand, tugging me to her side.

"Lead the way, Alexandre."

With one last smitten smile at her, Alexandre turned and led us around the crowds to the doors of the lift. When we stepped inside and started our ascent, I reached out and grabbed Sylvie's hand. Her soft brown eyes traveled from the exceptional views and locked with mine. Even though she was the newest member of the Wilder Widows club, I felt like I'd known her my whole life... like a lifelong friend who had been at my side through all the ups and downs of my existence. She reassured me with a look, squeezing my hand tight.

When we arrived at the second story landing, Alexandre led us through the crowds for a peek out over the views sweeping across Paris.

"This isn't even the top?" I asked while watching the tiny dots moving in the city below. Boats puttered down the river, the glow of their lights reflecting on the darkening water they floated across. The last sliver of sunlight crept beneath the horizon, and Paris glowed with a sea of lights flickering on below, fighting the darkness closing in around them.

"Cripes. That's almost as beautiful as Roxy," Marge said on a sigh.

Each time she mentioned Roxy, her eyes sparkled brighter than the lights multiplying below. While I stared at her face once again aglow, I felt envious she'd found someone else. A new love to reignite her even in her later years. It hadn't occurred to me until this trip that perhaps there *was* still time for me to find someone else of my own. Perhaps I wouldn't have to spend the rest of my life alone. Perhaps, just perhaps, I could find someone in this world who would need me once again. With a heart swelling at the thought, I turned away from Marge and let the idea start to glow like the lights of Paris.

"We'd better hurry if we're going to catch the lift to the summit." Alexandre waved us onward, and we filed through the crowd to the next lift.

As it rose higher and higher in the sky, my anxiety rose with it. Was I really doing this? Me? Doris Miller? A God-fearing housewife from Minnesota was going to stand at the summit of the Eiffel Tower and show my tatas to the world? I said a silent prayer and asked for early forgiveness while I waited for the doors to open.

"Holy shit. Look at it. Paris." Alice opened her arms, embracing the breathtaking site stretched out for what seemed like eternity.

"Incredible," Sylvie breathed. "It's absolutely incredible."

Alexandre looked at his watch. "Light show starts in a few minutes. Enjoy."

Like a trained actress suddenly in the spotlight, Alice flipped on her charm. "Alexandre." She stepped in front of him, pressing a palm to his chest. "You are my hero. A true knight in shining armor."

Even in the dim light, I could see the flush fill his cheeks. "Anything for you, Miss Addington."

"Please. Call me Alice. We'll be back to the lift in a little while."

"I'll be waiting."

With a soft kiss on his cheek, she sent him on his way. As quickly as it came, her charm flipped back off again. "Okay ladies, we're doing this."

We all nodded though mine didn't have the same certainty as the others. "So, do we just walk up to the ledge and," I leaned in so the other spectators couldn't hear, "lift up our shirts for a second?"

Rolling her eyes, Alice took my hand and pulled me to the edge. "We'll do it in a more spectacular fashion than that. This isn't a water tower. It's the Eiffel Tower. What do you ladies say we do it when the light show starts?"

Sylvie nodded fast, and Marge shrugged. "Works for me. Too bad I don't wear dresses. If I did, I could just lift it over my knees, and you could still see my tits."

We erupted in laughter loud enough to draw the stares of the couples surrounding us, enjoying the romantic views.

"Sorry," I apologized to them between snickers. Here they were enjoying a romantic moment, and the Wilder Widows showed up to ruin the mood. If only they knew what would transpire when that light show started.

"I wish I was wearing a dress as well." Alice sighed and waved a hand over her pencil skirt.

We all turned to look at her, and Sylvie said, "Why? Your tits are still up where they belong."

"Well, of course they are." She cocked a hip. "I wish I was wearing a dress so I could hoist it up over my head and give Paris the best show it's ever seen."

Her wiggling eyebrows sent us back into stitches and drew more attention from the couples taking selfies.

"Sorry," I mouthed again.

One couple just behind Alice smiled at me, then went back to their snuggling. While I watched her rest her head on his shoulder, a protective arm around her waist, a knot tighter than a knitting ball should be formed in my stomach. Once upon a time in my life I stood on a ledge with a man's arm around my shoulder. His soft kiss pressed against my cheek while I stared out into what I'd thought was the whole world. And now, even though I missed my life with Harold, I wondered if maybe someday I could feel another man's arm wrap around my waist again. Feel the stubble from his chin brush against my cheek. Feel the way that young woman looked like she felt right now.

Wanted. Protected. Needed.

"Get up here!" Alice waved me forward, and I noticed the group already lined up along the fence wrapping around the summit.

With one last longing glance at the happy couple, I stepped in between Sylvie and Alice. "I can't believe I'm doing this."

"You're just finishing what you should have decades ago." Sylvie's warm smile soothed me again.

Decades. How was it possible that much time had gone by? An entire lifetime in the blink of an eye. As I grabbed the railing in front of me and squeezed, I saw the same white knuckles I'd stared down at all those years ago. But this time, when I looked up, it wasn't a sea of ranch-style houses and parks stretched in front of me. It was Paris. Bigger. Better. Grander. And suddenly, I wondered if that was what this second act in my life would be. No longer an afterthought, biding my time alone until God called me home. No. This act of my life was going to be my Grand Finale. My Paris.

Bigger. Better. Grander.

Suddenly the tower lit up with thousands of flickering lights. I gasped in awe as the space surrounding us sparkled and glowed while the lights raced around us.

"Oh my God!" Sylvie squealed as she spun in circles. "It's like magic!"

And it *was* like magic. Like the flickering lights, I felt my own desires sparking to life. Hope and possibility coursed through me like the lights surging around us. And this time I wouldn't chicken out. I wasn't going to turn away from the possibilities because of fear or insecurity. Not in this act of my life. The rest of my life had been lived for others. This time it was just about me.

I stepped back up to the railing and glanced to the women at my sides. Reaching behind me, I unhooked my bra and watched their eyes turn into orbs as I grabbed the bottom of my shirt. "Are we doing this?"

"Hell yeah!" Alice unhooked her bra and grinned.

"I feel like we're at Mardi Gras!" Sylvie laughed while she followed suit and got into position.

Marge struggled to unclasp her bra. "I think I should go to the other side. I don't want to knock anyone out with my big swingers."

"You're not going anywhere. Wilder Widows on three." I arched a brow and eliciting a nod from each of them.

My hammering heart rattled my ribcage once again, but this time I didn't let it deter me. This time I let it invigorate me and fuel my desire to live this next part of my life to the fullest. I inhaled a deep breath, and when I released it, I also exhaled all my fears and limitations. With one last apology to God, I smiled.

"One... two... three!"

"WILDER WIDOWS!"

We screamed in unison as we hoisted up our shirts. The shock from the freedom and the cool breeze blowing across my bare chest sucked the air from my lungs. Breathless, I closed my eyes and tried to burn the feelings coursing through me into my mind.

Fearless. Brave. Free.

They were feelings I never wanted to go away. Feelings that were now the soundtrack to my new life. My second act.

After what felt like an eternity of freedom, Sylvie laughed and lowered her shirt. "Holy shit! You did it!"

I pulled down my own, saddened to feel the fabric brush against my breasts again. "I did it." I grinned so wide I was sure it was brighter than all the lights sparkling around Paris.

"Way to go, Doris! The Old Maid is no more!" Marge tucked her breasts back into her oversized bra then clapped me on the back.

Alice still stood with her unnaturally perky breasts exposed, continuing to hold the eyes of the slack-jawed crowds surrounding us.

Sylvie tapped her on the shoulder. "We're done, Alice. You can put your shirt down now."

"One more second," she said, closing her eyes and inhaling a deep breath. When she blew it out, she pulled her shirt down and smiled at the people still gawking. With a flourish, she took a bow before turning back to us. "There. That ought to have given them enough of a show. And Doris! I'm proud of you! I didn't think you had it in you."

Neither had I. But now that it was in me, I never wanted to let it go. I wanted to hold onto this feeling and wrap it around myself like a warm blanket and never take it off.

"How do you feel?" Sylvie asked, and the Wilder Widows stared at me, awaiting my answer.

"Alive."

For the first time since Harold died, leaving me all alone, I felt alive again. Heck, it may have been the first time in my life I'd ever felt this alive. My whole life I'd had mapped out by the time I was ten. Graduate. Get married. Have babies. Raise a family. Die. What I hadn't taken into account was what would happen after I'd raised that family, the time between the life I'd chosen and the death that awaited. And now I had a fresh new chapter in the book of my life, and I got to choose what went in it—a new story filled with more adventure than I'd ever dared to dream.

Their smiles matched my own, and they closed around me, pressing me between them as they squeezed their arms around each other.

"Thank you," I whispered into Alice's shoulder. "Thank you."

"Welcome to the rest of your life, Doris." She kissed my head before they gave me one last hug and we broke apart.

The crowds finally stopped staring at us and went back to watching the light show that continued sparkling around us.

"Well, that's two wishes down," Alice said, reaching into her oversized bag and pulling out the little knitting basket. "Are we ready for three?"

Sylvie and Marge exchanged excited glances, and we all nodded.

"Doris, since this was your wish, it's your turn to pick."

She shook the basket and lifted the lid I'd crocheted myself. With a deep breath, I reached inside and felt around until a piece of paper touched my fingertips. I plucked it out and unfolded it quickly, my new spark for life demanding more adventure. More of this feeling. More excitement. I read the words on the paper, and suddenly my newfound drive for adventure fluttered away on the breeze that wafted between us.

"What? Why does your face look like that?" Sylvie asked, stepping to my side.

I looked up at Marge and saw the tight-lipped smile forming on her face.

"No. No way!" I waved the paper in her face while I shook my head. "I can't run! I have bunions!"

"What is it?" Alice ripped the paper from my hand and gasped. "Run with the bulls? Are you nuts?"

"Run with the bulls? Holy shit," Sylvie whispered as she ripped away the paper and read the words herself.

Marge crossed her arms and smiled wide. And from the look on her face, I knew she wouldn't take no for an answer. This was her wish, and we'd promised to make it happen. With one last look over the sparkling lights of Paris, I tapped back into those newfound feelings of bravery and adventure. I took a deep breath and turned back to her. It seemed the first chapter in the new book of my life would take me to Spain. "Looks like we're running with the bulls, ladies."

MARGE

CHAPTER THIRTEEN

"You ready, Doris?" I called through the bathroom door of our hotel room in Pamplona.

"One second!" she sing-songed back, her new joyous outlook on life highlighting her tone.

"Hurry up! I need to touch up my makeup." Alice shouted over my shoulder, then grumbled under her breath. "The last time I had to share a bathroom with three other women was back when I was a showgirl. And even then, I got my own bathroom at the end when they chose me as the lead."

After spending a week in our luxury hotel rooms in Paris, Alice hadn't shut up since we arrived in this rundown hotel last night.

"Cripes. Can it, Alice. You'll survive a few days shoved in this sardine tin with us. It's a hell of a step up from the accommodations back in 'Nam. This may as well be the Ritz in comparison. You'll live."

She answered with an eye-roll. Since finding out this was the only room we could get in Pamplona during San Fermin Festival on such short notice, and at a price as high as our suites in Paris, it seemed like her eyeballs were in a constant state of rotation, and her breathing reduced to only long sighs and huffs. What a pansy.

Looking around the tiny room, I felt more at home here than I had this entire trip. Alice's insistence on luxury hotels and fine dining every step of the way was a far cry from the life I'd spent seventy-three years living. Between growing up in a two-bedroom apartment with my Italian immigrant grandparents, my parents and older brother, and my tent in 'Nam, I was used to cramped quarters. This dingy hotel with the stained orange carpets and two twin beds taking up most of the space made me feel at home. In fact, the carpet was the same shade as my mother's, so maybe that was why it felt so familiar.

Sylvie sat on the edge of the tiny bed, picking a piece of lint off her white pants. The room was so small with our bags of luggage crammed inside, she used my suitcase as a footrest.

"Sorry I took so long. I wanted to put on a little extra make-up for the party," Doris said, emerging from the dilapidated bathroom.

Doris wearing make-up. It still looked odd to me to see the Old Maid I'd known for years sporting her fashionable new hairdo, eyeshadow, and pink rouge on her cheeks. While the other three widows enjoyed their makeovers from Las Vegas, I was still content to look the way I always had. I'd never swiped a make-up brush across my face before, and I wasn't about to start now. Even when they'd told us we needed to wear makeup in Vietnam to help perk up the soldiers, I'd railed against it, relying on my nursing skills and winning personality.

"Took you long enough." Alice pushed past her but paused before stepping into the bathroom. Lines crinkled along the bridge of her nose while she tipped it up in disgust at the sight of the less-than-ideal space. "It may as well be an outhouse. And I don't do outhouses."

"Cripes, Alice. It didn't kill you going in it last night. and it won't kill you now." I gave her a shove, and she skidded to a stop in front of the cracked mirror.

"What time does the opening ceremony start?" Sylvie stood and stretched.

"It's already started. But the main celebration starts at noon. That's when they fire the rocket to signify the start of the San Fermin Festival. We need to get there early, though, or we'll never get anywhere near Plaza de Castillo, and that's where the party is... and where we need to be."

"It's all so exciting!" Doris clasped her hands together, the anticipation sparkling inside eyes tipped with dark mascara. "A Spanish festival. The perfect start to my new chapter."

"You're just lucky the timing worked out," Alice called from the bathroom.

But it wasn't luck. I knew this festival was coming up when I made my wish. I'd wanted to attend since I'd first heard about it back in 'Nam. After learning about San Fermin at a club at our military base, we'd made a pact to come to this festival and run with the bulls after we got out. But like most things in life, it never happened. "All that matters is that we're here. And I want to see it all, so hurry your skinny ass up and let's go."

Alice stepped out, her perfect silver hair shaped into place, and her makeup flawless as always. I suppressed my chuckle, knowing something about this festival that my better-looking counterparts were unaware of. And it was something I would let them find out themselves.

"How do I tie this on?" Sylvie asked, holding up the same red scarf we'd each bought when we got to town. Along with our white pants and white shirts, the red fabric completed the costume everyone wore to the San Fermín Festival and for running with the bulls. I'd insisted we each buy two pairs of white pants and shirts, as well as two scarves when we arrived. Even though they'd thought only one outfit was necessary, I knew they would thank me for the fresh change of clothes after today ended.

"You don't tie it on yet." I pulled mine out of my pocket. "It's tradition to wait until the rocket fires at noon and the festival starts before putting it on. Just hang onto it and follow my lead when it's time."

Doris tucked her scarf into her purse. "You sure know a lot about this festival, Marge."

"I've been waiting my whole adult life to do this. I've studied all the traditions and watched every National Geographic episode on Running with the Bulls. And if my shows are right, we're running late, and I don't want to miss the opening ceremony. So, let's hop to it, soldiers."

Bumping her hand against her head in a salute, Doris gave a sharp nod. "Yes, sir!"

One by one, they filed out of the room after me. Even in the hotel, the energy pulsing around us was palpable as other guests dressed head to toe in white filed into the hallways—all heading to the square, no doubt. Me and my three comrades, and tens of thousands of other visitors, would soon converge in Plaza de Castillo.

When I opened the door and stepped outside, the July heat and humidity shocked me to a stop. But after a moment,

I adjusted and continued trudging forward with the swarm of people pouring down the stone streets. With each step bringing us closer to the square, the din of the crowds increased to a low rumble. As we turned the corner and spilled into the square, the widows and I stuttered to a stop. A sea of bodies covered in white stretched in every direction. Music filled the electrified air and vibrated the stones beneath my feet.

"Holy shit," Sylvie said, stepping to my side. "That is a *lot* of people!"

"How are we even going to fit?" Doris stood on my other side, eyes widening while she swept her gaze across the crowd.

"I bet it smells like B.O. something fierce in there." Alice brushed a piece of her hair back into place after a welcomed breeze blew through and tousled it. "It's hot, there are way too many people for that space, and Europeans aren't known for their hygiene."

Though I'd seen videos about the festival, the sight of so many bodies in one place overwhelmed even me.

"Maybe we should sit this one out," Alice said, continuing to look at the crowds in disgust. "Go find a nice little restaurant somewhere and grab a martini or two."

Shaking my head, I took a breath. "No. This is part of the festival, and we're going." Without another word, I pushed into the sea of bodies, reaching back and grabbing hold of Sylvie's hand. She did the same with Doris, and soon the four of us were linked together, weaving our way deeper into the celebration.

When the wall of bodies became too compacted to pass, I stopped and pulled them up to my side. "This should work."

"What exactly happens now?" Doris rose on her tiptoes to try and see over the crowd.

"Now the celebration begins. They'll fire a rocket, and then all hell breaks loose."

"Hell?" Worry lines creased along Doris's forehead. "What kind of hell?"

"Not actual hell, Doris. Just one of the world's biggest parties. Don't worry, your soul is safe. Actually, this whole festival is to celebrate a Catholic saint. So, you can think of it like church." I grinned, knowing that while there was truth behind the words, the debauchery awaiting us when that rocket exploded was a far cry from an afternoon in the pews.

"Oh! Wonderful! I'm Catholic." She smiled and exhaled a breath ripe with relief, losing the terrified look. The same excited look she'd worn daily since we flashed everyone from the Eiffel Tower returned.

The crowd cheered when the mayor stepped out onto the balcony. My Spanish wasn't good enough to understand his words, but listening to the crowd's responsive roars rise and fall told me we were closing in on the moment I'd spent decades waiting for.

"Take out your scarves," I said to the girls when I saw the other festivalgoers raise theirs high in the air. One by one, the widows lifted their scarves along with me. We held them up while the noise of the crowd softened into near silence.

"Pamploneses, Pamplonesas, Viva San Fermín! Gora San Fermín!" A voice shouted over the crowd.

"Viva San Fermín! Gora San Fermín!" the crowd cheered back.

A loud boom echoed through the square, but the sound paled in comparison to the deafening roar of the crowd. It shook me to the core, rattling my old bones while it traveled through us. With a grin as wide as it was after the first time I kissed Roxy, I shook my scarf and cheered with them.

Music started back up, and the crowd began to move, bouncing and dancing as they screamed in unison. A rush of liquid blasted me in the face, and I tossed my head back, opening my mouth, allowing the champagne to flood in and bubble along my tongue.

"My hair!" Alice screamed. Opening my eyes, I turned to see her taking a champagne blast to the head. My laughter erupted harder than the champagne bottle as the bubbly liquid pelted the widows in the face. When the stream stopped, and they stood soaking wet, wide eyes blinking hard, I rolled forward and clutched my stomach, still struggling to catch my breath.

"What the hell was that?" Sylvie wiped the smeared mascara from below her eyes.

"Welcome to the San Fermin Festival, ladies!" I laughed as I opened my arms and took a spin around, more champagne spraying me while I danced a little jig.

"That is a waste of perfectly good alcohol!" Alice huffed and surveyed the surrounding scene. More champagne sprayed, and this time she stepped toward it and opened her mouth, smiling when she successfully captured some on her tongue.

"This is crazy!" Sylvie screamed over the crowd, her laughter mingling with the songs breaking out around us. "Absolutely crazy!"

"It's amazing!" I shouted back.

It was everything we had hoped for and more: Percy, Manz, Stilts, and me. While I stood in the middle of the celebration we'd talked about so many times sitting around a campfire in Vietnam, I fought off the sadness they weren't here with me experiencing it.

"This is *not* church!" Doris shouted into my ear, leaning back to scold me with a look. But before she could pierce me all the way, another blast of champagne to the head caused her to snap her eyes shut.

Laughter rolled through my belly like waves along the beach. I knew if Percy had been alive to be here, he'd be the one spraying champagne. But instead of Percy, Manz, and Stilts, I stared at the three widows who now took their places. My comrades from a different time in my life.

"Well, when in Pamplona!" Sylvie gave in to the energy of the crowd, and though soaked in champagne, began dancing with a young Spaniard who could have passed for Antonio Banderas back in the nineties. He grabbed her by the waist, spinning her in circles before hoisting her onto his shoulders. Another man handed her a bottle of champagne, and she grinned wider than the Cheshire Cat before popping the cork to the roaring approval of the crowd. A waterfall of champagne exploded around us, along with the sounds of her laughter.

When I glanced to my left, Doris and Alice held hands as they bounced in circles. Even with her flattened hair and smeared make-up, Alice still maintained her air of grace as she twirled Doris beneath her arm. They'd all argued every step of the way to Pamplona, calling me crazy, telling me I'd lost my mind, but seeing the joy they each radiated while we flowed with the crowds convinced me I'd been right to dig my heels in and force them here.

A firm squeeze enveloped my waist, and I squawked as my body hoisted into the air. The jarring movement stopped, and I settled onto the shoulders of a man who grinned up at me with a smile that would have weakened my knees if I was straight. But if I'd learned one thing on this trip, the most important thing, it was that I was about as straight as Staff Sgt. Adam's nose after he took a blow to the face with the butt of a rifle.

When I'd locked eyes with Roxy, I'd known it was then or never. One chance to find out if I really *was* a lesbian or if I was just asexual. Later that night, when she'd reached up and touched my face, drawing me in for a soft kiss, I'd been more terrified and exhilarated than any other time in my entire life. Those moments before our lips touched dwarfed any of the fear I'd felt in 'Nam with bullets whizzing past and bombs shaking the ground. But when her lips had touched mine, all the fear melted away. All the puzzle pieces snapped into place. The unanswered question screamed out its answer, and for the first time in my life, I knew who I was. I'd lost myself in her kiss, only to find myself for the first time in my life.

"Marge! This is wonderful!" Doris called up to me. My handsome steed pranced me around in circles and grabbed a bottle of sangria being passed around. After taking a chug, he passed it up. Tipping back my head, I let the pink liquid pour into my mouth. It slid down my throat, and some of it missed, running down my chin and pooling onto my shirt and the head of the man below me. I mouthed an apology, but he only laughed, taking the bottle of sangria and dumping the rest on his head.

Our white clothes turned pink while it splattered and sprayed around us. Doris squealed as she caught a few drops on her shirt. While she assessed the damage, another spray of sangria collided with her chest, leaving a pink burst across her left breast. Gasping, she looked at her breast and then back up at me.

"My shirt!" she shouted up. "It's ruined!"

"Mustard! Someone hit me with mustard!" Alice said, pushing into the group. Her sangria-soaked pink clothes displayed a large splotch of yellow. "It doesn't even match the pink!"

"I told you, ladies, we needed two outfits!" I called down while my ride continued dancing around with me. "Wait until they start throwing flour!"

"They did!" Sylvie pulled up beside me on the shoulders of the man she still rode. Her face and clothing were a mosaic of pinks and yellows, and the only thing on her face I could see behind the wall of white was her eyes. But behind the flour mask, they still sparkled with joy.

"Viva San Fermin!" I screamed at the top of my lungs, letting the words rip through my throat. The crowd around me went wild, screaming back the sentiment. For just a moment, I pictured Manz and Stilts standing below me. Their faces covered in sangria and smiles instead of dirt and blood. Percy stood beside them, his youth restored as he grinned up at me, a gentle nod thanking me for following through on our dream. But when I blinked, three women stared at me, and they smiled and screamed it too.

"Viva San Fermin!"

CHAPTER FOURTEEN

"That was the craziest experience I have ever had!" Sylvie settled into the chair at the restaurant we'd all piled into. We'd considered going back to the hotel to change since we were coated in more layers of food and booze than we could ever count, but a sea of people around the restaurant sported the same look, so we went in any way.

"Did you see me perform my high kick over that guy's head?" Alice laughed while she dabbed the mascara smeared under her eyes. All three widows resembled raccoons while they sat across from me. Now more than ever, I was grateful I wasn't one to wear makeup.

Doris nodded. "You had a whole section cheering you on!"

In true Alice form, she'd embraced the opportunity to dance for a crowd. After she began her routine, a group of people formed around her, clapping and cheering while she had kicked higher than any human's leg should go. At least it was a hell of a lot higher than mine could ever flex.

"You were a star out there," Sylvie said.

A proud smile tipped Alice's lips while she nodded. "I'm always a star."

"That you are." I laughed. "So, what did you ladies think?"

"At first, I was horrified," Doris said, but then her face softened. "And then I embraced it and had the time of my life!"

"Better than church?" My eyebrow rose.

Pursing her lips together, she nodded. "But don't tell Father O'Malley."

Pretending to zip my lips shut, I gave her a wink. "Secret is safe with me. Maybe you can encourage your church group to celebrate saints the way they do at San Fermin."

"Oh!" She fanned her face. "They would all keel over dead if they saw what I was just part of!"

"But you had fun?"

"Yes! So much!"

"Me too," Sylvie agreed. "It was incredible being in the middle of all of those young, wild partiers. We were twice the age of everyone there!"

"And twice as good looking." Alice smirked.

"I had no idea that there was so much history and festivity around the running of the bulls. I thought people just ran down the streets one day of the year, and that was it."

Shaking my head, I flagged the waiter. "No. It's a long tradition, and it spans an entire week."

The waiter arrived and perused us all with a questioning gaze before breaking into a smile. "I see you ladies took advantage of the opening ceremonies?"

"Hell yeah, we did." I grinned.

"Looks like you had a wonderful time! Can I get you something to drink? More sangria?"

"Ugh. Sangria." Alice faked a gag. "I've had enough of that to last a lifetime. I'll take a water."

All three of our heads swiveled toward her.

"Did you just order water instead of alcohol?" I asked, shock raising my naturally baritone voice.

"Holy shit." Sylvie mirrored my surprise.

Doris made the sign of the cross. "Praise, Jesus."

"Shut it," Alice warned, and I snapped my gaping mouth shut.

"Anyone else want a water?" the waiter asked while stifling his smile.

Sylvie made a circle around the table with her finger. "Four, please." He nodded and backed away.

The warm buzz from the multiple rounds of sangria and champagne still tingled through me. Even though we'd been doused in water from the balconies during the ceremony, I hadn't drunk any in hours. It felt like I'd swallowed razor blades after screaming 'Viva San Fermin' more times than I could count.

When the waiter returned with a pitcher of water, we took turns filling our glasses and guzzling it down. Each one of us moaned our relief as we downed the water. The waiter noticed the empty pitcher and picked it up to refill it while dropping off our menus.

Sylvie looked over the menu. "I love tapas."

"I've never had it." Doris squinted at the menu.

"Tapas just means small plates," Alice said. "We order lots of small plates and share with the table."

"Sounds wonderful!"

"Doubt they'll have hot dish, though," Alice teased.

Doris sneered from behind her menu then went back to mouthing the Spanish words I knew she didn't understand. In fact, none of us spoke Spanish, and I had no idea what we would be ordering.

When the waiter returned, we gave up on trying to translate the menu and asked him to bring out courses of his favorites. Excited to be in charge of our dining experience, he hurried away to get started.

"So, you still haven't told us why this festival was your wish." Sylvie wiped at her smeared eyes again.

A heavy sigh lifted my shoulders. They were right. I'd left out the real reason I was so intent on coming to this festival. It was something I didn't talk about often. Couldn't talk about. But the sangria and champagne took hold of my tongue.

"I made a promise back in 'Nam to Percy and our two best friends, Manz and Stilts."

Just saying their names sent me down a rabbit hole I'd spent a lot of years trying to step around. Sliding back in time, I once again sat around a campfire with my closest friends. I could still hear their laughter as if they sat beside me here in Pamplona.

The widows watched me quietly, and I knew how much pain must be apparent on my face.

"What happened, Marge?" Doris asked, reaching out to touch my hand.

"We met in-country."

I saw the confusion furrow their brows, and I realized they didn't know the lingo that had been part of my vocabulary since signing up for the Army. "In-country means we met in Vietnam."

"Oh, that makes sense." Sylvie nodded.

"When I signed up for the Army, I didn't know anyone. I was barely twenty, but I knew my skills and temperament would be helpful during the war. So, I did my duty and signed up for my first tour. I ended up in Saigon, and that's where I met them."

Once again, I was no longer sitting at a table with the Wilder Widows. I was standing on a tarmac in Vietnam surveying the surroundings that terrified me more than I had admitted, even to myself.

"After a whirlwind trip from the States jumping from one plane to the next, I landed out in the middle of nowhere. It was surreal climbing out of the Jeep on the base, knowing it would be my home for the next few days, months, or even years. As I walked to the tent that I would call home, a few GIs were tossing around a makeshift football, and an overshot throw sent it colliding with my head. Percy ran up apologizing, and right behind him, trailed his two buddies, Manz and Stilts."

I remembered Percy skidding to a stop in front of me, sweat beading his smooth brow. Barely twenty himself, he'd only been in-country for a few weeks, and the horrors of war hadn't deepened the creases on his face yet.

"After they apologized, they introduced themselves and offered to buy me a drink at the club to make it up for me."

"There were clubs in Vietnam?" Alice asked, leaning forward, perching her chin on her knuckles.

I snorted. "Well, we called it a club, but really it was a tent with warm drinks and an old jukebox with some American records. We spent a lot of time in that tent when we weren't on shift."

"I still can't believe you were in Vietnam. It must have been awful." Doris squeezed my hand a little tighter.

Shrugging, I tipped my head. "Sometimes. Sometimes not. There were plenty of times we had fun, lots of laughs, and I got to see a part of the world I never would have seen otherwise. Other times," I paused while memories flashed through my mind like lightning, "it was hell."

"So that's how you met Percy, then?" Sylvie asked.

Smiling, I remembered my sweet Percy. "Yes. We met when I was first stationed, and then after I was moved elsewhere, we met again. On and off for the first year, Percy, Manz, and Stilts kept marching back into my life. I made other friends there, of course, but those three were my best. They would get sent off on assignment, and I would be left behind with the other nurses, desperate to go with them. But because I'm a woman, I had to stay behind and just pray I would see them again."

"I can't imagine, Marge. It must have been awful not knowing."

Blowing out a breath, I nodded. "Torture. On any given day, you could hear the bombs going off, the gunfire exploding around us, and I would wonder if they were in it. I got in some tight situations myself, but luckily my boys had taught me how to handle a gun when we got stationed together again up in the central highlands."

Doris's eyes widened. "Did you have to... shoot anyone?"

"You did what you had to do to keep yourself and your patients safe, Doris."

Realizing I didn't feel like talking about that part of my memories, Doris clamped her mouth shut and waited for me to go on.

"So, the boys and I kept getting stationed together, and each time we got closer. During my second tour, one night, we were in a club on our base in Cu Chi, and we heard about the Running of the Bulls. Manz just thought it was the greatest thing he'd ever heard of." I laughed, remembering his excitement when he'd put his fingers to his head like horns and chased me around the tent. "And Stilts, who we called that due to his long legs and height of six foot seven, decided he could outrun any one of those bulls with his long strides. So that night, with a little more alcohol than we should have had, we all made a pact that once the war ended, we would meet up in Pamplona and run with the bulls together."

Chuckling to myself, I continued remembering that time in my life. "I awoke the next morning with a headache and wondering why the hell I'd agreed to run with a pack of bulls. But that day, when I saw them again, they were just as excited about the pact, and instead of backing out, I'd decided if I could survive Vietnam, I could survive some bulls. So that is how it began."

"And you never did it?" Alice asked.

"No," I answered, and it felt like someone sucked the wind right out of my sails. "A few months later, just one week before my tour ended and I was going to reenlist, the sirens went off. We hunkered down in the bunkers for a while, but nothing happened. But then the familiar sound of the helicopters descending on the base forced us out of hiding to treat the wounded. I hadn't seen my boys in weeks, and I didn't even know they were in the area until I saw them carry Percy off the helicopter in a stretcher. The sight of him slammed me to a stop. My worst nightmares came true as I saw them race past with him, blood pouring from a wound on his head. I was in a daze when Manz came past on the next stretcher, burned so bad I almost didn't recognize him. And then Stilts."

I stopped and closed my eyes, fighting back the tears. "He was DOA. I saw them take him the opposite way. But I knew." I stopped and blinked, drawing in a ragged breath as the emotions overwhelmed me. "His long legs didn't fit on the stretcher."

"Oh, Marge. I'm so sorry." Sylvie took my other hand and squeezed.

"It took a few moments and a sharp order from my commanding officer, but I came back to my senses and raced inside to work on them. Their platoon ended up under heavy fire. Guns, grenades, mines. It was a bloodbath. Stilts got killed, and Manz and Percy survived the attack, but the injuries were bad. Manz especially."

"Did he make it?" Sylvie whispered, her eyes boring into mine.

"No. He didn't." I slipped further down the rabbit hole until I landed back at his bedside, holding his bandaged hand. "He was severely burned and only survived a few hours. I stayed by his side the entire time. He knew he wasn't going to make it, and yet he was still telling jokes right up until the end. I penned a letter to his mother for him and promised I would see that she got it. And before he died, he made me promise I would go to the San Fermin festival and run with the bulls... and bring him with me. So, he gave me his dog tags."

I reached under my shirt and lifted three sets of dog tags concealed beneath it.

"Percy's. Manz's. And these were Stilt's." I fingered my way through the tags I'd slid over my neck in the bathroom this morning, determined to make sure they experienced every second of this adventure we'd all been determined to share with each other.

The widows teared up along with me, but I sniffled hard and shoved the tags back down inside my shirt.

"I stayed with Manz until he died, and then returned to Percy, who I knew was doing alright. He had a nasty head wound, and his legs were badly damaged and full of shrapnel, but he would survive. However, the injuries were too severe for him to stay on, and without any family to take care of him, I decided right then and there not to sign up for another tour and to go home and take care of Percy. He proposed to me in his hospital bed a few days later, and I accepted. We flew out together a month later, and I nursed him back to health in the States. We talked about coming here often, but he had a severe limp and leg pain from his injuries. I knew he couldn't make the run. And a few years after we got back, we decided we wanted a child, so we got pregnant and had Martha. Between his limp and the fact that we were now responsible parents, trips to Spain to run with the bulls became a long-lost dream. Our adventures and wild days were long past."

"Why didn't you just say so, Marge? If you had just told us why this was so important to you, we wouldn't have griped every step of the way."

Shaking the sadness off, I smiled at them. "What? And miss all that time listening to you complain you couldn't run because of your bunions?" I looked at Doris. "Or your plantar fasciitis?" My gaze landed on Alice. "Or your trick hip?" I grinned at Sylvie.

"I do have a trick hip." Sylvie crossed her arms. "I really have no idea how I'm going to run."

"And I really do have bunions, Marge." Doris pointed at her foot. "But I'll certainly try."

"I may have issues with my foot, but like I said after Vegas, I can handle it. A dancer pushes through pain every day. I pushed through it just fine today, in fact. I'll run with you."

"I'm not exactly in running shape myself, to be honest. We'll figure out a way to get us down those streets and keep ourselves alive in the process. Trust me, ladies. I think I have a plan."

"Care to share?" Alice arched a brow.

"Nope." I smiled and sat back, allowing the waiter to drop the plates on the table in front of us.

"Oh my! It smells heavenly." Doris wafted a hand toward her nose and closed her eyes, inhaling the spicy smells.

"Enjoy, ladies. I'll be back with the next course when this one is finished." His thick Spanish accent caressed the words and made everything sound a bit dirty.

"Wait!" Alice lifted a hand and stopped his departure. "Can we get a bottle of champagne, please?"

"Of course." He folded into a half-bow and disappeared around the corner.

"Already drying out?" I teased. "Gonna start shaking?"

"Shut it, Marge. I just wanted to celebrate."

"What are we celebrating?" Sylvie asked.

"Us, of course." Alice smiled. "And Marge. This is her wish, and we should stop to acknowledge it."

"I'm surprised you didn't write 'kiss a woman' on that piece of paper." Sylvie waggled her brows at me. "Although, you did it anyway."

"Honestly? I almost did. But then I thought about my promise all those years ago and knew if I had you ladies at my side, I would finally see it through."

"That's sweet, Marge. We're glad to be here."

"I only wish Roxy could join us. She would have loved this." I smiled, thinking about my wild woman still working back in Vegas. From the stories she'd shared about her life in Vegas, she would have fit right in at this crazy festival.

"Did you talk to her today?" Alice asked.

"Yep. Every day. And when we aren't talking, we're texting. She taught me how that night before we left. Being a younger woman and all, she is more technologically savvy than me." A proud grin stretched across my cheeks.

"Marge is a cougar." Alice gave me an appreciative nod. "Wait? Is it still a cougar if you're a lesbian, or is there a different term for it? Like a lion? Or maybe a panther?"

"Cougar works for me. And I'm a proud cougar with a hot little dish back in the States."

As much as they teased me about Roxy, and as much as I joked back, having found her brought me a joy like I'd never known.

Sylvie finished chewing her bite of food. "And Percy really never knew?"

Shaking my head, I shrugged. "Hell, I didn't even really know."

"What do you think he would say if he was still alive?" Doris asked.

"I've actually thought about that a lot since I met Roxy. What do I think he would say? I think he would hug me and tell me how happy he was for me. He was my best friend, and I don't think he would have been upset at all. In fact, I think he would have come right out and admitted he was gay, to both himself and me simultaneously, and then we would have gone out to find him his own Roxy."

I took a bite of the tapas and moaned my pleasure. "Amazing."

"It's so good! Spicy." Doris swigged down her water.

"You know," I said, "I am sad that Percy didn't get his own Roxy. He was the most wonderful man. Kind, sweet, funny. He would have made some man very happy, and I just wish we'd been born in a different time where we wouldn't have felt the need to hide it. Nowadays, it's as normal as putting cream in your coffee."

"Well, at least you have Roxy now." Sylvie smiled. "Are you going to see her again soon?"

"As soon as we're done with our Wilder Widow's wishes, I'm hopping on a plane straight back to Vegas to see her."

"Good for you, Marge. You deserve to be happy." Doris smiled.

Our waiter returned, holding a bottle of champagne and four flutes threaded through his free hand. After setting them on the table, he popped the cork and filled them up. One by one, we took a glass, holding them in the air.

"Here's to the Wilder Widows," Alice said. "To our wild adventure, finding new love, and finding ourselves. And here's to Percy, Manz, and Stilts."

Tears brimmed my eyes while I nodded at her and clinked my glass against hers.

Even though they weren't here physically with me, I would make sure I finished out the promise I'd made to them all those years ago. "To Percy, Manz, and Stilts," I said.

CHAPTER FIFTEEN

"Where did you go?" Doris asked when I stepped back into our tiny hotel room.

"Don't you worry about where I went. Just worry about where we're going." Looking at the digital alarm clock on the nightstand between the beds, I gave it a nod. "T minus two hours until go time. And I want to make sure we have time to see the bulls in the pen."

"It's so early," Alice grumbled while she dragged herself out of the bathroom.

Rolling my eyes, I stepped up against the wall to allow her to pass through. "You could have slept longer if you hadn't insisted on full Oscar-worthy makeup and hair for five minutes of running down the streets with bulls on your ass."

Spinning around, she cocked a hip, perching a hand upon it. "I could die today, Marge." She leaned into my face. "Die. And if I am going to die, I'm going to look damn good doing it. I want the coroner weeping over the loss of such a beautiful face, not cringing at the site of my rigid corpse. And if I die, there is no doubt someone along the streets will capture it on video. When it's playing on repeat back in the States after news releasing that a beautiful American dancer was gored to death, I want to look *good* while I'm being impaled on the big screen."

Pressing up the bottom of her short, sleek hair, she spun and walked over to her bag, pulling out a pair of red pumps.

"Alice, you can't run in heels." Sylvie shook her head and gestured to the tennis shoes she wore.

"I'm not dying in sneakers."

"Well, you would have a better chance of surviving if you wore sensible shoes, Alice." Doris pointed to the same hot pink sneakers she wore every time we walked back on Wilder Lane.

"I'll take finishing the race impaled on the horn of a bull before I put those things on my feet."

"Suit yourself," I said, leaning down to fasten my own Velcro closures. With one last tug, I made sure my trusty shoes were ready for what awaited us today.

"If I die today," Alice said. "Make sure they use the photo of me in my showgirls' outfit as the photo in the news story. That and the one where I'm in the sapphire dress at the fundraiser from last year. They're framed on my mantle."

"I'm going to find the worst picture of you I can find." I grinned. "One with a double chin and one crossed eye."

Gasping, Alice pressed a palm to her chest. "I've never had a double chin in my life!"

"Then I'll have one of our kids Photoshop it in."

"You wouldn't!"

"I would. So, use that as an incentive not to die. I don't want you getting any ideas of going out in a blaze of fame and glory."

Glaring, she pressed her heel down into the red shoe with extra force.

I looked around at our little group, all of us wearing our secondary white outfits and our red scarves tied around our necks. Turning to the door, I touched my scarf and felt the outline of the dog tags underneath my fingertips. Percy, Manz, and Stilts were with me, and I could only hope they would help keep us all safe.

"Alright, Widows. It's showtime." I turned back and gave them the same look my Staff Sgt. would give us just before a chopper loaded with wounded would arrive.

Fear filled their eyes, but one by one they lifted their chins, straightened their shoulders, and fell into line behind me.

We got outside, and even at six in the morning, the streets buzzed with energy from the people excited to run with the bulls or watch from the stands. Everyone up early to get the best spot. Many still partying from the night before, even a man asleep on the streets I had to step over. I walked the girls down the road and turned the corner away from the direction all the other bull-runners were walking.

"Isn't it that way?" Sylvie asked, pointing down the street.

"It is. But we're making a quick stop."

"For what? Breakfast?" Doris asked. "I don't think I can eat. I'll toss my cookies if I try to run with something in my stomach. I don't think I've run since gym class in high school."

The scooter rental place came into sight, and I smiled and turned back toward them, opening my arms to showcase the colorful scooters lined up behind me. "I told you I would come up with a solution, ladies. And here it is. None of us are in any condition to run, so I rented scooters!"

"What?" Alice stepped around me and cringed at the small orange scooter with the basket in front. "A scooter?"

"So smart!" Sylvie smiled and walked over to the pink one.

Crossing her arms, Alice shook her head. "I'm not riding a scooter."

"Alice, you're limping. And you're in high heels. You need a scooter," I said.

Shaking her head harder, she scoffed. "These aren't even cute, chic travel scooters! These are mobility scooters! Old people scooters! I don't do tater tots, and I don't do old people scooters. I'll run."

With a shrug, I shook my head. "Suit yourself. But I'm riding this bad boy." I patted the orange one, and Doris stepped up to the turquoise one.

"I've never ridden a scooter." Doris climbed on hers, taking a look around.

"I know. It's why I didn't rent the regular two-wheel kind. These sweet rides have three wheels, so we don't need to worry about tipping over and getting trampled. More stable." Pride swelled in me because I'd even thought that part through.

"I'm all about the scooter." Sylvie climbed into the seat and put her feet up on the floor in front of her. "I was not looking forward to running. How fast does this bad boy go?"

"Ten miles per hour, baby." I slid a hand along the sleek orange lines of my scooter.

"And how fast do bulls run?" Doris asked.

With a snort, Alice answered. "A hell of a lot faster than that."

"We'll be fine," I argued. "We just need to stay out of their way, not outrun them. No one outruns them."

"I'm scared." Doris pushed out her lower lip.

"Me too," I admitted. "But I made a promise to my friends. Even if you all decide to back out, I need to do this."

"We're with you, Marge. You made a pact with them, and the Wilder Widows made a pact with you." Sylvie smiled.

"Do people die during this thing?" Alice asked.

"Rarely. Some gorings most years, but there are ambulances all along the route, so we'll be fine."

"Just remember... the good picture." Alice pointed at each one of us, making sure her point hit home.

"I paid for these when I went out this morning. Keys are in the ignition. Just turn it on. Right handle is gas, left handle is brake."

"When the bulls come, just keep squeezing the right." Sylvie laughed while she fired up her engine. It whirred to life, and she squeezed the right handle, creeping forward with much less thrust than she seemed to anticipate. "Okay, they are slow to get going. We need a good head start before the bulls reach us!"

I turned my key, and the scooter vibrated beneath me. "Follow me, ladies. We're going to see the bulls before we run. Want a lift, Alice?"

Turning up her nose, she sauntered away down the street, and I laughed before zipping past her. We filed down the streets of Pamplona on our scooters with Alice trailing behind until we found the pen the bulls were being kept in. A small crowd gathered around them, staring at the animals before they began their famous run through the city.

We parked our scooters and climbed off, joining Alice along the wooden fence.

"They're huge!" Sylvie said, stumbling to a stop at my side. "We're running with *those?*"

"It's only the black ones you really need to worry about." I pointed at the six black, muscular bulls who huddled together in the back. "The brown and white ones are just steers. They train them to run this route, so they help keep the black ones, the fighting bulls, on course."

"It's staring at me." Doris locked eyes with a particularly fierce black bull.

"It's not staring at you." Alice laughed.

"No. It is. It's staring right at me. He's memorizing my face so he can find me in the pack."

"Doris," I laughed, "that bull isn't singling you out. He's just—"

Before I could finish, it launched forward. Head down, eyes locked, it charged straight at Doris.

"Holy shit!" I shouted, and we all jumped back while it skidded to a stop in front of the fence. A deep snort shook us to the core, and it pawed at the gate, its eyes fixated on Doris. I traced my eyes along the deep scar running down his face and ending between his huge white horns.

"El Diablo," she whispered, holding its intense gaze.

"What?" I asked, stepping to her side and pulling her back. She stared at it as if she was in a trance.

"El Diablo." She made the sign of the cross, and the bull snorted one last time before trotting back to its herd.

"That was intense!" Alice joined us from where she'd taken shelter behind a small building. "That thing *is* gunning for you, Doris! Stay the hell away from me when we run."

"Can it, Alice." I jabbed an elbow into her side. "No one is gunning for Doris. And we aren't separating during the race. All for one, one for all."

"All for one, one for all." Sylvie placed her hand over mine. Doris and Alice followed suit, and together we did a cheer before turning back to look at the bulls one last time.

"You stay the hell away from her, El Diablo," I whispered to him before we hopped on our scooters and headed toward the place the other runners gathered.

When we reached the area where the crowds were congregating, we wound our scooters through the bodies, trying to get a good spot. A policeman lifted his hand, stopping us as we tried to get past. At first, he said something in Spanish, but when I said I didn't understand the language, he responded in English.

"You can't ride those during the run," he said, his dark brows pushing together while he stared down his nose to where we sat on our scooters.

"Says who?" I stood up, closing in on him. "I didn't see a damn thing about no motorized vehicles in any of the literature."

"You just can't. You'll get hurt. Turn back." He shook his head, pointing over my shoulder.

"Are you discriminating against the disabled?" I sneered.

"No. Now turn back." His mustache twitched as he snarled.

"Yes, you are." I rose on my toes to get closer to eye level. "You're discriminating against us!"

"Turn. Back," he warned, and this time his tone meant business.

Just when I was ready to go to blows, briefly wondering what prison in Pamplona would be like, I remembered I had a much more effective technique to get us past that barrier. Spinning on my heel, I marched over to Alice.

"Handle it," I said, and she answered with her signature smile.

"Consider it handled."

Just like a switch turned on, Alice's eyes narrowed into seductive slits. Stepping around me, she sauntered past the scooters, landing in front of the officer. Her height and her heels brought her to eye level, and she placed her hand against his chest. I wished I could hear what she whispered in his ear. As if transfixed under the weight of Alice's allure, the stern expression on his face transformed into one of shock, and then a pink hue traveled across his bronze cheeks. This time when his mustache twitched, it was from the smile Alice's words induced.

Sitting back on my scooter, I awaited the verdict. Even if they didn't allow it, I knew I still had to run. I touched the dog tags beneath my shirt, remembering my vow. Alice brushed a soft kiss against his cheek and turned back toward us. The victorious smile tugging up her lips told me she'd been successful yet again. That woman could charm the pants off any man on the planet.

"Go," she said, waving me forward.

I twisted the handle on my scooter and slowly accelerated, glaring up at the cop as I rolled past. His smitten expression turned into a scowl as he watched me go by.

"That was close," Sylvie said, pulling her pink scooter up beside me.

"Thank you, Alice," Doris said when Alice strutted up beside us. "I don't even want to know what you said to him, but I'm glad he's letting us ride our scooters. There's no way I could make the run."

She beamed. "Walk in the park."

"So, what happens now?" Sylvie asked.

"Now we wait," I answered. "First, they have the runners spread out along the route. Some of them will run all the way to the end and skip the running of the bulls."

"Oh! Let's do that!" Doris clapped.

Scowling, I shook my head. "No. We run *with* the bulls. We're not ninnies. So, after the runners spread out a little to keep the congestion down, there will be a prayer to San Fermin, and then at eight o'clock, the rocket fires, the bulls are released, and we scoot for our lives."

"Jesus, help me." Doris placed her hands together and prayed.

My own silent prayer went up as well, but this time it was to my lost friends. I prayed they would watch over us all and maybe even come along for the ride.

CHAPTER SIXTEEN

"Is this really happening?" Sylvie asked.

I looked over to where she was parked on her pink scooter and gave her a sharp nod. "Widows, this is it. In less than a minute, they will fire that rocket. When they do, I want you to pull that handle with everything you have. Don't slow down. Don't veer. People will go down in the streets. Run 'em over."

"What? Run people over?" Doris gasped. "Shouldn't we stop and help them up?"

"Only if you want a bull's horn up your ass. We don't stop for nothing. You just keep on scooting. The runners know what they signed up for."

"Oh my." Alice sucked the air through her teeth.

"When we get to the arena, just keep scooting. We'll find a safe place to stop. Everyone clear?" I barked, my military background rising up.

"Yes, sir!" they mirrored and then broke down, giggling.

"And keep your eyes peeled for El Diablo. He looks like one nasty son of a bitch."

They nodded, terror moving across their faces. The runners spread out around us bounced up and down while they stared behind us, waiting and prepared to bolt the moment that rocket went off and the bulls were on their way. With one last touch to the memories hanging around my neck, I inhaled a deep breath and prepared myself. The same feelings I had when the sirens went in 'Nam off flooded me again. The waiting. The watching. The unknown. But this time, I wasn't hunkering down in the bunkers. This time I was out in the fray, out where Percy, Manz, and Stilts would be. And when the rocket went off, I felt them with me.

"GO!" I screamed, twisting the handle of my scooter as I crept forward. Rocking back and forth, I tried to get it to top speed faster than the manufacturer intended. The roar of the crowd shook through me, and the runners at our sides took off. The energy coursing through those streets fueled my adrenaline, and I grinned wide while I finally reached top speed.

"Holy shit! We're doing this!" Sylvie screamed as she rolled up beside me.

"Heavens to Betsy!" Doris called, pulling up on my other side. "This is crazy!"

Alice kept up with a jog, but I could see her wincing in pain with every step. Her red high heels click-clacked against the stones our scooters bumped along. "You okay?" I called up to her.

"Just worry about yourself!" she called down, huffing hard already. "I'll be fine!"

We wove between the runners, the crowds cheering us on from the balconies above as we passed by. When I heard the soft cheers rise into screams and shouts, I knew it was happening. They were here. The bulls were coming.

"Incoming!" I shouted, glancing over my shoulder to see the pace of the runners pick up to racing. Panic stretched their faces tight when they pumped their arms to move faster. I squeezed the handle of my scooter, begging it to pick up the pace. A pace as fast as my hammering heart would be ideal.

The cheers reached deafening levels, and I looked back over my shoulder. A bull charged through the runners, sending bodies launching out of its way. Some men jumped over the barricade while others leaped up to dangle from the balconies above. Alice's wide eyes looked back at the bull and then down to me. I could see her faltering, her limp exaggerating with each stride.

"It's coming!" She panted, fear crackling in her voice. "It's coming!"

"Run, Alice! Run!" I commanded, but with each step, she slowed down.

"It's a brown one! I'm okay!" she called.

Looking again, I saw it was indeed one of the steers charging our way. It blew past, its hooves thundering the ground while it ran by.

"One down, eleven to go!" I yelled, and my lips stuck to my bone-dry teeth from the smile I'd been wearing since we started this race. Exhilaration and pride wove through me. This experience everything my buddies and I hoped it would be. The adrenaline. The excitement. The feeling of being alive. So, so alive.

The cheers rose again, and I looked back over my shoulder. A body flew through the air to the chorus of gasps from the onlookers. When he disappeared back into the terrified crowd, I began to question this decision for the first time since we arrived. Screams peppered the air around us, and the runners took off at breakneck speed, blowing past us on our scooters.

The runners parted, bodies launching and diving out of the way. I saw the black shadow emerge from between them—muscles rippling as it charged our way. The deep scar across his face identified the snorting, angry wall of dangerous muscle headed our way.

"El Diablo!" I screamed, and the widows spun back to look. The huge bull headed straight for us, and I squeezed my handle tighter. Sweaty palms threatened to slip, but I tightened my grip and willed my scooter to impossible speeds.

"El Diablo! El Diablo!" Alice panted and pushed herself harder, but her speed slowed even more.

"Run, soldier! Run!" I commanded, but she continued losing pace as the bull closed in.

"I'm not gonna make it!" She puffed. "I can't run anymore! Don't forget! Use the good picture!"

"No man left behind! Hop on, sweet cheeks! Hurry!" I leaned back, opening my arm and waving her in. The huffing of the bull's deep breaths grew louder, and I could hear his thundering hooves approaching. "Now, Alice!"

With a shriek, she launched herself into my lap. Her red high heels kicked in the air as she struggled to balance on my lap. The roar of the crowd drowned out El Diablo for a moment, but soon I could feel his hot breath on my neck. I looked behind me and saw eyes lit with fire boring into mine.

"Holy shit!" I screamed, turning back to stay on course. A man fell down, and I gunned the gas while we bumped over his legs. The jarring movement nearly dislodged Alice, but she wrapped her arms around my neck and held on tight.

The bull veered away from me, locking onto Doris beside me while she leaned forward on her scooter and tried to get away. "He's coming for me!" Her blood-curdling scream rivaled the cheers around us. The bull bore down, his horns low while he barreled up behind her.

Holy shit. I killed Doris.

I prepared for the impact and the guilt that would forever haunt me while Doris tried to scoot away.

"Doris!" Sylvie screamed.

But instead of impaling her with his horns, he stayed just behind her, his body following her scooter everywhere she went as she tried to get away. The crowd roared again, and I glanced back to see another black bull coming our way. "Incoming!"

This one moved with speed, like lean marathon runners who'd trained for this their whole lives. Faster than El Diablo, and from the look in his eyes, even more dead set on turning Doris into a shish kabob. He locked onto her, moving up alongside El Diablo.

White knuckled, Doris glanced over her shoulder one more time. I could see her mouthing a silent prayer while she veered again.

"Do something!" Alice shrieked.

"Hey! Hey!" I shouted at the bulls, trying to get their attention while I beeped my horn.

"Well, don't bring them over here!" Alice shrieked again.

Ignoring my attempts to dissuade them, they continued after Doris. The lean bull moved up on her, head lowered, and eyes locked on.

This was it. Doris was toast.

As the bull charged forward, El Diablo grunted, swinging his huge white horns through the air, blocking the blow from connecting with Doris. The lean bull stumbled for a stride, righting itself before turning its attention to a man tearing down the street ahead. It dug down hard, racing after the man in front of us and sending him flying through the air to the chorus of the crowd's screams. It left him lying on the ground and galloped on, disappearing around Dead Man's Corner.

El Diablo cantered away, bypassing Doris but slamming a man into the wall before he too, disappeared around the corner.

"Whoo! You're okay!" Sylvie cheered, and we all looked at Doris, whose ashen face looked like they'd successfully skewered her, leaving nothing but a corpse still bumping along on her scooter.

"I'm alive!" she called over.

"You're alive!" I yelled back, grinning so wide I thought my face might tear. The pounding of my heart drowned out the sound of the screaming crowd.

We skidded around Dead Man's Corner, heading down the final stretch before the arena. The onlooker's cheers rose, working like a warning siren, and I looked back to see the herd of bulls boring down on us again.

"Incoming!" I yelled. We moved our scooters closer together, and Alice gripped me tightly. The raw power from the herd of bulls rushing past sucked the breath right out of me. I watched them go past, and for a moment, I envisioned Stilts racing ahead of them. Taunting them while he covered the ground with long, elegant strides. His boyish smile stretched wide across his face while his laughter echoed through the streets. Manz raced beside them, ducking and darting between them, using his small size and agility to dodge their swinging horns. And Percy.

Percy was by my side, holding my hand while he grinned down at me. Staying with me. Keeping me safe. Always keeping me safe. My partner through life. My best friend. My soul mate. And then I felt his grip slip as he raced ahead, his laughter mingling with his friends' while they disappeared into a sea of black bulls. My heart fluttered in my chest. Tears brimmed my eyes as I closed them, holding their memories close while I finished the final stretch we'd vowed to run together.

The red banner signifying the end flapped just up ahead, and I followed the bulls under the tunnel and out into the arena. Cheers shook the walls while bulls, runners, and my Wilder Widows poured into the sand. And once again, I saw my boys. As if time had stopped back in 'Nam, they looked the same way I remembered them the first day I saw them tossing around the football. They stood in the center, grins wide, while they waved at me one last time.

"We did it, boys," I whispered as I reached up and squeezed the tags around my neck. "We did it."

"We did it!" Alice screamed, mirroring my sentiments and shaking me from my visions. I glanced back to where I'd last envisioned the boys, but they were gone. Our pact fulfilled.

I smiled and drove my scooter to the edge of the arena. The widows pulled up beside me, and those same smiles I'd pictured on my boys were now stretched across their faces instead.

"That was amazing! What a rush!" Sylvie hopped off her scooter and jumped up and down.

"It was." I smiled and looked back at the arena one last time. But this time, instead of the boys waving at me, I saw a black bull charging our way.

"Incoming!" I shouted. "Over the fence! Over the fence!"

With mirroring screams, we launched over the fence surrounding the arena. The bull slammed into the wall just as we cleared the other side. We landed in a pile, our shaky bodies collapsing in a heap.

Puffing hard, I tried to catch my breath, but the weight of their bodies pressing down on me made it impossible to expand my ribcage. "Can't. Breathe." I managed to sputter out.

"Oops! Sorry." Doris climbed off me while the other girls rolled off to their sides. One by one, we stood up, Sylvie grabbing my hand and pulling me back to my feet.

"That was close!" she said while wiping the dirt off my backside.

Together we peered over the wall separating us from the bulls and the crowd still racing around the arena in front of them. There was no doubt in my mind Manz, Stilts, and Percy would have still been in there, laughing while they dodged each charge and going back around for more.

"Does it feel good?" Alice asked.

With a soft smile, I nodded. "Better than you can imagine. And they were right here with me." I tapped the dog tags under my shirt. "And even more importantly, you girls were right here with me."

They all smiled down at me, and I realized for the second time in my life, I had 'people.' Percy, Manz, and Stilts had been my first true friends. And now, in this second act of my life, I had three more—my Wilder Widows.

"So, what happens now? Do we need to get the scooters back?" Doris asked, peering down at our scooters that had been tipped over when the bull slammed into them.

"Screw the scooters. Just leave 'em." I shook my head. "They'll find 'em eventually. I got insurance."

"Are we sticking around for the bullfights?" Alice asked.

"Bullfights?" Doris furrowed her brow. "What bullfights?"

"The running of the bulls is the tradition to get the fighting bulls to the arena. Later, the matadors will fight them."

Doris's eyes grew wide. "What happens to the bulls when they fight them?"

"What do you think happens?" Alice snorted.

"They kill them?" Doris shrieked.

"It's their culture and tradition, Doris." I placed a hand on her shoulder. "I don't have a taste for it either, but they say even though it looks brutal, the bulls live much better lives than any other cow, and the fight is over fast."

Tears bubbled in her eyes, overflowing and slipping down her cheeks.

"I don't want to see this part, either." Sylvie shook her head. "I know this is part of their culture and that they even feed the meat to the poor, but I can't watch it."

"But El Diablo!" Doris wailed. "He saved me!"

"It's okay, Doris," I said, pulling her in for a hug. "They say it is the greatest honor for them to go out fighting. El Diablo was bred for this. His destiny."

"No!" She pulled back. "They can't kill him. They can't! He's... my friend."

"Your friend?" I arched a brow.

"Yes. My friend. You all saw it. He saved me." With a quivering chin, she wiped more tears streaming down her cheeks.

She wasn't wrong. That bull, the one we thought had it in for her, had defended her against an attack.

"We have to do something. Please." Pleading eyes searched through us.

"Oh, Christ." Alice blew a breath. "Stay put. I'll be right back."

"What are you doing?" I called after her as she trotted away.

"Just stay put!"

We waited for an hour and watched the bulls tearing after the runners. Some successfully dodging the charges, while others took a ride through the air or felt the horns tear through their skin when they didn't get out of the way in time. And El Diablo reigned his fury down on them all. One after another, he sent bodies flying through the air. His pride apparent after every hit. He trotted past us, slowing down while bending his neck and locking eyes with Doris as he went past.

"He can't die," she cried as he trotted back out to charge another taunter.

"He won't," Alice said, and we all spun around to see her standing behind us. "I just bought a fucking bull. And even with my skills, he cost me more money than a Mercedes."

"What?" I choked on the word. "You bought him?"

"Alice!" Doris clasped her hands over her mouth. "You saved him? Did you really save him?"

"He's safe. He'll be kept in the stables tonight, and I have a month to figure out where we're sending him to live out his days in pasture."

"Oh, Alice!" Doris flung her arms around her neck, holding her tight. "You *do* have a heart! A huge one! I knew it!"

Stifling her smile, Alice hugged her back. "Don't tell anyone. Don't need people knowing I've got a soft side."

"You are amazing, Alice," Sylvie said. "A beautiful, talented, kind woman... who owns a fighting bull."

"I own a fighting bull. What the hell did I just do?"

"You did a wonderful thing, Alice," I said. "You did it for Doris."

"And for El Diablo," she said, looking out at him as he knelt on a runner, grinding him into the sand. "He deserves a second chance... just like us."

"To second chances." Sylvie slung her arm over Alice's shoulder, and we folded into a group hug.

"So, now what? Looks like we have one wish left."

"Give me the basket." I stepped out of our embrace, cracking my knuckles while Alice leaned over the edge of the railing and grabbed her purse from the basket of my moped. We held onto her feet and pulled as she struggled to slide back over.

El Diablo tore at us, skidding to a stop just as Alice made it over the edge.

"Easy there, tiger. I haven't paid for you yet, so if you kill me, you're toast yourself!" She laughed, shaking her finger at him. His nostrils flared, and my gaze traced the long scar along his face up to a fierce pair of eyes I was grateful wouldn't be lifeless tonight.

"Ready?" Alice asked, lifting the lid of the basket.

With a nod, I reached inside and pulled out the last wish. Sylvie's wish.

When I read it, I smiled. "Well, this I think I can get behind."

"What are we doing?" Doris asked.

Sylvie smiled and took the note. "I used to ride horses when I was a kid. And I always had dreams of going out west to a dude ranch."

Alice groaned. "Oh no. Please say we aren't—"

I cut her off, grinning wide. "We're going to a dude ranch!"

SYLVIE

CHAPTER SEVENTEEN

"Ugh. Horse shit. All I smell is horse shit, Sylvie. Didn't we have enough time with the big smelly beasts in Spain?" Alice grumbled as we climbed out of our limo at the Dude Ranch.

"You'll live, Alice." I inhaled a deep breath saturated with fresh air and the smell of horses I'd missed so much.

"I love horses," Doris cooed and mimicked my deep breath. "I've always wanted to learn to ride. Great wish, Sylvie!"

"I don't mind 'em, but I've only been on a couple times." Marge came up to my side, dragging her bag behind her. "But if we can run with the bulls, I don't think we'll have any issues herding 'em."

"I hate horses." Alice huffed.

"Didn't you grow up on a farm?" I asked, remembering her mentioning that at some point in our travels.

"I did. And yes, we had horses. And cows. And pigs. And I swore I would never be around them again. Yet... here I am. And there are pigs." She pointed to the pigpen I hadn't noticed. Big, pink pigs meandered around together, oinking and rutting in the mud.

"Oh, they are so cute." Doris squealed and wandered over, cooing at each of them while they came up to investigate her.

"They aren't cute," Alice said. "They're dirty. And they can eat an entire human, bones and all."

"What?" Doris stepped back in shock but then turned and shook her finger at Alice. "Quit pulling my leg. Pigs don't eat people."

Marge shrugged. "Actually, she's right. Pigs will clean up a corpse in record time. Not a trace left behind. They are my go-to in the event I ever need to hide a body. Chop it into pieces and toss it in with some pigs. Cops will never find it."

We stood blinking at Marge and then turned and stared at the pigs. "That's just dark, Marge," I said.

"Dark, sure. Smart, absolutely. No coppers are gonna catch me if I need to off someone. My daughter's a cop. She knows how to get these things taken care of. Pigs or lye... that's how you get away with murder. The smart way." Marge tapped on her head with a finger.

"Remind me not to piss you off." I smiled.

"But know if you ever need to get rid of a body, I'm the first call you should make."

"Good to know." I laughed.

"I still think they're cute." Doris peered back over the fence.

Alice waved a hand toward them. "Disgusting. They're disgusting."

"Well, hello there!" a voice sing-songed and pulled our heads in its direction. A woman about our age sporting a cowboy hat, dirty jeans, and a flannel shirt headed our way. "I'm Madeline Walker, and I'm the owner here at Stone Creek Ranch. Welcome!"

I stepped forward, meeting her with a handshake. "Hi Madeline. I'm Sylvie, this is Doris, Alice, and Marge. We have a reservation."

"Of course! Thank goodness for that last-minute cancellation so we could accommodate you ladies. We're thrilled you're here. Follow me, and I'll take you to your cabin and show you around." With the wave of her hand, she gestured us to follow.

We grabbed our bags and started after her. Alice tipped the limo driver and hurried to catch up. I couldn't suppress my smile while we wound our way through the ranch. It was everything I had dreamed about and more. A childhood fantasy I now walked through. Horses grazed in the lush green pastures, and a small herd of cattle shifted in a portable corral. They looked far less frightening than the bulls we'd just seen in Spain.

"This will be your cabin for the weekend," Madeline said, opening the door to a small log building.

"It's charming!" Doris stepped in first, and I followed. Rustic but clean, I'd imagined a cabin on a dude ranch would look just like this. Antlers hung along the wall, perched above the log bed frames. A large bearskin rug stretched across the floor in front of the stone fireplace situated below a mantle holding framed black and white photos of cowboys and rodeo riders.

"I'm glad you like it," Madeline said, taking Doris's bag and setting it in the corner. "You ladies can set your bags over here."

We walked over, setting down our bags one by one.

"Normally, we like to give you a night in the cabin before we head out on our cattle drive, but since you are coming in a day late due to your travels, your first night will be out under the open country sky."

"Wait..." Alice lifted a finger and closed her eyes. "Camping?"

Madeline smiled and nodded.

"No one said anything about *camping*." Alice spun around and pierced me with a glare.

Giving her a sheepish smile, I chuckled. "Did I forget to mention this was a *working* Dude Ranch, and cattle drives and camping are part of the experience?"

Narrowing her eyes, her lips faded into a thin white line. "Yes, Sylvie. You forgot to mention that."

"Oops, I must have forgotten," I lied.

"I'm feeding you to the pigs," Alice growled.

"I love camping." Marge stretched and then sat down on the bed, giving it a bounce while she felt it out. "Fresh air and stars are good for the soul."

"We think so too," Madeline said. "Don't worry. We supply tents, and there will be three home-cooked meals every day. But why don't you ladies rest for an hour, settle in, and then come out and find me. I'll finish showing you around, and you can pick out your mounts."

"Thank you, Madeline."

With a curt nod, she backed out the door and closed it behind her.

"I love it here!" Doris flopped on the bed beside Marge. "I've never ridden a horse or been on a ranch. But I think it's wonderful!"

Alice only arched a brow and crossed her arms.

"Oh, come on, Alice. At least camping is better than the room in Barcelona, right?" Marge teased.

"I'll be at the Ritz if you need me." Alice reached for her bag and lifted it up.

"Okay. Stop." I demanded but struggled to conceal the laughter. "I ran with the bulls for Marge. I flashed my tits to all of Paris for Doris. I *kidnapped a woman* for you. Now the least you can do is suck it up and go camping, Princess."

With a scowl and a long exhale, she dropped her bag. "Fine. But I'm not going to like it."

"You don't have to." I stepped forward and patted her on the shoulder. "But you'll do it anyway because we're the Wilder Widows, and we have a pact. And this is something I've dreamed of doing my whole life."

"We're with you, Sylvie!" Doris stood.

"You know I'm in." Marge joined her.

Alice huffed another breath. "Fine. I'm in."

I clapped, stopping just short of jumping up and down. "Yay! We're going to have so much fun!"

****

After taking a short nap and recovering from the flight from Spain, we pulled out the clothes we'd purchased at the country store on our way here.

"Do I look like a cowgirl?" Doris asked, modeling her jeans, pink cowboy hat, pink plaid shirt, and hot pink cowboy boots.

"Like a real authentic cowgirl," I lied, and she squealed her excitement.

Marge and I had chosen sturdy brown boots, jeans, muted flannel shirts, and simple cowboy hats. Practical. The kind of outfit Madeline was wearing when we met her. Alice stepped out of the bathroom wearing a stark white cowboy hat, designer jeans, a white button-down blouse, and bright red alligator boots. Her boots alone had cost more than all our outfits combined.

"If I'm going on this stupid cattle drive, I'm going to look damn good doing it."

Marge snorted. "Yeah, for about five minutes until you fall in a pile of horse shit and ruin your white shirt."

Glaring at her, Alice strutted out the door. We followed after her, but as we started down the steps from our cabin, Alice skidded to a stop. One by one, we slammed into her, then fanned out, looking to see what caused her abrupt halt.

It only took a second to see what had all of Alice's attention.

"Holy shit, is that Sam Elliot?" I whispered while I took him in.

Long silver hair tied in a knot beneath his cowboy hat brushed along bare muscular shoulders. As he swung the ax against the firewood, every muscle in his impressive physique flexed beneath tanned skin.

"Heavens to Betsy," Doris whispered on a breath.

Another swing of the ax showcased his bulging biceps, and I struggled to swallow.

"Is it just me, or is he moving in slow motion?" Alice asked, her own jaw failing to stay shut.

"Not just you. He's in slow motion."

Doris clutched her chest. "He's magnificent."

"Save a horse. Ride a cowboy." Alice broke her stare and smiled down at Doris. "Did you just have a hootie?"

The smart remark shook Doris from her trance, and she swatted at Alice's arm. "No!"

Her shrill retort caught the attention of the cowboy across the yard. Setting down his ax, he lifted his tan hat and swiped a muscular forearm across his forehead.

Tongues tied and mouths agape, we stood in a row while we watched him snatch up his flannel shirt and start toward us. One by one, his arms disappeared inside the fabric as he made his approach until only the silver hair across his chest and the rippled abs were still visible.

"Howdy, ladies," he said, tipping his hat as he came to a stop at the bottom of the stairs. He started working on closing the buttons of his shirt, and I had to stop myself from racing down there and ripping them back open.

"How — Howdy," I sputtered.

"I'm Axel. Axel Walker."

Walker. Damn it. Must be Madeline's husband.

"Is Madeline your wife?" Alice cut straight to the chase while she struck her sexiest pose.

"No, ma'am," he answered. "She's my sister. Never did marry myself."

Even though our gasps were inaudible, I felt all the air around us disappearing into our lungs.

"Is that so?" Alice crooned.

"Yes, ma'am," he answered, but instead of fixating on Alice like every other man in the world, his amber eyes drifted to Doris. His piercing gaze locked right onto her shocked one. "I'm single."

As we all glanced at Doris, the hue in her cheeks transition until it matched her brand-new boots.

"May I escort you to the stables? Madeline said you ladies need to pick out your horses for our cattle drive today." He extended an elbow to Doris, and Alice scoffed softly beside me.

"Why... thank you. Howdy, I'm Doris." She slid her hand into the open crook of his arm. Together they walked down the stairs and left the three of us frozen to the floorboards in shock.

"Did that... just happen?" Alice whispered.

"Did Doris just steal a handsome cowboy out from under your surgically created perfect nose?" Marge craned her neck around me. "Why, yes. Yes, it did."

"Good for her," I said while I watched her walking away with him.

"That is a bonified silver fox." Marge blew out a breath. "Not my type of silver fox, but a rare silver fox indeed."

"He's gorgeous," I added. And he was. Even at his age, probably close to ours, his body rivaled those meatheads I'd seen pumping iron at the gym the few times I'd tried working out. But I imagined Axel's muscles didn't come from lifting weights and rowing machines. No. His muscles came from real ranch work like I'd just witnessed as he chopped that wood.

"I've had better." Alice flipped her hair and started down the stairs. Marge and I exchanged a glance, stifling our chuckles while our friend walked away on a wounded foot that mirrored her wounded pride.

"Are you ladies coming?" Doris called back over Axel's shoulder.

"Coming!" I answered, and we hurried after her and her smoldering cowboy.

CHAPTER EIGHTEEN

"Now, I want you ladies to take a few moments and just watch the horses." Axel stood perched on the wooden split-rail fence surrounding the pasture. "A lot can be determined about you by the horse you choose... or maybe I should say the one that chooses you." His bright white smile flickered in the sunlight, and my knees wobbled again.

"How do I know which one chooses me?" Doris asked, leaning on the fence beside him.

"You'll know. And I have a hankering you're going to get the best one out there." His quick wink had Doris giggling again.

"Just make sure mine isn't a nag." Alice shielded her eyes from the sun while she looked out over the colorful herd of horses.

"There ain't a nag in there," Axel said. "Nothing but the finest ranch horses this side of the Mississippi. Of that, I can assure you."

Madeline stepped up beside her brother. "The way this works is each of you gets a halter and lead rope. You'll head out into the herd and find your horse. When you've found it, slip on the halter and lead it back over here. Then we'll teach you how to tack up."

I already spotted the one that was calling to me. A beautiful blood bay with four white socks and a long stripe down his face. He looked just like Pete, the gelding I learned to ride on when I took lessons as a kid.

"Can we go in there?" I asked, excited to get started.

"Have at it. Just watch out for the piles on the ground, and don't walk behind 'em." Axel climbed off the fence and swung open the gate.

The widows and I marched inside, each going our separate way while we moved through the herd of grazing horses. A few lifted their heads and snorted at my presence, trotting away when they spotted my halter. But they weren't the ones pulling me toward them. I continued moving through them until I reached the bay gelding at the back. Lifting his head, he looked at me, and I stopped.

"Hey, buddy," I said, offering him my hand just like I'd been taught. "How are you doing today?" He stepped forward, pricking his ears at the sound of my voice. The lush grass bent beneath my gentle steps as I walked toward him, and he started toward me.

When we reached one another, I pressed a hand into his neck, closing my eyes while I inhaled his scent. A scent that had filled a large part of my childhood and one I hadn't smelled in years.

"Hey, buddy," I whispered into his mane. "You want to go for a ride with me?"

A soft snort was my answer, and I slid my lead rope around his neck to hold him steady while I slipped on the blue rope halter. After tying the knot and securing our bond, I stepped back and smiled. Warm brown eyes searched my face, and I remembered how I always felt a horse could see straight into my soul. The way he stared at me now did nothing to shake loose that belief.

"That one's Whip!" Madeline called over the fence, and I turned toward her. "He's a good one!"

I looked back at my horse. "Whip, huh? Let's hope you aren't too fast. It's been a lot of years since I've ridden, so be careful with me, okay?"

Heaving a deep sigh, he tugged at the rope and went back to munching at my feet. Even the sound of his grazing flooded me with memories long since gone—memories of lying in the pasture with my schoolbooks beside Pete. Or summer days at horse camp with my girlfriends, giggling in the fields while we shared our crushes with one another as the horses grazed around us.

"Got one!" Marge cheered, and I turned to see her standing beside an older appaloosa holding her lead rope tight. His sparse mane and scraggly tail moved in the gentle breeze, and a long roman nose pushed against Marge while she grinned beside him.

"Appaloosas are notoriously stubborn!" I laughed and shouted to her.

"That's Cochise, and he ain't no exception!" Madeline cupped her hands to call over the increasing breeze.

"Well, so am I!" Marge patted him on the neck and started toward the gate. The stubborn gelding leaned back against her, digging his hooves into the grass while he pinned his ears in response. "Oh hell, come on. If I gotta go, you gotta go."

Tugging harder on the lead rope, she leaned forward, and finally, one reluctant foot after another, Cochise followed.

"He's stubborn," Axel said. "But he knows his job. When we're working the cattle, all you gotta do is sit tight, and he'll handle the rest."

Alice stepped out of the herd of horses with a beautiful white mare at her side. Not a speckle of color was present on the horse beside her dark brown eyes. "Look! It's a clean one! And we match." Grinning, Alice led the mare to the gate.

"You sure do have an eye for the fancy one," Axel said. "That's Lady, and she's just that. She's a bit fiery from time to time, but she'll take good care of you."

"Clean, fiery, and beautiful. A perfect match." Alice smiled, and I saw her soften for a moment while she and the mare exchanged a look. As expected, Alice was all talk, and deep down, I knew she would enjoy this as much as me.

"Well, well, well." Axel grinned and looked past us all. "I told you the best one of the bunch'd pick you!"

Doris beamed while she towed a small buckskin paint behind her. Gold and cream colors swirled around the horse's body, the gold glistening in the bright sun. A long black mane and tail matching the black on her legs and face blew up in the wind. Doris indeed had picked a beautiful mare.

Axel stepped forward and met Doris as she approached the fence. "That one's Norma. Such a beauty we named her after Marilyn Monroe." He slid a hand along the mare's long, muscular neck and then looked back over his shoulder at Doris. "It's a no wonder she picked you. Beautiful women sticking together and all."

The energy crackling between Doris and Axel would have set the prairie on fire if it had been any dryer.

"Look at her go," Marge whispered to me as she dragged her gelding up beside mine. "Looks like someone is starting to open herself up to the possibilities after all."

We exchanged a smile as we watched Doris and Axel walk back to the barn together with Norma in tow.

"That she is." I sighed and let the ideas of possibilities for myself start to blossom as well.

****

"Mine's busted!" Marge growled while she thumped her legs along the sides of Cochise. "Damn thing won't move!"

After our lesson on tacking up, mounting and basic riding skills, Alice and I didn't need assistance since we had plenty of experience. Marge and Doris needed extra help, and Axel willingly devoted extra attention to Doris. Now we stood at the edge of the pasture getting to know our horses while Axel, Madeline, and some wranglers rode off to rustle up the cattle we would be transporting fifteen miles across the countryside.

"Give a little cluck and a squeeze," I said, riding up beside Marge.

"I'm squeezing so hard I might shit myself!" she groaned, and her reddened face shook while she squeezed even harder. Giving up, she slumped forward and let out a defeated sigh. Cochise continued chomping on the grass, paying no mind to the determined rider on his back.

"You need to take charge. Show him who's boss." Alice rode up on her other side and gave him a swift tap on the rear. Cochise only flicked an ear and continued eating. "Wow. That really is a stubborn horse. Should we find you a new one?"

Marge inhaled a breath, furrowing her brow while she straightened back up. "Nope. This one's mine. He may be stubborn, but so am I. I'm not giving up that easy." With renewed determination, she began bumping at his sides again while she tugged unsuccessfully on the reins to lift his head.

"This is amazing!" Doris bounced in the saddle as she trotted up beside us. "I'm on a horse! I've always wanted to ride a horse, and now I am. And she's so beautiful!" Norma came to a stop beside me, and Doris shifted in her saddle to regain her balance.

"I spent so much of my youth on horseback," I said. "From the time I was five, I took regular lessons at a stable down the road."

"You were so lucky." Doris ran a hand along Norma's neck. "I was too busy taking care of my little sisters, and we didn't have any extra money for things like riding lessons."

"I had to do a *lot* of chores to convince my parents to keep paying for lessons. I even got to do some shows a few times. Mostly western pleasure, but I rode English sometimes, too."

"I rode as a kid," Alice said from where she sat perched on Lady. "We had a dozen horses on the farm. Then I found boys in middle school and never got on again."

"I'd take horses over boys any day." Marge scoffed.

"Of course you would." Alice rolled her eyes. "You're a lesbian."

"True." Marge shrugged.

"I picked horses over boys," I said. "But then I stopped riding during college and never got going again. I missed it." I patted Whip on the shoulder, and he responded by bending his neck around and sniffing my new boot.

"We're ready!" Madeline called. She and Axel led a herd of cattle behind them. Three wranglers moved behind the herd, whooping and cracking bullwhips to keep the animals moving forward. "Just ride on over here, and we'll teach you how to wrangle cattle as we go!"

Excitement fluttered through my stomach—a real cattle drive. I'd seen an advertisement in one of my horse magazines as a child and had dreamed of doing this ever since. And now I was on one. Clucking my tongue, I spun Whip toward the herd. Doris and Alice fell in beside me, and we looked back to see Marge frantically kicking her gelding.

"Come on, Marge!" I shouted over my shoulder.

"I'm trying!" she called back, but Cochise ignored her pleas.

"When he sees he's the only one left, he'll come running," Alice said with certainty. Having been on the left-behind horse on trail rides myself, I knew she was probably right. We kept on moving until we heard Marge squeal behind us. We whipped around to see Cochise barreling toward us, Marge clutching the horn for dear life while he cantered up beside us.

"Cripes!" she shouted when he slid to a stop at my side. "You son of a bitch! You could have killed me!"

"Stubborn. Obstinate. Unpredictable," Alice said, looking over at them. "I'd say you picked just the right horse for you."

"Can it, Alice!" Marge answered, huffing for breath. "He's an asshole!"

"Like I said..." Alice smiled.

Our laughter mingled while we rode up to Madeline and Axel at the front of the herd.

Madeline tipped her hat as we pulled up. "You ladies getting comfortable up there?"

"Yep," I answered.

"Good. We got about fifteen miles of rough terrain to cover. Your jobs are to keep moving along the side of the cattle, making sure none of 'em wanders off. If you see one make a break for it, don't run after it yourself. Just holler up to us, and one of us will go retrieve it."

"Got it," I answered, and the Wilder Widows all nodded their understanding.

"Now, just kick back and enjoy the ride and keep an eye on those cattle. Holler if you need anything."

I spun Whip away and fell in line on the flank of the sea of colorful cattle moving beside me. Their rainbow of earth tones blended together, and I had to blink periodically to make out the different longhorns in the herd. A small calf trotted up beside me before bucking wildly for a moment and racing back to his mother's side. The little creature made me smile, and I tossed up a grateful prayer that those widows had knocked on my door that day.

Instead of spending my days alone in my quiet house after Bruce died, I was on the adventure of a lifetime. I was finding myself again, stepping back in time to reintroduce myself to the girl I once was. The one before the big job, the child, the husband. The one who laughed with her whole body and dreamed big. The one who loved freely and with her whole heart.

Our ride took us over terrain more beautiful than I could have imagined. Whip followed the herd across the river, and I stopped to take a mental picture of the small waterfall spraying along the rocks. Mountains stretched up in the horizon casting long shadows over the grassland. Even the sky looked bluer here. The girls were unusually quiet while we rode. Each of us seemed to be tongue-tied by the surrounding sights. Only Doris chattered away the whole time, laughing and talking with Axel while she rode up ahead at his side.

All of us had changed on this journey, but Doris had blossomed more than I'd expected. When she'd first knocked on my door, someone's grandmother had stood there. But now, the woman on that horse, flirting and giggling beneath the gaze of a handsome cowboy, was so much more than just a grandmother. She was beautiful and alive. Free to be herself for the first time in her life. I was proud to have been at her side while she broke down the barriers holding her back. Broke through the loneliness I knew I would have experienced had I not had the Wilder Widows waiting on my doorstep.

"We got a runner!" Joe, one wrangler, shouted. A cow bolted past us and headed for the hills to our west. Before I could blink or call up for help, Marge screamed, and I spun to see her gripping her horn tight while Cochise barreled across the grassland after it.

"Holy cripes!" she hollered, her voice fading with the increasing distance between us.

Madeline started toward us, but she was far off on the other side of the herd, and that meant I was the closest.

"Marge!" I shouted, spinning Whip toward her and kicking him forward. Alice appeared at my side, Lady's long strides keeping up with us as we raced behind Marge.

"Pull on the reins!" I screamed, but the wind carried my voice away. "Marge! Pull back!"

Marge yanked on her reins, but Cochise shook his head, pinning his ears as he raced after the rogue cow. Bouncing and flailing, Marge screamed while she clung to her saddle, giving up her fight to stop the runaway horse.

"Hold on, Marge! We're coming!" Alice screamed, and I saw her riding skill shine through while she and Lady launched over a fallen log. It may have been a lot of years since she'd been on the back of a horse, but she had a natural riding ability I would have killed for.

Cochise swung wide, circling back in front of the cow. Determination burned inside his mottled eyes as he charged toward it. Marge screamed again when he went low, spinning on his hocks and cutting off the cow's attempt to escape again. Again and again, Cochise spun and cut, each time sending the cow back toward the herd.

"Just keep holding on, Marge!" Alice called, trying her best to steer Lady up beside them. But Cochise's quick movements were impossible to predict, and every time Alice reached for their reins, he spun and loped away again.

Finally, the cow gave up his rebellious run, spinning on his hoof and galloping back to the herd. Cochise chased him for several seconds before realizing his job was done. As fast as he started, he slammed on the brakes, sending Marge slamming into the leather horn.

"Ugh!" she grunted when it collided with her stomach. Puffing hard, Cochise pulled the reins from her hands, lowering his head and going back to munching on the grass.

"Marge! Are you okay!" I rode up to her side, reaching down and snagging the reins in my hands.

"Cripes! This thing is insane!"

"Are you hurt?" Alice asked, huffing herself while she pulled up on the other side, sandwiching the horse between us.

"No. Not hurt," Marge sputtered, and slowly the color returned to her face. As it came back, her shoulders started shaking. Thinking she was about to cry from the fear of her harrowing experience, I reached out to touch her shoulder. But instead of sobs, laughter floated out of her mouth. A rough, raspy laugh filled the charged air around us, and tears started flowing down her cheeks.

"Did you see me?" She sputtered between oxygen-stealing laughter. "I was like John fucking Wayne!"

The contagious laughter swept over me, and I started laughing with her. Alice followed suit, and soon matching tears streamed down our cheeks.

"John fucking Wayne!" Marge rolled with laughter.

"Well," Alice said, gasping for breath to form words. "Cochise was John Wayne's horse, so it only makes sense."

When Madeline arrived, she and her horse huffed for breath, and I saw the concern tightening her face soften at the sight of us clutching our sides in stitches.

"Everyone okay?" she asked.

"We're fine. Everything is fine," I answered, struggling to catch my breath.

"He's a madman!" Marge laughed, pointing down at the spotted gelding casually grazing beneath her.

"Yeah, he knows his job. Sorry, I didn't see the cow break for it, or I would have warned you. Cochise never lets a stray get away."

"I can see that!" Marge roared with laughter, wiping away the last of the tears.

"You sure you're okay?" Madeline asked.

"Okay? She's John Wayne, baby!" Alice nearly tumbled off Lady with the force of her laughter.

"You girls can ride." Madeline gave Alice and me a smile. "Color me impressed."

"What about me? I was a freaking bonified cow-wrangler!" Marge lifted her chin.

"I think that was all the horse, Marge," I teased.

"Yeah. But I stayed on." Pursing her lips, she arched her brows.

"That you did, Marge. Well done." Alice leaned over and patted her on the shoulder. "Well done."

"Why don't you ladies come on back, and we'll try to keep a better eye on you until we reach camp in a few hours." Madeline waved us forward.

Alice and I clucked our horses on, and they went willingly. Marge gave Cochise the same encouragement, but just like before, he ignored her pleas and continued munching on the grass while she flailed above him, a stark contrast to the galloping steed she'd been on just minutes before.

"Oh cripes! Come on!"

Alice and I exchanged a glance and dissolved into laughter.

CHAPTER NINETEEN

"Wait, where does this go?" Alice asked, staring at the tent pole in her hand.

"I think it was supposed to go in there." Pointing to the center of her tent, I grimaced. As we stared at it together, we watched it collapse on itself and fold into a crumpled pile of yellow fabric.

Tossing the pole on the ground, she crossed her arms. "I hate camping. I'm sleeping in yours tonight."

Chuckling, I placed a hand on her back. "That's fine, Alice. I don't mind the company."

"Aren't we paying them to do this for us? I mean, shouldn't they be setting up the tents?"

"It's part of the experience. Fishing for our own food. Setting up our own tents. Building our own fires. It's what makes it so fun!"

She blew out a puff of air that tousled her hair. "Says you."

"Yeah. Says me. Just go find a place by the fire. Axel has been teaching Doris how to start one. I'm sure it's going by now."

"Have you seen those two? That fire has been burning all day."

Doris had spent the entire day glued to Axel's side. Or perhaps it was Axel who was glued to her side. It was impossible to tell who was following who while they crossed the fifteen miles of lush terrain today. And Doris had never looked happier. Radiant, in fact. Doris looked downright radiant basking in the glow of Axel's attention.

"Caught one!" Marge walked up holding a dead fish. "This sucker didn't know I used to catch 'em by hand back in 'Nam. Tried getting away. Psht."

"Atta girl, Marge. You're really getting the full wilderness experience," I said.

"I was made to rough it." She looked at Alice. "Unlike Princess Pansy over here."

"I was made for the stage, Marge. Lights. Cameras. An audience. Not trees and squirrels." She pointed to the squirrel scurrying across a branch overhead.

"Just go sit by the fire and let the rest of us handle the dirty work."

"Fine by me." Alice held up her hands and crossed the small clearing in the woods, then headed toward the fire crackling through the trees.

"Pansy!" Marge called after her. Alice just lifted her middle finger and kept on walking.

"I love razzing her up." Marge smiled and set her fish down on a log.

"Don't I know it." I smiled. "You need anything?"

"Nah. Just gotta filet this up and give it to Madeline to add to our dinner menu tonight."

"I look forward to trying it. I'll see you at the fire."

Leaves and sticks crunched beneath my feet while I walked away, taking my time to appreciate the fresh air and smell of pine surrounding us. It mingled with the smoke from the campfire, creating a bouquet of earthy scents I wished I could bottle up to take home with me. A perfume I could spray around my home so I could be transported back here any time I needed to clear my mind.

"Hi, Sylvie! Pull up a log." Doris waved at me, and right beside her, where he'd been all day, sat Axel. "He showed me how to make a fire. Look! I made this!" With a triumphant smile, she waved a hand over the crackling flames and clapped.

"Nice work, MacGyver," I teased, pulling up a seat on the fallen tree by the fire.

The embers flickered and burned, drifting up into the darkening sky. I watched them rise high, burning out and fluttering back down as ash that landed around us.

"Want some?" Alice pushed a silver flask toward me.

"What is it?"

"Whiskey." She grinned.

"Isn't that what got us into this situation in the first place?" Arching an eyebrow, I took it anyway. Pulling one long swig, I choked it down, sputtering and coughing while I handed it back.

"Doris?" Alice asked.

Her gaze shot to Axel as if awaiting his judgment, but then her face stiffened, and she gave a sharp nod. "Just one sip."

Good for her. It was time for Doris to make her own decisions and wander off the clear, worn path she'd followed her whole life. This was her chance to taste freedom and find out what else life had to offer besides going to church, raising kids, and taking care of her husband. As she pulled the flask to her lips, I chuckled to myself that it seemed drinking whiskey was now on the menu.

"Ooh!" She scrunched her face while she smacked her lips. "Eventually, I'll be able to drink that without puckering up like a prune."

Alice took a swig, her face stoic and smooth as she downed another gulp. "You'll get there," she said with a smile after she pulled it away.

"So, Doris says you ladies are on some kind of an adventure?" Axel poked the fire with a long branch, sending more sparks flying into the air.

I nodded. "We are. We're traveling the globe while fulfilling all of our wishes."

"And who's wish was this?"

"Mine."

His eyes drifted over to Doris. "Well, I'm sure glad you're here."

It inspired the same giggle from her I'd heard all day.

"And what was your wish?" he asked Alice.

Straightening her shoulders and lifting her chin, pride radiated from within. "To be a Vegas showgirl again."

"Is that right?" he laughed. "And were you?"

"Of course. I was the star."

"We may be wanted fugitives back in Las Vegas, but we made it happen." I laughed.

"And I ran with the bulls." Marge came out from the woods and settled down beside me.

Axel's wide eyes glowed across the fire. "The bulls in Spain? You ran with the bulls?"

Marge grinned wide. "Damn straight we did."

"Wait? All of you?" Axel's mouth fell open while he looked across our little group of widows. "Even you?"

Doris gave him a quick nod. "It was exhilarating! I almost got gored, but a different bull saved me! Well, the bull and Jesus, of course."

"Yeah, and then I had to buy the damn thing because Doris couldn't stand to see it slaughtered. Now I've got to find someplace to keep a freaking bull."

Axel lifted a hand and closed his eyes. "Are you trying to tell me you own one of the famous Spanish fighting bulls?"

Alice gave him a dismissive shrug. "I do. And I have no idea what to do with the damn thing, but I couldn't watch Doris cry."

"El Diablo saved my life." Doris furrowed her brow. "He didn't deserve to die."

"I didn't even know you could buy those. They are supposed to be very special bulls bred just for the yearly fights. I've heard they're treated like kings up until the day of their big fight."

"It took all my God-given charms to convince them to sell him, and even with those, he still cost a fortune."

"But you saved him. For me." Doris smiled. "Thank you, Alice."

"You're welcome, Doris. Now we need to hurry up and figure out what we're doing with your damn bull. It's not like we can bring him home to live in the backyard." Alice lit up and turned to Axel. "Hey! You've got cattle. You want a fighting bull?"

Axel spit out the sip of beer he was taking. "What? Are you serious?"

Alice lifted a shoulder. "I need to find someplace to keep it. I promised Doris I would send him out for retirement somewhere. I could have him shipped here if you want him."

Dimples deepened on his face while his lips stretched into a wide grin. "A real live Spanish fighting bull? Here? On my ranch?"

"He's yours if you want him."

"Oh, Axel!" Doris exclaimed. "He would be so happy here! All this beautiful countryside? El Diablo would be in bull heaven."

Axel turned to Doris and brushed a piece of hair from her eyes. "Well, any bull with the brains to save this beauty has earned himself retirement on my ranch. I'd be happy to take him and give him the life he deserves for saving this little lady."

"Really? You'll take El Diablo?" Doris blinked fast.

"If that's what you want."

Reaching out, she squeezed his hand. "It would be a miracle."

"Then make the arrangements and send him here. I'm not sure if he'll fit in with the herd since those bulls are notoriously territorial, but I've got one cow who's a real pill, a nasty thing, and I think she may get along with him just fine. I can have a little family of fighting bulls someday."

"El Diablo is getting a girlfriend!" Doris squealed. "Saved from death's door and delivered to paradise. A true miracle." She made the sign of the cross, pressing her hands together in a silent prayer.

"Anything to see you smile like that." Axel brushed a finger across her cheek, and the sparkles in her eyes exploded like a light show. "I'm going to check on Madeline and see if they made it up here with supplies yet. I'll leave you ladies to relax."

We sat by the fire and chatted while Madeline and Axel cooked up dinner. When they called us over to grab our plates, I was delighted to see a traditional camping spread cooking on the fire they'd made by the supply tent. Hamburgers, boiled potatoes, and baked beans were set out for us to self-serve.

"Beans?" Alice crinkled her nose, whispering over my shoulder. "Don't give any to Marge."

"Beans!" Marge said as she stepped into line behind us. "I love me some good baked beans. Just gotta warn you ladies, though. I wouldn't want to be in the tent with me tonight."

"You're an animal," Alice grumbled and stepped in front of me, placing extra space between herself and the grinning Marge.

"Just giving you a heads up." Marge tossed an oversized scoop of beans on her tin plate.

We finished filling our plates and found our seats back by the fire. Axel ate with Madeline and the wranglers at the other fire, leaving the widows and me a little time to ourselves.

"So, this is your big wish, huh?" Alice said, lifting the top of her bun and pulling a face. "Beans, dirt, cow shit, and burned burgers?"

"Well, it's the only wish I can actually do, so yes... this is my wish."

"Wait a minute," Marge said. "This isn't your actual wish?"

The moment the words slipped out, I wished I could shove them back inside. "No. I mean, yes. Yes, this is my wish."

Three sets of eyes bore through me, and I shifted on the log, looking away to the flames licking at our feet.

"Sylvie..." Marge warned. "What aren't you telling us?"

"Nothing. It's nothing." I forced a smile and tried to shake the tension from my shoulders.

"If I'm sitting here in the middle of the fucking woods eating beans, this had better damn well be your wish, Sylvie," Alice growled.

"It is!" A laugh more fake than I'd anticipated slipped out. "It is."

Doris set down her plate and scooted to my side. "Sylvie, I can tell you're holding something back. What is it? What aren't you telling us?"

His face flashed through my mind. A smile so bright it had lit up my entire life.

"Sylvie. Spill," Marge commanded.

Heaving a deep sigh, I set down my plate and turned to them. "My real wish, the one I *can't* do, so this is my wish, is to see the man I loved with all my heart before I married Bruce."

Memories smashed back into me as if I'd been run down by one of the bulls in Pamplona. I saw flashes of his face, his eyes, and our naked bodies pressed together while he told me he loved me.

"Who is he?" Marge asked, pressing closer.

Who is he? My great love. My soul mate. The one man who cracked open my soul and stepped inside, refusing to vacate almost forty years later. But instead of telling them that, I just answered, "His name was Thomas Connolly."

"Thomas Connolly, huh? So, who was he?" Alice asked, offering me a swig of whiskey.

Knowing I needed some liquid courage, I took a big swig, letting it burn a hole through the wall I kept his memories hidden behind.

"I was just out of college and engaged to Bruce."

"You were engaged?" Alice grinned. "You scandalous thing, you!"

Rolling my eyes, I shrugged off her comment. "Yes. I was engaged. And yes, I cheated. And yes, it was scandalous. I'm not perfect."

"No one is perfect, Sylvie." Doris pressed her lips together in a sympathetic smile. "We all make mistakes. Now, quit interrupting, Alice!" Doris swooshed at her. "Go on, Sylvie. Tell us what happened."

I let the crack the whiskey made in the wall open all the way up. "Bruce and I had been together for several years, and we were about four months out from our wedding date. It was then I started to see the dark side of the man I was about to marry. Fresh out of college, he was struggling to find work, and his temper and bad attitude showed through for the first time. In college, he'd been happy. Funny. Full of life. But now, the man I said yes to was only a memory, and the man I was marrying wasn't anyone I wanted to tie myself to. But I wasn't sure how to end it. Bruce went out of town for a week on job interviews, and I decided to head out to the bar one night to meet up with some of my girlfriends. We had some drinks and some laughs, and then half-way through the night, I saw a set of amber eyes staring at me from across the bar. I'll never forget the intensity of his gaze. It seared right through me."

Doris clutched her chest and sighed. "Like Axel's."

Nodding, I pushed a stray rock back onto the fire with my foot. "He was gorgeous. Dark hair, big muscles, and a smile that nearly took me to my knees. He sent me a drink, and even though I knew I shouldn't, I couldn't stop my feet from taking me to him. It was like he sucked away my common sense and ensnared me with his looks."

"He was a fox?" Marge asked, wiggling her brows.

Blowing out a puff of air, I nodded. Hard. "More like a lion." I grinned. "A powerful, sexy, strong lion of a man. And I was powerless to resist him. Not that I wanted to." Laughing, I remembered how he'd reached out to touch my hand and how I'd tried to remember Bruce and pull it away. Instead, my fingers entwined with his, holding tight as he'd rubbed the pad of his thumb across my palm.

"After spending hours laughing and talking, we ended up back at my place. One thing led to another, and I ended up having the hottest sex of my entire life."

"Ah, this would be the partner you mentioned envisioning from time to time to get your hootie?" Alice gave me a sly smile, and I laughed.

"Yes, Alice. This would be him."

"He sounds delicious."

Closing my eyes, I pressed my lips together, remembering the taste of his kiss and the smell of his sweaty skin as it slid against mine. "Absolutely delicious. I was irrevocably in love with him in a matter of hours."

"So, what happened? Why did you marry Bruce if you fell in love with someone else?"

"Tom and I spent the whole week together, most of it in bed. I told him I was engaged, and he begged me to break it off. The feelings for each other were mutual, and I can't explain it, but I just knew... *knew* this was the man I was supposed to spend my life with. So, I agreed. I would end my engagement and be with him."

"So, what happened?" Marge asked, pressing her elbows into her knees while she leaned forward.

"He was a Marine."

"Ah. A military man. My kind of guy." Marge slapped her knee.

"And he was on leave, but that Monday, he got called back in for some conflict."

"What conflict?" Marge asked.

"He didn't say. All he said was that he loved me, to end my engagement, and as soon as he got back, he would find me."

"But you married Bruce anyway?" Doris asked, sadness pulling her eyes down. "But Tom loved you. And you loved him."

With a deep sigh, I admitted the one thing I never told another soul. "A couple months after he'd left, I still struggled for the strength to end it with Bruce. I hadn't heard from Tom at all, and I had started to wonder if I was just some fling he had no intentions of returning to. That maybe the feelings between us were one-sided, and he was already shacked up with some other gullible girl. Even though I lost hope he was coming back to me, I still decided I couldn't marry Bruce. I was going to end it anyway. It was then I found out I was pregnant." I paused, searching for the strength to say it. "And it was Tom's."

Three gasps conjoined and ripped through the crisp air.

"Wait. So, Rachel isn't Bruce's child?"

Biting my lip, I shook my head.

"Did Bruce know?"

I shook my head harder.

"Does Rachel know?"

"No. Not a soul in the world besides you three knows that truth. Rachel is Tom's daughter."

"Holy shit," Alice breathed.

"Holy cripes."

"Heavens to Betsy."

I nodded, agreeing with their sentiments. "Holy shit, cripes, and Heavens to Betsy is right. I can't believe I just told all of you that."

"And you never told Tom? Or Bruce? What happened?" Alice stared at me with wide eyes.

"I found out I was pregnant and panicked. And I mean *panicked*. I knew it was Tom's. There was no doubt in my mind with the timing after I had talked to the doctor. Not to mention Bruce and I were always careful, and Tom and I had been anything but. When I sat there in that doctor's office, I couldn't even fathom what to do. My wedding was less than a month away, I was knocked up, and Tom was nowhere to be found. So instead of calling off the engagement and ending up pregnant and alone, I made a choice right then and there to pretend Tom never existed, my baby was Bruce's, and I was going to march down that aisle no matter how much I already hated him."

Doris scooped my hand in hers. "Oh Sylvie, you must have been so scared."

"Sad. Scared. Guilty. So many emotions. But I swallowed them down and did what I needed to do to make sure my child would be cared for and raised in a family. I married Bruce and let him think Rachel was his. And, of course, he never questioned it."

"And you never saw Tom again?"

The most painful memory of my life resurfaced, ripping me back open as it did each time it broke free and crept up inside my mind.

"Once. Four months later." I closed my eyes and remembered the emotions slamming into me when I opened the door to see him standing there. "He showed up at my apartment, the one I'd been living at when he and I were together, that was now my apartment with Bruce."

"What happened? Why was he gone so long?" Doris's eyes looked like they were ready to pop right out of her skull.

"I opened the door and almost passed out when I saw him. I was pregnant, almost six months. Luckily, I wasn't showing a ton. I also had on a baggy sweatshirt, and I remember holding my breath while I waited for him to notice the swell in my belly, but instead, he swept me into his arms, crippling me with a kiss and apologizing for being gone so long. He said he was away on important military business, and he couldn't get back any sooner. Then he saw my ring and stepped back."

"What did he say?"

"He was shocked I was married. Angry even."

"Psht." Alice scoffed. "Figures a man would just expect you to wait around for him."

"That's what I said! It was a dizzying blend of anger and regret I felt when I stood in that doorway staring at the man I had loved. Still loved. He could have called or written. Sent a messenger. A carrier pigeon, for crying out loud! He just kept telling me it was impossible based on where he was and what he was involved in. But it was too late. I was married. Bruce thought the baby in my belly was his. It was just too late."

"So that was it?" Marge's gruff voice softened. "You just said goodbye."

Tears brimmed my eyes while I nodded, remembering the searing pain that traveled through me when I'd watched him walk away. "Yes. I told him it was too late, I was sorry, and I couldn't be with him. He told me he would always love me and walked away. It was awful. I wanted to race after him, tell him I was pregnant with his child, and we should run off together. But instead, I stood in that doorway sobbing while I stared at my wedding ring and rubbed my belly. I had made my choice. It was too late."

"Oh, Sylvie. I can't imagine carrying that with you all these years."

"It's been hard. So many times when Bruce was awful to me, I wanted to scream in his face that Rachel wasn't his and I was still in love with another man. But each time I opened my mouth, I thought of what it would do to Rachel, and I choked the words back down. I had made my bed, and it was my penance to lie in it. At least until she was grown and could handle hearing such shocking news."

"But you still never told her?"

"No. By the time she was grown, it was too late. I didn't see the point. She and Bruce were never close. His temper and bad attitude were hard on us all. He was never abusive or anything like that, but the minute she turned eighteen, she moved out. I also figured Tom was already married with a family of his own. There was no sense in blowing up my family to run after a man who probably had forgotten all about me."

"It sounds like he really loved you, Sylvie. I can't imagine he forgot about you." Doris sighed.

"My love for him hasn't faded in almost forty years. He's like a torch that just won't go out no matter how hard I try to extinguish it. But I can't imagine he feels the same way. I made my choice. Now I need to live with it."

"So, that's what your wish would have been? To see him again?" Marge asked.

With a deep sigh, I nodded. "Just one more time. But it's not possible. I don't even know where he lives... or *if* he lives. A couple months after I saw him, Bruce got a job a few hours away, and we moved. I don't know if Tom still lived in Valley Hills or if the military took him away. I never saw him again. And it's all just too late. So instead... dude ranch." I grinned. "And this is a wonderful wish, and truly something I've always wanted to do. Thank you for making this possible, ladies."

"Thank you for sharing all that with us," Doris said. "I hope it feels better having some of that weight off your shoulders. We're happy to help you carry it."

"It means the world to me to have each of you in my life. Thank you for knocking on my door."

We all exchanged a smile, and then Axel stepped out of the woods and into the firelight.

"I don't mean to bother you ladies, but it's a beautiful night, and the stars are out in full force. It's not often you get to see them like this when you're in the city. I wonder if I might borrow Doris to accompany me on a walk? That is if she would like to."

Doris nearly leaped to her feet. "I would love to accompany you on a walk, Axel. It's a lovely evening."

She stepped to his side, and with a quick wave over her shoulder, we watched them disappear into the darkness.

"She had better ride that cowboy tonight, or I'm gonna hop on him myself."

"Alice!" I laughed, swatting her in the arm. "You get enough men. You leave this one to Doris. It's about damn time she had a romantic tryst."

"Touch Doris's man, and I'll spear you myself." Marge poked at her with the metal skewer she used to roast marshmallows.

"I'm just kidding!" Alice laughed, lifting her hands in submission. "But really, I hope she hops on that. I bet he gives one hell of a bronco ride."

We burst into laughter, leaning in together and giggling while we sat together by the warm fire.

CHAPTER TWENTY

"Oh, Marge!" Alice choked, waving her hand in the air. "Come on!"

Marge snickered from beneath her sleeping bag. "I told you not to share a tent with me."

"I didn't share a tent with you. You're the one who crawled in here with us last night," Alice grumbled.

"I thought I heard a bear. Figured you ladies would need someone to protect you."

"Well, it's morning, and we're all alive. The only thing we need protecting from right now is you. If you don't get your stinky ass out of here, we won't be alive for long. Now go!"

Laughing from beneath my sleeping bag, I listened to Alice smack Marge with the pillow. "I slept like a log last night." With a big yawn, I stretched my arms as I emerged from my cocoon. "All that riding really wiped me out."

"My ass hurts." Marge mirrored my yawn.

"I bet it does." Alice laughed, waving a hand in front of her face.

"I meant from the riding."

I sat up and groaned. "Are you two starting up this early? I haven't even had my coffee yet."

"Oh, coffee. That sounds amazing." Alice stood and stretched.

We dressed quickly and stepped outside, passing by Doris's tent as we walked to the food tent.

"Where's Doris?" Marge asked, stiffening while she lifted the flap to find it vacant. "Where the hell is Doris?"

"I'm sure she's fine. Probably beat us to the coffee."

"No. She wasn't there when I checked before bed last night, and her sleeping bag is still rolled up. She didn't sleep in there." Marge stood, her military background snapping to the forefront. "Split up, soldiers. We've got a man down."

"I'm sure she's—"

"Good morning!" Doris sing-songed and we spun to see her standing behind the fire, pushing bacon around on the cast-iron skillet. "I hope you all worked up an appetite. Madeline let me do the cooking this morning. I'm so excited. It's been ages since I've gotten to cook for a group of people! We've got bacon, eggs, and I made hash browns from the leftover potatoes last night. Come on up and grab a plate!"

"See, a bear didn't snatch her up. She's doing what Doris does best. Taking care of people." I smiled and headed toward her.

"Isn't it a beautiful day?" Doris sighed when I got to her. "The most beautiful day in the history of days." With a languid smile, she broke into a hum while she flipped an egg sizzling in bacon grease.

A quizzical look passed between Alice, Marge, and I, and then recognition lit up our faces.

"Doris, you dog, you," Alice said, leaning in. "Did you?"

A pink hue rose across her cheeks. "Did I what?"

"You know what." Marge pushed. "Have a hootie."

"Stop!" Doris lowered her voice, waving at us with her free hand.

"You trollop!" Alice laughed. "You did!"

Stiffening her chin, Doris fixated her gaze on the bacon. "A lady never tells."

"You did!" Marge howled. "You did, didn't you?"

Struggling to keep my mouth shut, I stared at Doris as she tittered while flipping another egg. Finally, she looked up and peeked over her shoulder each way before leaning in. "I did. I had a hootie." Her voice dissolved into giggles.

"Whoo hoo!" Marge whooped, pumping her fist into the air.

"Get out!" I laughed, struggling to keep my voice down.

"Shhh!" she shooshed us. "Don't let anyone hear you."

"And? Did you love it?" Alice's eyes lit with excitement. "You did, didn't you?"

Doris giggled again, then nodded and gave us a sheepish grin. "It was incredible! I can see now why you all were so set on making sure I didn't die without experiencing that."

"Ahh." I smiled. "Now she gets it."

Marge bumped her on the shoulder with a fist. "Good for you, Doris. You got laid."

"What?" she gasped, looking over both shoulders again. "We didn't... you know. We're not married, so we can't. But he did... other things. Good things. Down there." She cupped a hand over her mouth while she said it and pointed to her crotch.

Alice gave her an appreciative nod. "Proud of you, Doris."

"I think I love him," Doris whispered. "Like, really love him."

"You just met him, Doris." Alice shook her head. "That's the hootie talking."

Doris's face slid down into a frown.

"Hey now," Marge defended. "I knew I loved Roxy the minute I saw her."

"And I knew I loved Tom the second I saw him," I added, knowing the power of love and that it didn't always take days, weeks, or years to grow. Sometimes it slammed into you like a Mack truck. And from the way Doris lit up around Axel, it was clear to see she felt it too.

"Well, I *do* think I love him. And he seems to really care about me." Doris stood her ground. "In fact, he's asked if I'll come back soon."

"Oh, you'll *come* back again." Marge snorted, eliciting a glare from Doris.

"Don't tease me! It was special. We walked along the river, and then he laid out a blanket so we could lay back and watch the stars. So romantic." Another sigh hummed through her.

"I'm sure it was, Doris. I'm happy for you." I tried to put a stop to the teasing, and I gave her a quick wink.

"Now plate up some food. Coffee is over there. We've got a long ride back today, and you ladies will need your strength."

"Yes, ma'am," Marge said, falling into line and grabbing a plate, and we all followed suit.

After enjoying our breakfast, we tacked up the horses and mounted back up for the long ride home. Doris rode alongside Axel the whole way; their stolen glances and subtle touches caused my heart to swell. She looked happy. Radiant. In love. And from the starry-eyed gaze her silver fox continued giving her, it was clear the feeling was mutual. A new love resembling the one I'd experienced only once in my life.

I was quieter than usual on the ride home. Without cattle to herd since we'd left them on the prairie to graze, the ride back went at a much quicker pace. Despite the beautiful scenery, my mind continued leaving and traveling to an apartment I hadn't seen in over thirty-five years. It kept returning to the arms of the man who still held my heart, and it continued reliving the happiest days of my life. It kept returning to Tom Connolly. The love of my life.

****

After we returned to the dude ranch, we limped back to our cabin. Two days of hard riding had taken the wind out of our Wilder Widows sails.

"Hot tub. Now." Alice sat back, kicking off her dirty red boots.

"Count me in." I groaned, rubbing my aching lower back.

"I'll meet you ladies there in a minute. There's something I need to do," Marge said, disappearing into the bathroom.

We pulled on our swimsuits and scurried across the lawn in our bare feet to where the hot tub on the deck of the main hall sat. One by one, we slid inside, each *oohing* and *aahing* as the hot water enveloped us. Alice pushed the button on the wooden post beside her, and it sent bubbles tumbling through the steaming water.

"Now, *this* is my kind of getaway." Alice closed her eyes and pressed her head back into the headrest. "Next time we do this, you ladies can do the whole cowgirl thing. I'll just be here in the hot tub."

"I loved it out there," Doris said. "I never knew how much I would enjoy being out in the wilderness and with the animals. And getting to cook for you girls this morning was wonderful."

"Maybe you should stay on as the cook." Alice snorted. But I looked over to see Doris chewing on her bottom lip.

"What? Why are you making that face, Doris?" I asked, scooting closer to her.

"Because Axel asked me to do just that."

"He what?" Alice and I echoed as we flew up to sitting.

"You're kidding," I breathed, but Doris only smiled and shook her head.

"No. We talked about it a little on our ride home. I told him how much I loved this and couldn't wait to get back. And when I told him there was nothing waiting for me at home, he asked me to stay. They need a cook since Madeline hates doing it, and they've been getting busier. It sounds like heaven to me spending my days on a ranch cooking for large families and groups that come to visit."

"Not to mention Axel?" I arched a brow.

Doris gave me a sheepish smile. "And Axel, too. I'm not sure what it all means, or if I'm just being a silly fool, but I really do love him. And if I stay on, I can see where it goes."

"And maybe you'll end up getting married and have the *big* hootie!" Alice teased.

"Maybe." Doris shrugged it off, but I could see the excitement flicker in her eyes. "He sure is handsome. I can't believe he's interested in me."

"I can." I touched her shoulder. "You're beautiful, Doris. And sweet. And funny. And caring and kind. You're a catch for any man. Even that silver fox of yours."

"He's got abs, Doris. Abs. At our age. You hang on to that man with everything you've got." Alice laughed. "Because if you don't I—"

"Can it, Alice," Marge said, stepping out around the corner. "He's only got eyes for our Doris."

Doris smirked and gave Marge a grateful smile.

"Did you hear that Doris may be staying on here?"

"I did," Marge said, sliding into the water. "I think it's a wonderful idea. We sure will miss you, but I don't see any reason you shouldn't give it a try. What's waiting for you at home?"

"Nothing." A flicker of pain traveled across Doris's face, but then it lit up again. "Is this crazy? Me staying here?"

"Not even a little bit," I said. "I would stay in a heartbeat if I were you."

"You're absolutely right! Why shouldn't I stay? At least give it a try? All that's left for me at home is knitting. At least out here, I can be useful. Have people around who need me. And El Diablo! He'll be here too!"

"And have hootie after hootie." Alice grinned.

"Amen to that." Marge lifted a bottle of wine in the air.

"Ooh! Wine!" I took it from her, taking a pull straight from the bottle before passing it over to Doris.

"So, our Wilder Widows group is breaking up?" I asked, just realizing the ramifications of Doris's new adventure.

"Not yet," Marge stated, and I looked over to see mirth flashing in her eye. She reached out of the hot tub, and when her hand emerged, it clutched our knitting basket.

"What are you doing, Marge?" I said. "We pulled the last wish. This was it."

She gave the basket a shake, and I heard something moving around inside. The three widows exchanged a mischievous smile and looked back at me.

"What? What's going on?" I asked.

"I think there was a mistake," Alice said after taking a big swig of the wine. "There was a mix-up with the wishes. There's one more left. Go ahead. Take a look."

Furrowing my brow, I slid forward in the water and reached into the basket. Sure enough, I felt a piece of paper at the tips of my fingers. Careful not to get it wet as I pulled it out, I unfolded it, gasping when I read the words. "Find Sylvie's true love."

"That's your real wish, and to hell if we're giving you your second choice. Our work isn't done yet," Marge said.

"I... I can't." I folded it back up and put it back in the basket. "Thank you, ladies, but I just can't."

"Why not?" Doris sat forward. "You deserve to have your happy ending, Sylvie. I have Axel. Marge has Roxy. Alice has... well, Alice has herself and about a hundred lovers."

She grinned. "Why settle for just one?"

"It's your turn, Sylvie. We talked about it today, and we aren't going to stop until we find him."

"I don't even know where he lives. Or if he lives. Or if he lives and doesn't want to see me. What if he's married? What if he hates me for breaking his heart?"

"And what if he doesn't?" Marge asked, and the weight of her question nearly pushed me under the water. "What if he still loves you and you can finally be together?"

"You owe it to yourself to find out." Doris crossed her arms. "And we're going to be right at your side while you do."

"What about your new life here?" I waved a hand around me.

"It will be here when I get back. We Wilder Widows are sticking together until *all* our wishes have come true. And yours was to see him again, so that's what we're going to do."

"But how do I even go about finding him?" Just the thought of seeing him again sent my heart racing faster than it had when I'd seen that bull charging up behind me in Pamplona.

"You leave that to me." Marge slid to the side of the hot tub and dried her hand on a towel. Pulling out her cellphone, she pushed the buttons and held it to her ear. "My daughter is a cop. She'll find him."

Holding my breath, I waited to find out my fate. Was it possible I could see Tom again? Did I want to see Tom again? What would he say when he saw me? Questions collided through my mind while I waited.

"Martha, it's mom," Marge said into the phone.

Oh, God. She answered. Was this happening?

"No, I'm fine. Sorry, I should have called. I was on a trip." We listened while Marge paused.

"No, a big trip. Vegas, Paris, Spain, now I'm in Wyoming. I'm fine. Sorry I worried you."

Still waiting. Watching.

"I know, I know. I'll tell you all about it. But right now, I need a favor. I need you to find someone for me. A man."

More waiting. More watching.

"No, nothing like that. He's not for me. Turns out I'm a lesbian."

I choked on the air as my eyes shot open.

"Yeah. Roxy. I'll introduce you someday. You'll love her."

Waiting. So much waiting.

"Yep. She's a real hot mama. I want to tell you more about her, but first I need you to find that man. Thomas Connolly. Last known whereabouts were," she placed her hand over the speaker, "Where was he last living, Sylvie?"

"Valley Hills," I said back.

"Thomas Connolly. Marine. Valley Hills."

Waiting. More waiting.

"You did? Great! Is he alive?"

Holy shit. She found him already? Is he alive? Waiting…

"Single?"

Holding my breath.

"Great. Get me an address. Thanks, sweetheart. I'll call you when I get back."

Marge hung up and turned to where we all sat stunned and staring. "He's alive. He's still there." She slipped back into the water without any more words, and I struggled to form my own.

"He's alive? And still living there?"

"Yep. Seems we didn't even need the cop computer. She found him on Facebook."

"You're kidding," I breathed. "He's really still there?"

"He sure is. And she thinks he's single."

Even though I was outside, I felt all the air suck out of the atmosphere.

"Buckle up, ladies. We've got one more adventure to go!" Doris said, and I almost passed out.

CHAPTER TWENTY-ONE

"This is crazy," I said as I climbed back into the front seat of the car, pressing my oversized sunglasses up onto my nose. "We look ridiculous."

"Speak for yourself. I look fabulous."

Looking over my shoulder into the back seat, I looked at Alice sporting her rhinestone sunglasses, red scarf wrapped around her head, and red lipstick to match. She was right. Even in her costume, she still looked fabulous.

"Now *I* feel like the old maid."

I turned sharper to see Marge sitting behind me. The floral scarf and purple sunglasses didn't have the same chic effect as they did on Alice, and it caused me to snort.

"So, where are we going?" Doris said from the driver's seat, and I turned to stare at her as well. A pink scarf tied tight around her chin matched the pink sunglasses she'd picked out at the dollar store we'd just left.

"Home. This is nuts." I shook my head and felt my headscarf loosening. I didn't need to look in the mirror to know I didn't look as elegant as Alice. The purple scarf and oversized black sunglasses I'd tossed in our cart weren't something I would ever wear if I wasn't planning on stalking an old lover.

"It's not nuts. It's true love." Doris smiled. Ever since meeting Axel, all she could do was smile and talk about true love. Her newfound love had her more driven to get me back to mine than even the other motivated widows.

"It's stalking. That's what it is. Stalking," I grumbled.

"Not true." Marge leaned forward into the space between the front seats. "Stalking is defined as 'a course of conduct directed at a specific person that involves repeated, at least two or more occasions, visual or physical proximity, nonconsensual communication, or verbal, written, or implied threats, or a combination thereof, that would cause a reasonable person fear.'"

Staring at her in the rearview mirror, I only blinked.

"I asked Martha. She told me we're good." Marge shrugged and fell back into her seat.

"Well, okay then, Encyclopedia Britannica. So, we're not technically stalking. *Yet*. But it sure feels like stalking."

"Nope. Not unless we do it repeated times and, if he's a reasonable person, cause him fear."

"Have you looked at us?" I waved a hand around the car. "If I saw us on the street in these getups, I'd be scared."

"You three may look ridiculous. But I still look good." Alice sat back against the plush grey seat of the car we'd rented at the airport.

"Can we just forget about this? Seriously. I don't need to see Tom again. It's been too long. And what would I even say?"

"Well, first we need to find him and make sure he hasn't turned into a troll in his old age," Alice said. "Because if he has, we're on the first plane outta here."

"Can we just be on the first plane outta here, anyway?" I pleaded.

"No," they echoed, and Doris started the car.

"Are you sure you won't let me drive?" Marge asked. "I've seen you drive at home once, Doris. You nearly took out that group of school kids crossing the street."

Doris puckered her lips and glared at Marge in the rearview. "That was once. There was a sunspot. I'm a good driver!"

"Tell that to the people you're about to mow down." Alice snorted.

"We drew straws, and I got the one saying I can drive. Now just buckle up and tell me where we're going."

"Does this thing have double seatbelts back here?" Marge asked while she clicked herself in. "Extra airbags? A roll cage?"

Doris just huffed and put the car in drive. "Just tell me where we're going."

According to Martha's research, Tom now lived on Walnut Lane. Since I'd spent my entire youth running around this town, I didn't need a map to tell me where it was. It was only three blocks over from the house I grew up in. "At the stoplights up there, take a left."

"Got it," Doris said, pressing the gas and pulling out of our parking spot. A horn honk caused us all to jump, and Doris slammed on the brakes. The car she'd pulled out in front of whizzed past, and a middle finger greeted us from the driver as he blew by.

"Oops." Doris gave us a sheepish shrug.

"Cripes, Doris! Careful!" Marge shouted. "You may get off easy anyway, Sylvie. Looks like Doris will kill us long before we solidify our stalker status."

"For the first time in my life, I'm praying for death." I blew out a breath as Doris looked over her shoulder before creeping out onto Main Street.

Following my instructions, she drove us through the town I'd once called home. Each street we turned on brought back a flood of memories. I saw the old oak tree I'd learned to climb at my friend Sarah's house. Further down, we passed the street where I'd gotten that scar on my knee that I hated so much. I'd hit a rock while riding over to Trudy's house and gone ass over teakettle on my bike. Doris turned again, and this time I saw the house I'd called home for eighteen years.

"Pull over for a second." I rolled down my window to get a better look. "This was my house growing up."

The modest two-story home still looked remarkably the same with only a few minor changes. Dark green shutters framed the windows now instead of the blue ones from when I'd lived there, and the driveway had been newly paved and looked sharp next to the fresh coat of white paint.

"Wow. It's been years." I leaned out the window, closing my eyes to inhale the scents of my childhood. I could almost smell my mother's fresh cinnamon buns on a Sunday morning.

"It seems like a nice place to grow up," Doris said.

"It was." A soft smile lifted my lips. "Many happy memories here. I loved this town. In fact, I never wanted to leave. Bruce was the one who forced us to move away."

"Well, I'm glad he did. If you hadn't, we never would have met you." Doris tapped my thigh. "Now, tell me where to go so we can bring you home to your true love."

My inward groan turned into an external one. "Just go straight for three blocks. It should be on that street."

"I'm so excited!" Doris squealed as she pulled back out. Another horn honk caused her to slam on the brakes again. An old lady in a minivan raked us with a glare as she pulled around.

"Oops." Doris shrunk a little lower in her seat.

"Can we go back to running with the bulls? I think we were safer then," Alice said, and it caused me to laugh, loosening the fingers of tension tearing into my shoulders.

"I'm telling you. We need a damn roll cage to ride with her." Marge tugged on her seatbelt to make sure it was still on tight.

"Okay. Now we're off." Doris took an extra look in her mirrors and pulled back out.

It felt like an eternity as we crossed the last three blocks to Walnut Lane. Time seemed to slow down as our rental car rolled down the suburban streets.

"There! That's it! 2723!" Marge pressed her face to the window. "The white one!"

"Are you sure?" I asked, sinking lower into my seat as we rolled up in front of it.

Doris pressed on the brake, but I screamed and smacked her in the leg. "Don't stop! Go! Go!"

With a shriek, she stepped on the gas, and our tires squealed while we skittered away.

"Cripes! I've got whiplash!" Marge scolded. "What the hell?"

"We can't stop in front of his house! He'll see us!"

"Isn't that the point?" Marge said.

"No," Alice defended me. "The point is to find out if he's a troll *before* he sees her. That way, if it's a no-go, we can get the hell out of here without being detected."

"Thank you. Exactly," I said.

Despite my mini-meltdown, I didn't really care if he was still the gorgeous man I remembered. I loved Tom for Tom... not just his striking good looks. And God was he something to behold back then. Even if he was five hundred pounds and bald now, I doubted my feelings would subside even a little. As long as he looked at me with those eyes... those golden orbs that stared straight into my soul, my love for him wouldn't dream of fading. No. His looks didn't worry me. My hesitation had nothing to do with the superficial. When I thought of facing Tom after all these years – I just didn't know what to say. How to feel. How to process all the emotions racing around inside of me like the Indy 500. Tom... my Tom... was just a few hundred feet away.

"So, what do I do?" Doris asked, keeping the car moving.

Alice waved her forward. "Just keep circling the block. He's got to come out eventually, right?"

"Right. Good plan," Marge agreed. "Keep moving, Doris. It's harder to hit a moving target."

"We're not under fire, Marge." Alice laughed.

"You know what I mean. Just keep moving, Doris."

"Got it."

For an hour we circled around the block time and time again. Even with all the time that passed and the number of times I saw that house, the knot tangled up in my gut hadn't unwound even a little.

"Still nothing." Marge grumbled as we passed it again. "What the hell is he doing in there?"

"Maybe he's not home. Maybe he's at work. Or on vacation!" Yes. Vacation! Perhaps he wasn't home, and I could tuck my tail and run all the way back to Wilder Lane.

"Lights are on. See that?" Marge pointed to the bay window overlooking the yard. "He's home. Wish I'd brought my binoculars."

"I think that takes us one step too far in the stalker ladder," I said.

"So, you really don't know if you want to see him?" Doris asked while she continued around the block.

"No. I'm not sure about this at all."

"But why not? He was your true love."

"*Was*. That's the operative word here. He *was* my true love... but that was almost forty years ago. So much has happened. So much has changed. Like me, for instance! When he met me, I was young and gorgeous. A doe-eyed girl without a line on her face. Now look at me." I waved a hand over my head. "Well, right now all you see is my scarf and sunglasses, but beneath it is an old woman!"

"You are not an old woman!" Doris scoffed. "You're a chicken! A spring chicken! And a beautiful one at that."

Alice leaned forward and peered over her sunglasses. "You've still got it, Sylvie. No need to worry about that."

But I did worry about that. What would he think if he saw me? Would he judge my fading beauty and count his lucky stars he didn't end up with me? Or worse yet, would he even recognize me? Even see the young woman he'd once held in his arms, kissing her senseless between breathless admissions of his love?

"You're a stone-cold hottie," Marge said, and it caused me to erupt into laughter.

"A stone-cold hottie?" I laughed.

"That's what Roxy calls me." A proud smile lifted her lips. "It's the hip lingo."

"Well, thanks, Marge. Glad you think so. But the question is, will he?"

"It's been forty years, and you're still thinking about him," Alice said. "It's time to march your ass up there and see what happens."

I looked out the window as we passed his house again.

"What do you have to lose?" she kept on. "Him? You don't have him now, and you have no chance of having him unless you pull up your big girl panties and knock on that door. Forget what I said about stalking him to see if he's a troll. Let's just pull up, knock on the door, and if he's ugly as sin, just race back to the car, and Doris will be the getaway driver."

"Oh, cripes. Someone get me a helmet if Doris is going all Fast and Furious over here."

Alice's words settled in bone-deep. I had nothing to lose. What was the worst thing that could happen? He slammed the door in my face and I never saw him again? A life without him already awaited me if I didn't find the courage to face him again.

"Okay," I breathed, barely able to form the words. "Do it. Pull up."

"Seriously?" Doris turned toward me with wide eyes. "You're doing it?"

"I'm doing it. Pull up in front the next time we go by." As I said the words, the emotions I'd held behind the carefully constructed wall he lived behind bubbled up, threatening to topple it down. We turned the corner back onto his street, and Doris let the car slow down while we rolled up near his house. As I took a last breath to steady my nerves, I saw the front door open.

It only took a split second after my eyes clapped onto him for all the breath to leave my body. Steel grey strands of hair had replaced the raven ones from before. A salt and pepper beard trimmed short wrapped around the once-smooth muscular jawline that hadn't diminished one bit. Still strong and proud, and a perfect fit for the muscular body my eyes raked lower to take in. Even at this distance, I could see the Marine tattoo on his tanned forearm, and I remembered tracing my fingers along it at the bar the night we met.

"It's him!" I shrieked, scrambling to inhale my next breath.

"Where? Oh!" Marge said. "Another silver fox!"

"Hellooo, Tom," Alice crooned from the back.

"Where? Where?" Doris said, and I felt the car swerve.

The jarring movement caused the tires to screech, and the noise pulled his gaze toward us.

"Get down!" I screamed, diving into the center of the car.

"Incoming!" Marge screamed, and from the corner of my eye, I saw her grab Alice and drag her down onto the seats. "Stay down! Take cover!"

The car screamed forward, and my heart raced faster than the roaring engine. Had he seen me?

"Did he see us?" Doris asked, and when I opened my eyes, her face floated in front of mine.

"Doris! You're driving! You can't duck!" I screamed. The whites of her eyes shone for only a second before she shot back up to sitting.

"Oh no!" she cried out as the brakes seized up. I shot up in my seat just in time to feel the airbag explode in my face. The seatbelt gripped my chest, and I gasped while it slammed me back into the seat as we crashed to a stop amidst the sound of crunching metal.

In the blink of an eye, the car stopped shaking. Black smoke from the tires rolled in through the windows, and I coughed out the powder from the airbags burning my lungs and clinging to my skin.

"Is everyone okay?" I choked out the words while I assessed my own shocked body.

"I crashed!" Despite her sobbing, Doris looked relatively unscathed. The deflated remnants of her airbag dangled from the steering wheel, and her pink sunglasses were now cracked and crooked on her nose.

"We're okay," Marge said from the back seat as she pulled Alice back to sitting. "Any injuries? Everyone okay?"

"I think we're alright," I said, giving myself one last once over. Besides the burning in my lungs and the bruises I knew would form on my chest from the seatbelt, I knew I was okay.

"Cripes, Doris! I *knew* you shouldn't have been allowed to drive! What the hell did you hit?"

"I... I don't know?" She peered out the windshield, and all our gazes followed. "I don't see anything."

"Probably a decorative rock. Which is what your head is filled with," Alice said after straightening her scarf.

Suddenly I remembered our location. Where we were. Walnut Lane. Why we were in a rental car on that particular street. I spun around in my seat to see Tom racing our way, a cell phone pressed to his ear.

"Shit! Go, Doris! Go!" I screamed, ducking back into the seat.

Doris restarted the car and slammed it in reverse, but the tires only squealed as we spun in place.

"It won't move! It won't move!"

"Don't drive off! It's fleeing the scene! We'll be outlaws!" Marge barked, but Doris continued pressing on the accelerator. More black plumes of smoke rose around us as the tires dug into the pavement, but the revving engine refused to move us backward.

Panic rose inside me and threatened to choke the life out of me as Tom approached the car. Concern and confusion tightened his face as he tipped his head, gazing into my window.

"It's over. We're made." Marge let out a defeated sigh as she looked out the window to Tom. Doris stopped pressing on the gas, and the engine sputtered to a stop.

Covering my face with my hand, I tugged my scarf up tighter. The white powder coating my sunglasses blurred my vision, but even with the obstructed view, one glance up to

Tom's face pressing against the window, and I forgot how to breathe.

"Are you okay in there?" he asked, rapping on the window. "Is anyone hurt?"

With my pulse ripping through my veins at light speed, I nodded my head. "Yep. We're fine. Thank you and goodbye."

"Are you sure no one is hurt?" The window muffled his voice, but those low, velvety tones I'd remembered him whispering in my ear sent a surge straight through me. God, the man still looked exactly the same.

His hypnotic golden eyes.

That chiseled jawline.

Memories crashed into me, refusing to fade.

"We're fine, Tom. Just go."

Tom. Shit! I said his name. Peering out from behind my sunglasses, I peeked up to see his furrowed brow while he searched my face. Praying my dark sunglasses and old age would conceal my identity, I stared straight into those eyes I knew so well. And they stared straight through me.

"Sylvie?"

CHAPTER TWENTY-TWO

"Hi, Tom," I whispered, pulling down my sunglasses. The moment I got a clear look at him without my sunglasses between us, I felt the butterflies lift off in my stomach. Just like they had the first time I saw him forty years ago.

The widows sat in silence while Tom and I remained trapped in our stare. Emotions swirled inside his amber eyes while he stepped back, disbelief keeping his masculine jaw propped open.

"Is that you?" he asked, regaining his lost footing.

"It's me." I pulled the scarf off my head and brushed off the airbag dust.

"Sylvie?" he asked again, disbelief shaking his voice.

"Hi, Tom," I repeated, still unable to form any more complex words.

"Get out there," Doris whispered, giving me a little shove.

With a quick glance around the car, I caught all their encouraging nods. I let their confidence push me on, and I grabbed the door handle and pressed it open. Rising up, I stood in front of Tom. He towered over me, and I remembered how small I had felt beside him. How strong and powerful he was and how protected I felt wrapped inside his arms. How badly I wanted to step into them, wrap my arms around his waist, and bury my head in the chest I wish it had rested on every night for the past forty years.

Age had transformed the color of his hair, but it still flowed in the same thick waves I'd run my fingers through while we'd laid in bed and talked all night. So much of him had changed, but I still saw the same man I'd given my heart to all those years ago and never gotten it back.

"What... what are you doing here?" he asked.

"I, uh, was here visiting with some friends." It wasn't entirely a lie. I just left out the part I was here visiting him.

A siren echoed through the warm, summer air, and soon blue and red lights appeared as a police car pulled around the corner.

"Are you sure you aren't hurt?" he asked, looking me over.

Tom. Always looking out for me. Always protecting me. I could see the concern weigh down his brow.

"I'm okay. Just some bruises from the seatbelt, I think."

"Good. I, uh, good. Glad you aren't hurt."

The weight of our last interaction hung between us. The tears. The heartbreak. It dangled between us like an invisible barrier I didn't know how to pass through.

"Anyone hurt?" the police officer asked as he walked up behind me, shaking me from the locked stare Tom and I shared.

"No. We're fine, officer."

"All good, here," Marge said, climbing out the door and stepping to my side. "What did we hit anyway?"

"Fire hydrant," Tom said, pointing to the front of the car.

I turned around for the first time to see the damage we'd done. The bumper of the car had settled over the top of the fire hydrant, and now I realized why we'd been unable to back away.

"Is that what I hit?" Doris emerged from the car and craned her neck around. "Oh, yeah! Would you look at that."

"Were you driving?" the officer asked, and she gave him a sheepish grin. "I'm going to need your license and insurance information. Follow me."

Worry filled Doris's eyes as she walked back to the police car.

"I'm Marge. This is Alice." Marge stuck out her hand, and Tom gripped it with his. The force of her handshake started him, and he looked down at her with a smile.

"Helluva grip."

"First Lieutenant Marge Moretti... now Marge Burns. US Army. A marine?" she pointed to the tattoo on his forearm.

"Yes, ma'am."

"Glad to meet you."

"As am I. Charmed, really." Alice held out her hand and flashed him a coy smile. I felt the claws of jealousy ripping through me, but Marge caught her flirtation and snatched her by the back of the shirt.

"We'll be over here so you two can catch up." Marge leaned in. "When the coppers ask, the story is we swerved to miss a dog. Small. Brown. Came outta nowhere. Got it?"

I nodded.

"Good," Marge said, and Alice cast a sultry glance over her shoulder while Marge towed her away.

"Your friends?" he asked.

"Yes. My best friends," I answered. "The Wilder Widows."

"Widow?" he asked, and I saw his chest cease movement while he waited.

"Yeah. Bruce passed away. Cancer."

"I'm sorry to hear that." He said the words, but his voice held zero remorse.

"And you? Are you... married?" My own chest ceased moving while I waited.

"Divorced."

"Oh. I'm sorry," I said, but the same remorse was absent from my voice as well.

"So, what are you doing here, Sylvie? I thought I heard your parents passed away, and I didn't think you had any other family in the area."

Stumbling for an answer that didn't end with 'stalking you,' I bit my lip and took a breath. "I was just in town showing the girls where I lived. Didn't realize you still lived here."

"Is that so?" A dark eyebrow rose in a challenge. Lying was never my strong suit, and Tom's ability to see straight through me was doing me no favors right now.

"Yeah. Funny running into you here."

"So, you weren't circling the block for the past hour staring at my house?"

I opened my mouth to speak but instead ended up gasping like a dying fish. He'd seen us? Of course he'd seen us. He's a military man, trained to notice and observe everything. A scalding heat raced to my cheeks, and I tried to decide which way I wanted to run.

"I kept seeing the same car over and over again. Finally decided to come out and investigate. Imagine my surprise seeing it run over a fire hydrant and then finding you inside it."

A nervous chuckle shook my shoulders. "Yeah. Funny, huh? What are the chances? We were just lost."

"In your own neighborhood?" Mirth sparkled in his eyes while he watched me squirm.

"Ma'am, can you come over here and give me your statement?" the police officer asked me.

Thank God. Saved by the cop. "Sorry, I just need to chat with him really quick. I'll be right back."

"I'll be waiting." He smiled, and it almost dropped me to my knees.

I hurried over to the cop car and gave my statement. I left out the part about us being stalkers and circling Tom's house for an hour. Instead, I stuck to the story Marge had fed me.

"He just came out of nowhere," I said as we finished up.

"Yeah, that'll happen sometimes. But you should never swerve." A reprimanding look passed to Doris. "There could have been a small child or family walking on that sidewalk. Next time that happens, just hit the brakes and hope for the best."

"Sorry, officer," Doris said. "I'll be more careful."

If only he knew the truth.

"I wrote down your numbers if I have any questions. Tow truck will take care of getting the car out of here. Let me give you ladies a lift back to your hotel."

"Oh, thank you, officer." Doris hopped up from where she sat on the curb. "That would be wonderful."

I glanced over my shoulder to where Tom leaned up against a tree in his front yard.

"You going over there?" Marge asked.

"He saw us circling the house. I'm busted. Mortified. Horrified. It's over, Marge. I'm just going to wave goodbye, get in this car and never *ever* speak his name again."

"Bullshit," she barked loud enough I jumped. "You've got a second chance, damn it. And you're not going to be a chicken shit and take the easy way out this time. You did that once, and you lost almost forty years with that man. And I may be old. And a lesbian. But I can still see the love in his eyes when he looks at you." She stepped forward, pushing her nose into mine. With wide eyes, I swallowed hard as she pressed into me. "Soldier, you're gonna march your ass over there and ask that man out to dinner. Understood?"

I struggled to form words, but she rose on her toes and leveled me with a stern stare.

"I said... *understood*?"

"Yes, sir." Taking a big step back, I finally exhaled a breath of relief when I was out of range.

With the nudge of her chin, she encouraged me over. I turned to Tom, who watched us with a curious stare. Glancing back one last time, I saw my Wilder Widows watching me. Reassuring me. Supporting me. I let their smiles re-inflate my lost confidence, and I turned and marched over to where Tom stood.

"Will you go to dinner with me tonight?" I spit out faster than I'd intended.

"Dinner?" a dark brow rose along with the corner of his lip.

"Yes. Dinner. I would like to take you to dinner."

He brushed his fingers along his salt and pepper beard while he puckered up his lips. With each second he hesitated, the confidence seeped back out of me.

"It's fine if you don't want to. Just thought we could catch up or something, but it's fine." I started to turn on my heel, but he caught me by the arm. The second his skin touched mine, that familiar electricity traveled through me. A shiver snaked up my spine, and I hoped he hadn't seen my shudder.

"I was just teasing you, Sylvie. Of course, I'll have dinner with you. Where are you staying?"

I turned back, letting my eyes drift back to his. With every second his fingers remained on my heated skin, I felt all my fears melting away. "The Hyatt on Main."

That cocky smile I loved so much deepened his dimples. "I'll pick you up at seven."

Trying to mirror his confidence, I lifted my chin. "I'll be ready."

Emotions I'd suppressed for decades broke free beneath his heated gaze.

"See you soon."

"Bye, Tom." I turned on my heel and started away.

"Hey, Sylvie?" he called, and I stopped and turned back.

"Leave the scarf and sunglasses at the hotel. You look much better without them."

A girlish giggle slipped past my lips, and I gave him a quick nod. Trying to refrain from skipping, I hurried back to the widows waiting in the back of the cop car. I climbed inside, squeezing into the back with Marge and Doris. Alice spun around in the front, staring at me through the metal partition.

"Well?" she asked, and all three sets of expectant eyes bore through me.

"We're having dinner." I grinned so wide I thought my face may tear.

"Whoo hoo!" Marge hooted, punching her fist in the air.

I glanced out the window as the car pulled away, and Tom held my gaze as I passed him by.

CHAPTER TWENTY-THREE

The widows stood down in the lobby with me while I paced back and forth, the red high heels I'd borrowed from Alice click-clacking across the tile floor.

"Is this really happening?" I panted, trying to control my breathing. All the confidence I'd mustered for those few moments earlier had vanished the moment I was out from under his familiar gaze.

"You've got this, Sylvie." Marge took me by the shoulders and gave me a soft shake. "Just take a deep breath."

I inhaled and exhaled with her.

"You're going to have an amazing time, Sylvie. He's your true love." Doris smiled.

Alice nodded her agreement. "You'd better get yourself a hootie. That is one serious silver fox."

"Would you stop!" I laughed, tapping her on the shoulder. "It's just dinner."

"It's just dinner... with your true love." Sparkles filled Doris's eyes once again.

"You're only making me more nervous. I'm freaking out!"

"Sorry," Doris said. "But he is. He's your true love! I know it!"

"Doris," I warned. "Would you—"

"Hi, Sylvie."

I froze when his gravelly voice drifted over me.

Shit.

Doris's wide eyes stared over my shoulder, and I turned around to see Tom leaning against the lobby wall. Jeans that fit too well stretched over long, muscular legs, and a casual suit coat left open over his white t-shirt revealed the fit physique I'd been admiring earlier.

Did he just hear all that?

The amusement dancing in his eyes answered that question.

"Hi, Tom." Straightening my back like a rigid rod, I tried to pretend the last thirty seconds hadn't just been broadcast to the man standing only fifteen feet away. He was older now. Maybe he had hearing loss, I thought to myself, trying to stave off the panic.

"Hello, ladies," he said, casting that charming smile to the widows behind me.

"Hi, Tom," they echoed, and I could hear the drone of their voices. We were busted, and no amount of lying to myself would change that.

Shit.

"You ready?" he asked, pushing himself off the wall, slow, deliberate steps closing the distance between us. With every step that brought him closer, my already racing heart sped up. As he closed in, I noticed he'd trimmed his beard, smoothing down the straggling course hairs I'd noticed earlier today, and he had styled his thick hair into soft waves. When he extended an elbow, I slid my arm through, letting my hand settle on his forearm. Even though I couldn't see it through the grey suit coat, I knew my hand rested on that tattoo I'd loved so much.

"Ready," I said, and I hoped I meant it.

He escorted me to his truck, opening the door while I stepped inside. After he shut me in, I closed my eyes and tried to steady my breathing while he walked around the front. After climbing inside, he fired it up, and the awkward silence filled the cab, palpable enough to reach out and touch.

"Still like Italian?" he asked, and I nodded.

Speak, Sylvie! I tried to command myself, but my nerves held my tongue captive.

"Vincini's Italian is still in business. It's just around the corner. Sound good?"

"Mmmhmm," I mumbled. Words refused to form, but at least I managed to make some noise.

The one-minute drive felt like an eternity while we rode along in silence. All I wanted to do was stare at him until I could convince myself that he was real. Close enough to see. Close enough to touch. Maybe I'd gone down in the streets of Pamplona and been the latest victim of El Diablo, and everything since was just some bizarre coma dream. Maybe the ornery bull had hit pay dirt and finished me off. Perhaps I was dead, and I had made it to my heaven. Because heaven for me would be a lifetime with Tom.

Instead of openly gawking at him, I forced my eyes to the road. The truck pulled up in front of the restaurant I remembered so well. The one I'd begged my parents to take me to every year for my birthday. Tom tossed his truck in park and hopped out, and instead of waiting for him to open my door, I did it myself. When I stepped out toward the curb, I forgot about the height of the vehicle, and I misjudged the distance to the ground. With a shriek, I tumbled forward, reaching into the air for anything to grab onto to break my fall. When my fingers felt the solid wall of flesh in front of me, I grabbed tight, only to feel strong arms snake around my waist. I collapsed in his arms, suspended in his embrace... the embrace I'd envisioned every night I'd closed my eyes since we parted.

"You okay?" he asked, amber eyes boring down into mine.

Nodding, I tried to will my body to right itself. To stand up and pull myself from his embrace. But my body resisted, instead pressing deeper into his chest. Deeper into the one place that had once upon a time felt like home. *Still* felt like home.

Finally, my body responded to my mind's desperate pleas, and I pressed off his chest, smoothing my dress while I regained my composure.

"Still a klutz, I see?"

His white teeth flashed at me. That cocky smile hadn't changed one bit.

"Some things never change," I said, but actually, I was referring to his smile. And the feelings only Tom could evoke in me.

"Come on." He extended an elbow, and I took it. "Careful this time. Walking can be tricky." Laughter trickled through his words, and I chuckled in response.

The hostess seated us at a table in the back, and I was grateful they'd given us a dark, quiet corner. I didn't need the whole restaurant watching me bumbling like an idiot while I tried to learn how to speak full sentences again. Having Tom watch me struggle to speak would be embarrassing enough.

"Bottle of red?" he asked, and I nodded. "Pinot noir, please," he said to the waiter who set down our menus and walked away.

I buried my face behind the menu, trying once again to find the words to say. What did I even *want* to say? *I still love you? I'm an idiot? You have a daughter?*

That last thought nearly caused me to get up and bolt out of the restaurant. Should I tell him? And if I did, would he hate me forever?

"So, the Sylvie I remember was a chatterbox," Tom said, and I peeked up from behind my menu. "She was always laughing. Always talking. So many ideas running around inside that beautiful brain of hers. You look like her. You sound like her. But I'm not so sure you're her. You're too quiet. Are you her?" Leaning forward, he pressed his elbows into the white tablecloth.

"I'm still her," I managed to say. "I'm just nervous as hell."

His dimples deepened as he smiled. "And you don't think I am?"

Scoffing, I shook my head. "You're Tom. The most confident, cocky, self-assured man I ever met. Tom doesn't do nervous."

"Oh, I'm nervous, Sylvie." He chuckled. "More nervous than if I was lying in a trench with bullets whizzing over my head. But one of us has to speak, or this will be a long, awkward night."

"You are? You're nervous?"

Sitting back, he crossed his arms across his broad chest and blew out a puff of air. "The girl who broke my heart just waltzed back into my life. Yeah. I'm nervous."

Broke his heart? So he had loved me?

"A day hasn't gone by where I haven't thought about you," he went on. "So, imagine my surprise when I go out to investigate the suspicious car circling my block only to watch it slam into a fire hydrant, and the girl who got away is sitting in the front seat."

Sucking the air through my teeth, I slunk a little in my seat. "Sorry about that."

"Which part? The house circling, the crashing in front of my house, or the breaking my heart?"

The mirth in his voice floated away with those last words, and his eyes searched mine.

Exhaling a deep breath, I looked into his eyes. "All of it. I'm sorry, Tom. I'm so sorry about everything."

The waiter broke up our silent stare when he arrived with the wine. Grateful for the interruption, I smiled and sat back while he filled my glass.

"Are you ready to order?" he asked.

"I'll have the alfredo special, and Sylvie here will have the shrimp scampi." He arched a quizzical brow while he watched my face. "Right?"

"You remember." I smiled.

"Very good," the waiter said, backing away.

"I remember." Tom placed his napkin in his lap. "You may not have allowed me out in public to eat with you here that week we spent together, but you brought Italian home twice, and both times you had the shrimp scampi."

Laughing, I shook my head. "I still love shrimp scampi. And this is my favorite place to get it."

"It's funny actually, being out in public with you. You were so worried about being seen with me that I don't think I got out of your bed for a week."

Shame refilled that memory. I had still been with Bruce when we met, and even though I'd intended to end my engagement, I still hadn't wanted to risk being seen out and about with Tom. "I'm sorry I held you prisoner." I tried to laugh away the shame.

"I didn't mind." He took a sip of his wine, holding my gaze. "But being out in public with you is nice, too."

"It is nice."

"So, are you going to tell me what brought you home and circling my house?"

Heat flushed my cheeks, and it wasn't from the wine. "Can we skip over the part where I stalked you?"

"Not a chance." His smile widened, and it induced the familiar flip-flop in my stomach. "Spill."

"I don't even know where to start," I said.

"The beginning."

We drank wine and had dinner while I recounted the adventures of the Wilder Widows. With wide eyes and his deep laughter, he listened intently while I told him all about our escapades, right up to the moment we were sitting in the hot tub at the dude ranch.

"But if the dude ranch was your wish, then what brought you here?" he asked as he pushed his empty plate aside.

Maybe it was the wine. Maybe it was the way he still looked at me like the girl he once loved. Maybe it was the casual way we were together now that the fear had dissipated.

Whatever it was took hold of my tongue, and I admitted my truth. "Because my real wish was to see you again."

Shock settled in his eyes, and I waited for his reaction.

"I was your wish?"

I nodded and took a much-needed swig of my wine. "Yes. You have always been my wish. My one big regret."

He took a deep breath and blew it out. "Wow."

I exhaled my own breath. "Yeah. Wow."

"So, you haven't forgotten about me? All these years I figured you never thought about me once. And all these years I couldn't get you out of my mind."

"I have never, *could* never, forget you, Tom."

"You know, I married someone a few years after I met you. I thought maybe getting married would finally chase your ghost away."

The thought of him with another woman twisted my stomach into knots, but I had no right to feel that way. Not when I'd been the one who ended it. I'd abandoned what we had and married someone else.

"And did it?" I asked.

"No. In fact, it only made things worse. Made me miss you more, wishing she was you all those years. We only made it ten years, and I ended it."

"I'm sorry, Tom."

"And you? You really thought about me all those years?"

"Every day," I answered.

"Then tell me why, Sylvie. If you felt that way about me, the way I felt about you, why didn't you wait? Why marry that guy when I told you I was coming back?" Hurt darkened his eyes as he searched mine.

The truth swirled around on my tongue, and I opened my mouth, trying to find the right words to say.

"Here's your check," the waiter interrupted and placed our bill on the table. "Thank you for dining with us."

"Thank you for having us," I said, hurrying to my feet and grabbing my purse. *I'm not ready.*

Looking confused, Tom grabbed the check and rose along with me. I hurried to the door, panic pushing my feet farther and farther away.

He'll hate me if I tell him.

"Sylvie!" he called after me, but I rushed outside, stopping to inhale a deep breath of the sweet summer air.

I started toward the hotel. It was only a mile walk, and I couldn't face him... answer the question I knew he deserved to know the truth to. But I hadn't made it around the corner when he jogged up behind me.

"What the hell, Sylvie?" he asked, catching me by the arm. "What just happened back there?"

Shaking my head, I pulled from his grip. "This was stupid, Tom. I shouldn't have come here." I kept walking, stepping onto the bridge suspended over the little river I'd swam in as a child.

"Oh, hell no!" he shouted, racing in front of me and blocking me with his body. "You don't get to do this. Not again, Sylvie."

I looked up through tear-filled eyes.

"You don't get to blow into my life again only to leave me standing alone with a broken heart. Not again."

"I shouldn't have come here."

Reaching out, he brushed his thumb across my cheek, catching the tear as it trickled down. "But you did come. You're here, Sylvie. How? Why? Actually, I don't fucking care. All I care about is that you're here. And to hell if I'm letting you march back out of my life again."

When I opened my mouth to tell him this was a mistake, that I needed to go, his kiss forced the words back down. Strong hands cupped my face, and the weight of his lips crushed away all my doubts. With each swirl of his tongue, he transported me back through time to my happiest moments. The moments I'd been with him. He kissed away all my fears, my regrets, and the years I'd been miserable without him.

Wrapping my arms around his neck, I folded into his embrace. My tears slipped past my lips, and the salt mingled with the taste of his kiss. I inhaled his earthy scent, the one that was no longer just a memory. It was real, and so was he. And his kiss and the love for him that still lived inside me... it was all real, and I was holding it, tasting it, touching it.

"Sylvie," he whispered against my lips. "I love you. I still love you... never stopped loving you."

"I love you, too," I murmured into his mouth while the tears fell freely. "I have always loved you, Tom. I'm so sorry. I'm so sorry I ruined everything."

Softening his kiss, he brushed his lips against mine and then brought them to my forehead. They pressed into my skin while he wrapped his arms around me, pulling me tight to his chest.

"I missed you, Sylvie. Every day."

"I missed you, too." Burying my head in his chest, I pressed into his embrace.

"I'm not letting you go this time. You know that, right?" He kissed my head again.

I let myself linger in his arms, willing myself to find the strength to tell him what I should have told him all those years ago. The thing that could rip him from my arms once again. After squeezing him for a moment longer, I inhaled a breath and pulled back.

"You asked me why I married Bruce," I said, taking his hand in mine.

He nodded. "I never understood. I loved you so much, Sylvie. And I knew you loved me."

I squeezed his hand. "I loved you more than you could ever know. I loved you so much, Tom."

"So, why?" he asked, brushing a piece of hair from my face. "Why did you choose him?"

Closing my eyes, I dug down into my resolve and exhaled a deep breath. "When you left, I was planning on telling Bruce we were done. But I didn't hear from you. And I started wondering if what I was feeling was one-sided... that maybe you were one of those guys who makes every girl feel the way you made me feel."

"Never." He shook his head. "You're the only girl I'd ever felt that way about. Hell, you're *still* the only girl I'd ever felt that way about."

"But I didn't know that then," I said, tears welling in my eyes. "And after a couple months went by and I hadn't heard from you, I was sure I was just some passing fling to you."

"I'm sorry, Sylvie. I realize now I expected too much from you. I should have found a way to call or write or something. That was my fault."

"No," I shook my head. "I should have had faith in my feelings. I should have trusted in us. But I was young. Stupid. Scared."

"Scared? Of what?"

My breaths quickened while I stared into his eyes, hoping this wasn't the last time he'd ever look at me like that.

"Because I found out I was pregnant."

The silence settled over us like a damp blanket. Tom's wide eyes searched mine as I struggled to continue.

"I was pregnant, Tom. And you were gone. And I had no idea if I'd ever see you again. So, I made a choice, one I regret deeply, but I made a choice to stay with Bruce so my child could be raised in a family. I was too young, too scared, to risk being a single mother."

His shoulders rose and fell with his deep breaths. I waited. Watched.

"Was... was it mine?" he breathed.

I nodded, and the tears broke free. "She. Her name is Rachel. And yes. She's yours."

Stepping back, he raked a hand through his hair. "What?"

"I'm so sorry, Tom. I was so scared. And I didn't know if you were coming back. And I couldn't risk her growing up in a broken home with a single mom struggling to survive. I'm so sorry."

"Holy shit, Sylvie." He leaned forward, pressing his hands into his knees. "How could you... how could you keep that from me?"

I stepped forward to touch him, but he pulled away. "It all happened so fast, Tom. And it was a mistake. A *huge* mistake. A mistake I paid for every day until Bruce died. I was miserable with him. He was awful. I spent every day living with that choice, but it was a choice I made and one I had to commit to. I wouldn't let Rachel suffer for my choices, so I lived with them. Every. Single. Day."

Pressing his hands to the top of his head, he spun in a circle. "I have a daughter?"

I nodded.

"You knew she was mine, and you married him anyway?"

I nodded again. "I didn't know if I'd ever see you again."

"And when I showed up on your doorstep? You... you were pregnant?"

Shame settled deep in my gut as I dropped my eyes to the ground.

"Holy shit, Sylvie."

"I'm so—"

"Stop! Stop fucking apologizing. How could you? How could you not tell me? Wait for me? I would have been there for you, Sylvie. For her! I would have married you, like I wanted to, and taken care of you."

Sobs wracked my shoulders as I clutched the rail of the bridge for support. "I know that now, Tom, but I didn't know that *then*! By the time you came back, it was too late! Bruce and I were married, and he thought she was his. I was stuck! It was an awful situation, and I didn't know what to do when I saw you again. Please, you have to forgive me." I reached for him, but he stepped away.

"I... I can't even look at you. I can't."

The soft glow of the lamps illuminating the bridge showed the shimmer in his eyes. The hurt. The anger. The sadness. And all of it I'd put there.

He spun on his heel and walked away. I wanted to go after him, but I didn't deserve him. This. This is what I deserved after what I did. To be alone after a life tied to a man I never loved.

Listening to the soft rush of water beneath my feet, I let all my emotions rip out of me. Sobbing into my arms, I finally let the consequences of my decision sink in. I could have had an entire life with that man if I'd just been braver. Had more faith. Trusted. Instead, I chose the safe path—a path that took me away from the one man I'd ever loved.

As the pain broke me open, I welcomed it like a punishment I deserved.

"Fuck!" His deep voice startled me as it rumbled through the night, and I spun to see him at the far side of the bridge. He turned and stormed back toward me.

"Tom?" I whispered as I watched his long strides swallow the distance between us.

Fire burned inside his eyes when he stopped in front of me. "I'm mad as hell, Sylvie. Fucking livid, in fact."

Swallowing my tears, I shrunk beneath the weight of his stare.

"But I've already lost almost forty years with you. And to hell if I'm missing another minute more."

Before I could speak, his arm snaked around my waist, drawing me into him. His kiss crashed down on my lips, pain and pleasure twisting together while he claimed my lips again. Passion exploded between us while I surrendered, melting into his embrace. As he deepened our kiss, I let his love travel through me, creeping into all the cracks of the broken heart I'd nursed for all these years. It smoothed over the edges, sealing the holes and making my heart whole once again.

"I'm so fucking mad at you," he whispered between kisses. "But I love you, Sylvie. Always have, always will."

"I love you, too, Tom. Always."

Our lips drifted apart, and I pressed my head into his chest.

"Thank God for those Wilder Widows dragging you back into my life," he said as he pressed soft kisses to my forehead. "And now I'm never letting you go."

"Thank God for those Wilder Widows is right," I said with a smile.

CHAPTER TWENTY-FOUR

"Good morning, ladies," I said as I settled into the booth at the brunch restaurant I'd told them to meet me at.

Three sets of expectant eyes stared back at me.

"Well?" Doris said, leaning forward. "What happened?"

Marge leaned in next to her. "Your message last night just said you weren't coming back and to meet you here in the morning. So that means it went well?"

"Look at her face!" Alice grinned. "That's a hootie face. It went *very* well from the looks of that sex glow."

Biting my lip, I wiggled my brows and smiled.

They erupted in a unified cheer and startled the other diners around us.

"I knew it!" Doris practically screamed. "True love! It's true love!"

I could only muster a giggle while I sat back against the booth.

"Good for you, Sylvie." Marge grinned. "I'm so glad it worked out."

"Thanks to all of you," I said, reaching to the center of the table and opening my hand. They each leaned forward, and together we held hands. "It's all thanks to you."

"Did you tell him?" Alice asked.

Exhaling a deep breath, I nodded. "I did."

"And? How did it go?" Doris asked.

"He was mad." I sucked the air through my teeth. "Like, *really* mad."

"But?" Marge lifted a brow.

"*But...* he told me even though he was furious with me, he didn't want to miss another second of our lives together."

"Whoo hoo!" Doris whooped. "True love!"

Marge tapped my hand. "I'm so happy for you, Sylvie. Now you two can finally get the life you missed."

"It's so surreal," I said. "It was like no time had passed at all. We were just *us* again."

Doris smiled. "Because it's—"

"Yes, yes, Doris." Alice rolled her eyes. "True love."

"Well it is." She pouted. "Isn't it?"

Her eyes searched mine, and I smiled. "It's true love."

Her happy sigh filled the air surrounding us.

"It really is love. I can't even explain it. I couldn't explain it back then, and I can't explain it now. But I know he's the one for me. And this time, I'm not letting anything get in the way."

"Is he going to meet Rachel?" Alice asked.

"Eventually. We decided to let a little more time pass, and then I'll tell her. He said he wants things to be completely on her terms."

"Think she'll be mad?" Doris asked.

"Furious." I sighed. "But she's a smart, kind woman. I'm sure she'll understand the situation I was in and forgive me. At least, I hope she will."

"We all deserve forgiveness," Doris said.

"She will," Marge said. "She'll understand. It was an impossible situation, and you did what you thought was right at the time. You sacrificed everything for her."

"Thanks, Marge. I hope so."

"So, what happens now?" Doris asked.

"Well." I chewed on the side of my cheek while I searched for the words. "I'm going to stay here with him. We've spent so many years apart, we don't want to miss another minute. We're not getting any younger, after all."

"You're not going back to Wilder Lane, either?" Marge asked.

I shook my head. "Not right now. I'll be back, but I'm just going to stay here with him for a while and try to make up for lost time while we figure out our future. But don't worry, I'm not selling my house or anything."

"Me neither," Doris said. "I'm going to hold onto mine. It's our family home, and even though I'll be spending most of my time on the dude ranch, I'll still be back to visit you ladies often."

"Well, you'll need to tell me when you're going back. Otherwise, it will just be my mom, you see."

"What?" I asked. "Where are you going?"

"Vegas." She grinned. "Roxy asked me to come live with her instead of just visiting, and I said yes."

"Oh Marge! That's wonderful!" Doris exclaimed. "I'm so happy for you!"

"Yeah, like Sylvie said, I'm not getting any younger. I called Mom to see if she'd be okay alone, and she said go for it. She's looking forward to coming out for some gambling. So, what the hell, right?"

"What the hell." I smiled.

"Well, that's just great. Now I'll be stuck all by myself on that crappy lane." Alice sat back with a grumble.

"My mom will still be there. I'm sure she'll be happy to make you lasagna."

"Oh, Alice! We'll visit all the time. And you can come visit us any time you want." Doris rubbed her hand down the length of Alice's arm. "We will never just abandon you."

Alice grinned wide. "I'm just teasing. I won't be lonely. Hell, without you ninny's bothering me all the time, I'll have even more time for extracurricular activities with my pool boy."

We burst into laughter, and I leaned over, resting my head on her shoulder.

"Can we get some champagne over here?" Alice called to the waitress.

She responded with a sharp nod and disappeared into the kitchen. Alice's phone rang, and she flipped it over to look at the screen.

"It's my daughter. I need to take this."

I scooched out of the booth and let Alice slide past. When I settled back in, I couldn't suppress my happy sigh.

"I can't believe I'm with Tom. After all these years. It's a miracle."

"And I have Axel. And a new purpose. I get to feel needed again." Doris smiled.

"And I have Roxy. Never would have had the guts to go for her without you ladies at my side."

"Thank God for the Wilder Widows." Doris pressed her hands together in prayer. "You saved me."

"We saved each other." I tossed an arm around her shoulder and gave her a squeeze.

"Who knows how to pull up YouTube on my phone?" Alice shouted from the center of the diner. We all spun to look at her.

"What's going on?" I asked, hopping to my feet. Alice ignored me while her wild eyes searched the room.

"You! Hipster! You know how to pull up YouTube?" She hurried to the side of the lone man with the long beard and man bun in the corner and shoved her phone in his face.

"What?" he asked, looking up from his plate of eggs.

"YouTube! How the hell do I pull it up?" She snapped her fingers in his face, and he sat back with a start.

While he fumbled to take her phone, I stepped to Alice's side. "What's going on, Alice?"

Ignoring me, she leaned over his shoulder. "When you get to YouTube, look up the words 'Gammy Las Vegas.'"

He followed her orders, and I leaned over his shoulder with her. Doris and Marge squeezed in, and the four of us stared at the screen while he typed.

"What the hell is going on?" Marge asked.

"There!" Alice squealed. "That's it! Play it!"

My eyes widened as a video of Alice started playing on his small screen. There she was in all her showgirl glory. The video showed clips of her dancing on stage, running down the aisle with cops tearing after her. Then I gasped when I saw a clip of the four Wilder Widows tearing down the street, Alice's costume sparkling in the Las Vegas lights we blew past. And finally, a clip of her hanging out of the top of the limo streamed across the screen.

"Holy shit," I whispered while I watched the screen turn black.

"Six million hits and counting!" Alice clapped. "Celeste saw something on one of the Hollywood entertainment shows she watches about a viral video of a grandma stealing the spotlight at a Las Vegas show. When she saw the clip, she knew it was me... and it was! Is! It's me! And they're calling me 'Gammy' on account of my sexy gams! A grandma with gams!"

Alice did a spin and high-kicked over the top of the hipster's head. Her smile couldn't have been brighter if it was the sun.

"They're looking for me, ladies. The news said they are looking for Gammy so she can come back and have her own show!"

"What?" we mirrored, and I blinked back at her.

"Are you serious? They aren't looking for us to throw us in the slammer? We did kidnap someone, you know." Marge's stern expression gave off a silent warning, and the hipster beneath us flashed fear at her words.

"No. Not to arrest me. To make me a *star!*" Alice opened her arms and spun in circles. "I'm going to be a star again!"

"I can't believe it!" Marge clapped. "You're going to be a star! And wait! That means we'll be in Vegas together?"

"You're not getting rid of me that easily." Alice smiled, then ran forward, pulling us all into a hug while she hopped up and down. "My own show! All I need to do is call them up and tell them I'm Gammy, and I get my own show in Vegas. My dream come true!"

"I'm so happy for you, Alice," I said, squeezing her tight.

"And you know who else is said to still be living in Vegas?" Alice arched a brow. "Harry Hayes. I think I'll need to look him up again and give him his own personal show."

Laughing, I shook my head. It was all working out for all of us.

"Did you still want champagne?" the waitress asked, and we broke apart our group hug.

"Champagne for everyone!" Alice shouted, and the few patrons at the restaurant gave her half-hearted applause.

We hurried back to our table, sliding in one by one. Alice took the cheap bottle of champagne, popping the cork and sending it bouncing off the ceiling. Bubbles poured over the top as she hurried to fill our glasses.

We each grabbed a flute and lifted it into the air.

"Here's to chasing our dreams," Alice said.

Doris tipped her against mine. "To our second act."

"To true love." I smiled.

"To friendship. To the Wilder Widows." Marge pushed her flute against ours, and we all smiled.

"Wilder Widows!" we cheered together before taking long swigs of our champagne.

"I can't believe it's over," I said after setting my glass down. "I mean, I know we can't go on like this forever, but I can't believe it's ending."

A sadness settled over us while the weight of that realization sank in.

"None of us are going back to Wilder Lane." Marge pursed her lips. "I just realized that."

"But none of us are selling our houses, right?" I asked, sweeping them with a gaze.

"Right," they said in unison.

"So, what about this? We promise to visit often, and then what if we agree that one year from now, we all return to Wilder Lane and do this again?"

Three smiles glowed back at me, and they all nodded.

"Alice, do you have the basket?" I asked, and she lit up before reaching into her purse and pulling it out.

"Waitress? Can we get a pen?" I called. She hurried over and set one on the table.

I passed out four drink napkins, then grabbed the pen. After thinking about it for a moment, I lit up when I came up with my wish. I scribbled it on my napkin, folded it up, and dropped it in the basket. Doris, Marge, and Alice took turns writing down their wishes, each one smiling when it disappeared inside the basket.

Alice slid the lid over the top and pushed it to the center of the table. "So, we have a pact? One year from today, we open this up, and no matter what is on that note, we help each other do it?"

"We have a pact." I grinned.

"Agreed," Marge said.

Doris clasped her hands together. "Agreed!"

"And promise we won't be strangers the next year while we wait to open these up?" I said, beaming at the faces I'd come to love.

"Promise," they said.

Alice closed her eyes for a moment and let out a deep breath. "I know I don't say this enough, or probably even show it enough, but I love you ladies. With all my heart. Thank you for being the kind of friends I never thought I'd have. The best of friends. You're my family, and you always will be."

Doris clutched her chest as Marge's jaw slackened.

"Stop the presses," Marge said. "Did you just admit you love us?"

Alice narrowed her eyes and started to open her mouth with what I knew would be some sassy retort.

I lifted my hand and stopped her. "Don't ruin it, Marge. We love you too, Alice. I love *all* of you... with my whole heart. You changed my life."

"And you changed ours." Doris smiled. "I'm so lucky to have you Wilder Widows in my life."

"We sure are lucky we found each other." I lifted my champagne, and they followed suit. "To the Wilder Widows."

We clinked our glasses together, and our voices blended into one. "To the Wilder Widows!"

The Beginning

THANK YOU FOR READING

I hope you enjoyed *The Wilder Widows*! The greatest gift you can give a writer is your review. If you enjoyed this book, I would be forever grateful if you'd take the time to leave a review. Find out more about my other books and upcoming releases at **www.katherinehastings.com**.

You can also get new book releases, sales, and free book specials delivered right to your inbox by signing up for my Enews!
Sign Up Here!

Get social with me and join me on:
Passion Posse Reader's Group: www.facebook.com/groups/passionposse
Facebook @katherinehastingsauthor
Instagram @katherinehastingsauthor
Twitter @khastingsauthor
Follow me on:
Bookbub
Goodreads

Made in the USA
Thornton, CO
05/09/22 23:34:53

28411755-d481-4344-b3ff-ea7e1b9f7543R01